Thérèse and Pierrette

and the

Little Hanging Angel

a novel by

Michel Tremblay

translated by

Sheila Fischman

Talonbooks

1996

Published with the assistance of the Canada Council.

Talonbooks
#104—3100 Production Way
Burnaby, British Columbia
Canada V5A 4R4

Typeset in Palatino and printed and bound in Canada by Hignell Printing.

First Printing: September 1996

Thérèse et Pierrette à l'école des Saints-Anges was first published in French in 1980 by Leméac Éditeur, Montreal, Quebec. *Thérèse and Pierrette and the Little Hanging Angel* was first published in English in 1984 by McClelland and Stewart, Toronto, Ontario.

Canadian Cataloguing in Publication Data
Tremblay, Michel, 1942—
    [Thérèse et Pierrette à l'école des Saints-Anges. English]
    Thérèse and Pierrette and the little hanging angel

    Translation of: Thérèse et Pierrette à l'école des Saints-Anges.
    ISBN 0-88922-198-7

    I. Fischman, Sheila. II. Title. III. Title: Thérèse et Pierrette à l'école des Saints-Anges. English.
PS 8539.R47T4413 1996   C843'.54   C96-910516-9
PQ3919.2.T73T4413 1996

---

*"Imagining something is better
than remembering something."*

—JOHN IRVING,
THE WORLD ACCORDING TO GARP

While listening to
Brahms' Fourth Symphony

FIRST MOVEMENT

Allegro non troppo

The lilacs are finished already." Pierrette put her school-bag down on the step beside her. "They're all shrivelled up and brown." Thérèse was shuffling from one foot to the other in front of her friend. She really wanted to skip double Dutch but she knew they wouldn't have enough time before they left for school. She stood still for a moment and scratched her calf. "The lilacs are finished, but the bleeding hearts'll be out soon. I like bleeding hearts better." Pierrette's expression became obstinate. "They look nice but they don't smell. And flowers that don't smell ...." Thérèse uttered a little cry that cut Pierrette's remark in two, leaving the first part dangling useless in the morning sunshine. "Shoot, my garter came undone again!" She sat down beside Pierrette and both girls stuck their heads under her skirt. "Look at that! Gee, what a drag! I have to stop and do them up ten times a day!" "Won't your mother buy you new ones?" "My mother says there's nothing wrong with these, it's just me squirming all the time. Do you think I'm always squirming?" Now that the garter was fastened, Thérèse pulled down her skirt and looked at her friend. Pierrette seemed to be mulling the question over before she replied. "It's true, you squirm a lot. You never keep still for a minute." "How about you, don't you ever squirm?" "Maybe, but at least my garters stay done up!" Thérèse had straightened up while Pierrette was talking, and made as if to move away. She stopped to kick a stone, which took off in a direction completely different from the way she'd been aiming. "If she doesn't get cracking we'll all be late!" Both girls looked up at the window on the third floor where their friend Simone lived, their inseparable accomplice who had just got out of the hospital the night before and would be going out today for the first time in several weeks. Pierrette got up, went over to Thérèse and spoke very softly, as though she was telling a secret. "Maybe she's ashamed." "Ashamed?

About what?" "You know, her operation! Remember, she told us it might show for a while." "Maybe it'll *always* show, but it's still supposed to be better than before." The door to the inside staircase leading from the second to the third floor opened. Thérèse became silent. Pierrette put her hand on her friend's arm. "Jeepers, Thérèse, what'll we say if it looks as bad as before?" "We'll say it looks better and then we'll confess!" A tiny girl weighed down by a huge book bag was coming down the inside stairs, holding the rest of her gear at arm's length. "Hi, Simone!" Thérèse and Pierrette spoke at the same time, in exactly the same tone, in the same rhythm, in a single breath. The little girl stopped half-way down the stairs and put down her bag on a step. "Does it show?" Her voice was nasal, with a hint of barely controlled panic. For a moment, Thérèse and Pierrette didn't answer. Pierrette frowned and peered at Simone's face. Thérèse had started shuffling again, while she checked that her garter was still fastened. Pierrette was the first to speak. "You're too far away, Simone, c'mon down." A gentle morning breeze rose as Simone descended the last steps. It lifted the little girl's skirt a bit, uncovering her skinny legs and red knees. Thérèse started. "How come you're wearing knee socks? How come you haven't got your long stockings on?" Simone stopped short, holding her skirt against her legs with one hand. "Momma said she was so frazzled she forgot to darn them .... Anyway, never mind my stockings, does it show much?" Thérèse and Pierrette spent a long moment contemplating the narrow line of pink flesh running vertically from Simone's upper lip, too visible for their liking but not nearly as ugly as the hideous harelip with which their friend had always been afflicted. Simone sat on the steps with her elbows on her knees. "I know it shows. But momma said it'd go away, it's 'cause the operation wasn't very long ago, and that's why it's all red." Simone was on the verge of tears. She avoided her friends' gaze, which she knew was directed at her lip, the curse she'd been under since birth, the flaw in the very middle of a face that was still very pretty but had quickly made her the laughing-stock of the École des Saints-Anges, in spite of the compassion and magnanimity of some of the nuns, who went so far as to punish girls who made fun of her or gave her a hard time; she'd been promised that her deformity would disappear completely, but now there was a sort of red shadow as a reminder, an insinuation, whereas she'd been convinced that from now on she'd be able to plunk herself in front of any mirror and find she was pretty. But suddenly the childish sense of propriety that had held back Thérèse and Pierrette flew away and they literally threw themselves on their friend, squealing with delight, pinning Simone to the staircase, tickling her, kissing her, rumpling her hair and communicating to her the portion of their joy she was entitled to: their happiness at being together again. Thérèse, Pierrette and Simone, the inseparables, welcomed back their amputated centre: at last they were whole again, and they set off for school together, arm in arm, singing *"Mes jeunes années"* or *"J'irai la voir un jour,"* unconcerned about floppy garters or split lips and, most of all, savouring one another's presence, full, complete and enveloping, filled with promise and the certainty that solitude had been banished from their lives forever. "It looks terrific, Simone!" "It hardly shows!" "After the red fades you won't see a thing!" "I can hardly recognize you! You're really pretty now!" "You're beautiful, Simone!" Yes, it was the first time. And Simone sobbed with joy.

They left rue Fabre behind and turned left on to Gilford. It was only two blocks to the École des Saints-Anges: they would turn right on to rue Garnier and walk up to boulevard Saint-Joseph, which they would cross very carefully, looking left and right, smoothing their hair or flicking dust off their skirts for fear a nun might single them out at the entrance to the school yard if they weren't absolutely impeccable. Simone was back in her old place, between Thérèse and Pierrette, hugging her huge book bag, her friends' arms around her neck and waist. That's the way you always saw them strolling along rue Gilford, for several years now, the two big girls framing the smaller one, protecting her, guiding her as if she were blind or very frail. All three were the same age, eleven, and until two years earlier they'd been the same height, the same weight and had the same brownish blonde hair, which, in the case of Thérèse and Pierrette had gradually been transformed to gleaming auburn, while poor Simone, who hadn't grown any taller or gained any weight, still had drab and washed-out locks. And while Thérèse and Pierrette had suddenly developed, shooting up like weeds to the consternation of their families, who couldn't keep on providing the clothes and shoes they didn't even seem to want to take the trouble to wear out, so anxious were they to metamorphose, to leave the constraints of childhood and throw themselves headlong into the great adventure of adolescence, Simone was still resolutely small, as though protesting against the speed at which her two friends were being transformed and, in so doing, emphasizing her own fragility and ugliness. The energy that Thérèse and Pierrette used up becoming beautiful, Simone put into stubbornly remaining a pitiful little creature, born with a harelip and uncertain health, who faltered at the slightest provocation, so that she missed great chunks of the school year and was relegated to the back row, with the undesirables, though she actually adored school. Simone hadn't always been between Thérèse and Pierrette, submitting to their protection and pretending always to appreciate it; no, earlier, when all three first started school, it was often she who took Thérèse or Pierrette by the waist and subjected them to her authority, talking loudly and laughing hard to impress or dominate

10

them; but for two years now, since the day she realized that her two friends were taller, first by half an inch, then a whole inch and more, she had retreated to the centre of their triangle, hunching her shoulders and becoming sensitive to the cold, fishing for hugs and kisses, though deep down she was more inclined to dominate and even tyrannize the group. For Simone was a tyrant in a victim's skin, and like all false victims she exaggerated her inferiority, spitefully savouring her misfortune, even wallowing in it as she dreamed of suddenly being transformed and showing the world her true face, her strength and her frustrated authority. But this morning a good part of her masochism had dissolved in the tears, caresses and compliments of her two friends, and Simone seemed a little taller than usual when they turned the corner of rue Garnier, singing and keeping time by nodding their heads. Simone felt she could smile now without automatically becoming monstrous. Oh, the scar was there, of course, red and visible, but wasn't it just a negligible line where, for so long, there had been the disgusting hole that had ruined her entire childhood? This morning, Simone at last felt ready to grow up: soon the bright new creature would burst out of the cocoon. And people had better watch out. On rue Garnier they walked along the east side of the Saint-Stanislas-de-Kostka church, between Gilford and Saint-Joseph. It was one of the biggest churches in Montreal, proudly displaying its two steeples, its gilt and its famous sky-blue ceiling in the heart of a parish that was mostly very poor, but whose elite, made up of doctors, dentists, notaries and lawyers with prosperous practices along boulevard Saint-Joseph, tried hard to improve its reputation with personal donations, charity balls and excessive, flashy, vulgar fervour. High mass on Sunday at Saint-Stanislas-de-Kostka, with its pomp and over-long sermon, was an excuse for questionable courtesies, twisted civility and, most of all, grotesque pavanes during the course

11

of which decisions were made about the future of the parish, its line of action and its thinking, amid the dry coughs of the Ladies of Sainte-Anne and the booming voices of church-wardens looking for favours. So, while the ordinary people, embarrassed by the lavishness of ten o'clock mass, which made them seem even grubbier, were generally content with the sub-basement, vicars and a perfunctory mass, the wealthy sat imposingly in the midst of their gold, their curé, loud but off-key singing and the rumbling of the organ. Saint-Stanislas-de-Kostka was a wealthy trollop who brazenly revealed her milk-swollen breasts to the well-to-do from boulevard Saint-Joseph, and her square, nondescript ass to the poor from the rest of the parish. Once Albertine, Thérèse's mother, had asked her sister-in-law, the fat woman, why the front of the church was on boulevard Saint-Joseph rather than rue Gilford, and she had replied simply: "If the rich people had to go in the church through the back door like us, they'd stop going!" And Albertine had gone back to her work without arguing. "Maybe that's true ... but they're the ones that give the most." But from that time on, Albertine was often seen in her Sunday best and her Sunday uplift, entering the church through the door on boulevard Saint-Joseph, heels clattering on the white marble floor. Thérèse, Pierrette and Simone had to run to get into the school yard, because it was getting dangerously close to half-past eight and anyone caught on the street after the bell rang to announce the beginning of class would be severely punished. So it was that Simone returned to school running, red and out of breath, after the long absence that everyone had noticed, because for weeks now one part of the famous trio, Thérèse-'n'-Pierrette, had been missing. For that was the name by which all three were known at the École des Saints-Anges. Everyone knew Thérèse-'n'-Pierrette, but no one could have said why Simone's name wasn't in there, too. The answer would likely have been that "Thérèse-

'n'-Pierrette" was easier to say than "Thérèse-'n'-Pierrette-'n'-Simone," but then why wasn't it "Simone-'n'-Pierrette" or "Thérèse-'n'-Simone?" But there it was: Thérèse and Pierrette came first in class, were teachers' pets, adored by the nuns, and Simone was just a negligible quantity, a slowpoke, a mistake, a flaw for which the others would be forgiven the way you forgive a lisp or overly large freckles on a nose. Some of the nuns even maintained that Thérèse and Pierrette were only interested in Simone because they all lived on the same street and went exactly the same way to school. They couldn't accept that a genuine, deep friendship could exist between the elite of grade six – two little girls who were brilliant despite their poverty – and the plebian Simone with all her problems, a puny, ugly child who was like a stain between Thérèse and Pierrette. In fact, they considered Simone to be the lowest of the low: poor *and* hopeless in school. "The whole gang's back together!" Lucienne Boileau came running up, her pigtails flapping against her back as usual. She was somewhat fat and very jolly, and she would have loved to be the fourth wheel of their carriage, but, as Pierrette had put it so well one Saturday afternoon when Lucienne had left her native rue Papineau to try – in vain – to join their games: "Lucienne's okay, but you can't get rid of her!" In fact, Lucienne was what you might call pushy. Without knowing why and to her great sorrow, she systematically lost all her friends because she pushed them to the very brink. She didn't *like* her class-mates, she devoured them. At first they thought she was absolutely charming, but ten minutes later they'd want to strangle her because, in the end, such niceness was inhuman. Even the nuns, though they were very sensitive to flattery, had nicknamed her "ringworm," which shows how clinging she was! Still, she didn't despair, but kept hanging around the trio, probably nurturing a secret hope that one day she'd get her big chance. Lucienne was in Thérèse's

13

class and they often competed for first place in religion or arithmetic, while Simone was in Pierrette's class and was content to admire her friend from afar. Thérèse and Pierrette were never put together; they did too well and they'd have lowered the other classes' averages. At first this separation had upset them greatly, but they quickly realized that it was even more fun to get together at recess or after school, so they bore their pain with patience. None of the three friends could answer Lucienne, because the bell began to ring hysterically and silence fell over the school yard, though it had been so noisy, in less than four seconds. All six hundred little girls who filled the large asphalt square surrounded by a high wooden fence began to run at once toward the various places where their respective classes were to get in line. Simone and Pierrette kissed Thérèse. Lucienne would have liked a kiss, too, but she was pushed away, silently but firmly. Before she set off behind Thérèse, Lucienne suddenly became aware of the great change in Simone's face since the last time she'd seen her. She let out a strident cry that turned six hundred heads. "Holy cow, Harelip isn't deformed any more!" Mother Benoîte des Anges, the Principal, craned her neck slightly, recognized the guilty party and pronounced her sentence in an even voice that carried to the far end of the school yard: "One point off for Six B and a detention for Lucienne Boileau!" Sister Sainte-Philomène, the Six B teacher, looked heavenward while Lucienne, red with shame, took her place in line. Simone was smiling. Now everybody knew! Mother Benoîte des Anges always posted herself at the foot of one of the two enormous wooden staircases that flanked the school at either end, to watch the pupils go up in silent rows that were still noisy, because of the metal edges that protected the stairs from wear. She was a buxom woman, but her cold grey gaze belied whatever generosity might have been hinted at by her nicely rounded body. Your first

14

glimpse of Mother Benoîte's figure suggested a happy, affable woman, easy-going and warm, but once you'd seen those grey eyes, sharp and cold as a butcher knife, you were totally nonplussed and felt betrayed. In fact, this was the effect that Mother Benoîte aimed at: she was quite aware of the contradictory impressions given by her figure and her face, and she willingly made use of them, first gaining her interlocutors' confidence with her good-natured appearance and waddling gait, then disarming them completely with her impassive expression and toneless voice, every word of which was chiselled, perfectly pronounced and projected just enough to alarm or impress. She was, in fact, the terror of the École des Saints-Anges, and the greatest nightmare for each of the six-hundred-odd little girls who attended the school was to find herself alone with her. The children had nicknamed her "Mother Dragon Devil," but she didn't know about that. It was one of the few things she didn't know about life in the École des Saints-Anges: everyone was too afraid of her wrath to give anything away in her presence. In any event, Mother Benoîte des Anges (née Benoîte Trudeau, only daughter of an Outremont physician who had given up his practice as soon as he learned that his daughter was going into the convent: "What's the use of working if your money's going to end up as a dowry for a congregation that's got more power and money than you'll ever have?" and started to drink out of spite), had never been terribly fond of children. In fact, for her the pupils were the least interesting part of the task she'd been assigned when it was her turn to be named Principal, according to the hierarchy of her community. She liked to administer property, to be involved in big business, like the head of a company, but she tended to neglect the human element of her position. She was respected for her undeniable efficiency, but she was not venerated like her predecessor, Mother Saint-Pierre-André, who had left in the hearts of all the teaching nuns and all the grade-nine girls who had known the end of her reign, a blazing memory, firmly rooted and indestructible. Mother Saint-Pierre-André had been adored, while Mother Benoîte des Anges was endured. In the eight years she'd been there, Mother Benoîte had straightened out the school's finances, but in human terms she had been very disappointing. Even her great friendship with Monsignor Bernier, the parish priest, didn't fool anybody: they both loved money and power, and their monthly meetings nearly always ended with some sort of contract or deal, however trivial or insignificant. Priest and Principal traded favours solely for the pleasure of signing agreements, exchanging papers and suspecting each other of lying or cheating. Mother Benoîte had one hand on the metal post at the bottom of the bannister and she nodded slightly to each teacher as she walked past, savouring the fear she could read in the eyes of the nuns, even holding back a smile when an overly impressionable little girl tripped on the stairs. She frowned as Lucienne walked past. The poor child was so frightened, she took the pigtail she'd been fiddling with and nervously clamped it in her mouth. When Six A began to file past, the Principal looked for Simone. Everyone at school knew that Simone had been nicknamed "Harelip," and when Mother Benoîte heard Lucienne utter the name after the bell rang, she'd thought: "So, our little invalid's back .... Now we'll see what that hospital business was all about." Sister Sainte-Catherine, the Six A teacher, bowed her head as she passed the Principal, but Mother Benoîte stopped her by placing a hand on her arm. "Send Simone Côté to see me, Sister Sainte-Catherine. I want her in my office as soon as prayers are over." The whole class heard and their gazes turned toward poor Simone, who hunched down and grabbed a handrail to keep from falling. Pierrette bent over her friend and spoke to her softly, to calm her. Mother Benoîte didn't even raise her voice, but Pierrette started, then began to tremble, too.

"Pierrette Guérin, you may come first in your class, but I'll have you know you are not exempt from the silence that is required in this school! You will say your prayers on your knees this morning, and consider yourself lucky that your punishment isn't more severe!" Sister Sainte-Catherine turned around so abruptly that Mother Benoîte thought it wise to teach her a lesson, too. "Sister Sainte-Catherine, I'll have a word with you as well! Come to my office at recess, if you please!" Sister Sainte-Catherine didn't turn around to indicate that she had heard. The Principal frowned. "That youngster is a mite too insolent for my liking." As usual, Mother Benoîte waited until all the classes were inside the school before going to her office on the second floor, in the very heart of the school. She even waited to hear the droning voices of the pupils reciting their prayers before she closed her door. She sat in her green leather armchair and began to stare at the door. She knew that little Simone Côté would appear at any moment and she wanted the first thing the child would see as she entered the office to be her own gaze, which would penetrate to the depths of her soul.

Pierrette had said her morning prayers on her knees as the Principal had ordered, but she was too upset at what was in store for Simone to be humiliated by such a slight punishment. When a pupil was summoned by Mother Benoîte, all her class-mates were affected; little girls had often been seen coming out of the Principal's office completely undone, in tears, trembling and sometimes even with welts on their hands. The Principal's ruler was sadly famous throughout the parish, but the nun's authority was so categorical that no one had ever dared to intervene. When a pupil walked through her office door, nothing in the world could intercede on her behalf. And yet the teaching nuns were well aware that their Principal didn't know a thing about children, and that what she couldn't settle with affectionate words or judicious advice, she'd try to straighten out with her ruler; but they never butted in or protested. Mother Benoîte des Anges was their superior and they had taken a vow of obedience. Moreover, it was very rare for a nun to send one of her pupils to the Principal's office, though it was done in all other schools, and in the days of Mother Saint-Pierre-André no one had ever complained about the then widespread custom. Now the nuns waited until Mother Benoîte asked to see one of the girls. And when she called a pupil to her office it was always for some obscure question of decorum or money, rarely on a matter of discipline, since for all practical purposes the Principal knew nothing about what went on in the class-rooms. During morning prayers all the girls whose desks were near Simone's had, in turn, cast a glance both sympathetic and curious at their class-mate: sympathetic because of what might happen to her in the Principal's office, and curious because of the great trans-formation that had taken place in her. Harelip had changed, Harelip was almost beautiful! For Simone, the Principal's summons had come like a sledge-hammer blow on her head. So great was her terror that she stood there, frozen, unable to form a single syllable of her prayer, her brain empty of all images but that of Mother Benoîte, hand raised above her head to strike. "The old crow isn't going to punish me just because I had my operation! I don't care if she makes me repeat grade six, as long as she doesn't lay a hand on me!" When the prayer was over, all the pupils sat down at their desks except Simone, who remained standing. "Do I have to go right now, Sister?" Sister Sainte-Catherine slowly came over to Simone and took her by the shoulders. She tried to sound comforting, but her voice held a hint of concern. "Simone, there's no reason to be afraid. The Principal probably wants you to come to her office so she can find out how everything went in the hospital and how you feel now that you're back in school. Your operation was a great success, you know, and you're going to be very pretty when the scar fades." Simone was flushed with pleasure. Sister Sainte-Catherine had often defended her against her nastier classmates, but this was the first time she'd come over and actually touched her. Suddenly Simone felt relieved, and she could feel the other pupils' jealousy increase as the teacher spoke to her. "Everybody's looking at me! And they aren't laughing!" Her fear of being punished had vanished, her terror at having to confront Mother Benoîte evaporated. Simone was exultant. "I'm going to take you to the Principal's office, Simone, and I'll try to explain the wonderful thing that's happened to you. You must realize that Mother Benoîte doesn't know all the pupils, so sometimes we have to explain things to her." A deathly silence settled over the class. This was the first time a nun had taken the initiative of interceding on a pupil's behalf and, as a result, Simone's image had suddenly changed: by this one act, Sister Sainte-Catherine had turned Simone Côté from a dull and insignificant pupil into one who was privileged and respected. Simone was well aware of this and almost hugged the nun, but Sister Sainte-Catherine stepped aside just in time and walked toward the door, opening it slowly. "Come now, Simone, she's waiting for us." Simone left the class-room without a glance behind her, not even at Pierrette, who would have liked to give her a smile of encouragement. Before they went out, the nun turned to face her class. "I hope you'll behave yourselves and keep quiet while we're away." A resounding "Yes, Sister!" rose in the class-room, then silence fell once more as Sister Sainte-Catherine closed the door. A few heads turned toward Pierrette, who was puffed with pride. Her friend, who had been laughed at so often, had just been promoted to the ranks of the privileged, almost to teacher's pet, and no one would ever dare to call her Harelip again.

"Were you afraid she'd get lost?" Mother Benoîte des Anges had got up when she saw Sister Sainte-Catherine, but immediately regretted her petulant outburst: Sister Sainte-Catherine had spoiled her effect on little Simone Côté, which irritated her greatly, but she immediately realized that she shouldn't have shown her displeasure. After all, the Principal of a school ought to be able to get through anything without flinching, without showing the slightest emotion. Mother Benoîte was used to settling everything with her expression and her voice, and when she saw herself standing behind her desk, heart pounding, her hand about to begin shaking, when she heard the peevish question, so unworthy of her, "Were you afraid she'd get lost?" her anger intensified. She had lost control for barely five seconds, yet she felt this was evidence of great weakness. Particularly because Sister Sainte-Catherine hadn't been able to hold back a sardonic little smile that she'd allowed to surface just long enough to be an accusation. To put on a bold front, Mother Benoîte walked around her office and went to the door, something she did only rarely, either to greet an important person or to indicate to a visitor that there was no need to come in, she would follow him into the vast corridor. Very quickly, she regained control and looked daggers at Sister Sainte-Catherine as she approached. Simone, head down, was clutching at Sister Sainte-Catherine's habit and desperately clutching her hand. "And you've left your class unsupervised! I can see the commotion from here! In fact I'm surprised we can't hear it! I said, Sister Sainte-Catherine, that I wanted to see you at recess, at ten minutes to ten: come back here at ten minutes to ten, and not a minute

20

before! Go back to work and try to instil a little knowledge in your thirty-one imbeciles, if you can!" Sister Sainte-Catherine opened her mouth to answer her superior but judged it more prudent to be silent. She lowered her gaze in a gesture of submission, as the laws of the community required, then moved back two steps, leaving Simone between them like some precious article coveted by two sworn enemies. Then she walked away, her veil billowing behind her. "Come in, Simone." This was the first time Simone had entered the school's Holy of Holies. Everything in the Principal's office was intended to impress. Walls, floor and ceiling, all panelled in the same varnished wood, made the room so dark that even the light from a fairly big window wasn't enough to make people feel comfortable. The electric lights were always on (a powerful white porcelain ceiling fixture shed a pallid illumination that made people look sick), which often made the most courageous nuns say that for a principal with a reputation for being tight-fisted, Mother Benoîte was very generous when it came to her own office. But the many visitors who came to the school every day never failed to be impressed by the liberality that led them to think the Principal was a candid woman with nothing to hide, who lived permanently in a harsh light that made lying impossible. Thus the Principal could comfortably lie and shamelessly bamboozle, while her victims were blissfully unaware. In the very middle of the room sat imposingly a mahogany monster of sorts that served as a desk for Mother Benoîte, but could equally well have passed for a rich man's tomb. It took up a good third of the floor space, leaving only a cramped area between window and door for visitors to sit in. Moreover, in addition, the chair for them was small and hard, and not at all conducive to laziness or outpourings. Only Monsignor Bernier was entitled to a little more consideration: when he came to call, the Principal gave up her green leather armchair and humbly took the visitor's chair, a gesture that had the good fortune to flatter the priest and make him feel as much at home here as in his own presbytery. (Of course Mother Benoîte humbled herself before her priest the better to bring him to heel and to thwart him without his noticing.) Simone, then, entered the cenacle holding her breath, her eyes as big as soup-plates. She had heard so much about this place and the tortures that were inflicted in it that she almost expected to see metal rings on the walls, reddened with blood, a panoply of whips and daggers and, close to the window, a medieval wooden platform from which the Principal would dispense thwacks of her ruler and other forms of torture as passers-by looked on. She stood stiff and pale in front of the Principal's desk, prepared for the sky to fall on her head in the form of a nun driven mad by rage, who would spank her all over, like a big black bird hurling itself on its prey with furious swoops of its wings. But Mother Benoîte des Anges, sitting calmly in her chair, was scrutinizing Simone's face. She finally spoke, in the flat voice out of the nightmares of the six hundred little girls she enjoyed terrifying because she didn't understand them. "So that's it. Your little trip to the hospital was for *aesthetic* reasons!" Simone had never heard the word and thought it sounded like some particularly ugly disease, probably contagious and certainly fatal. "No, Sister, that wasn't what I had .... I just had a harelip and they fixed it." Her voice trembled, her eyes were brimming and a bit of snot was beginning to drip from her nostrils. "Blow your nose!" Simone started looking desperately for her handkerchief, couldn't find it and, feeling that the situation was becoming catastrophic, wiped her nose on her sleeve, thereby increasing Mother Benoîte's cold rage. "You dare to appear before your class with nasal mucus on your sleeve! And you dare to stand in front of me with your nose running!" She held out her own handkerchief to the little girl, turning her face toward the window. "Here, blow your nose and wipe your eyes! And tell your mother to wash it. Thoroughly! By itself! I don't want my personal things mixed up with your family's!" Simone had no alternative but to accept. She blew her nose for a long time, sobbing like a child who has just been wrongly punished. Then she stuffed the handkerchief in her pocket and felt it against her thigh like a burn. Mother Benoîte looked again at Simone's face, where the scar she had noticed earlier had turned redder during the little girl's outburst. "Well now, Mademoiselle Simone Côté, you're too poor to subscribe to *L'Estudiante*, but not so poor as to prevent you from undergoing a surgical procedure that was most assuredly useless and quite likely very costly." Simone had some trouble understanding the nun. The Principal's words weren't part of her vocabulary, and every time she heard an unfamiliar expression she caught herself wondering how her mother would pronounce it, or what simpler word she would have used. Mother Benoîte, who considered the pupils in her school frightfully ignorant and astonishingly lacking in curiosity, was well aware of this and almost enjoyed watching Simone reflect and attempt to translate her remarks into her own street talk. "At the beginning of the school year, we ask each of you for two dollars for your subscription to *L'Estudiante*, and you told us that your parents were too destitute. And we believed you! We gave you charity all year and now you come back, on the eve of final exams, after a long and suspect absence, with a new mouth that must have cost a fortune! What game are you playing, Simone Côté?" Simone started. Such an abrupt change of subject surprised her. In the midst of a pack of nonsense here was the Principal asking her about games! She pressed her hands against her heart and gathered all her strength before replying. "Well, my favourite game is ordinary skipping, but Thérèse and Pierrette, they'd rather play double Dutch." Mother Benoîte sprang to her feet, pale with rage, and Simone thought she'd had it, the ceiling was about to collapse around her. "Leave this room immediately, you insolent child! Get out of my sight before I choke you! Brazen hussy! I'm calling your mother. We'll see if the poor ignorant inhabitants of rue Fabre can laugh at a school Principal! Unless you bring the two dollars you owe us this very afternoon, you won't set foot in this school again! Do you understand? And you'll write your final exams some other year!" Mother Benoîte des Anges suddenly noticed that for a few moments now Simone had been staring fixedly, and she was afraid the child was about to have a fit. She quickly circled her office and ran to the door to call for help. Then she stopped suddenly, aghast. A thread of urine was running down Simone's leg and forming a puddle that was spreading over the waxed floor. Mother Benoîte ran out, screaming. "Sister Saint-Georges! Sister Saint-Georges! There's piss in my office!" Simone wanted to die. And as she fainted she thought she could see angels coming toward her with a gentle rustling of wings.

"If you ask me, she ate her!" Thérèse and Pierrette had met at recess, and Pierrette had just told her friend that Simone hadn't come back from the Principal's office. As usual, fat Lucienne had tried to worm her way into their conversation, but Thérèse put her in her place with a resounding "Beat it, creep, don't you know when you aren't wanted!" that left her somewhat stupefied. Usually, when she was brushed off, it was done with a certain tact, but this time .... Lucienne had gone away, head drooping, sucking on the end of her pigtail, and her big blue bovine eyes a little damper than usual. Thérèse and Pierrette had taken refuge on the steps of one of the cement staircases in the school yard. "You think she kept her inside to punish her?" Thérèse did up her garter, muttering, "What for? Simone couldn't have done anything to deserve a punishment yet, she just came back to school this morning!" Pierrette sighed. "Maybe Mother Dragon Devil's taking her around the school to show off her new mouth ...." "She'd've come out at recess. Besides, since when does Mother Dragon Devil care about us kids? She couldn't care less about anybody .... No, I'm telling you, there's some mystery going on in that office!" "Don't scare me like that, Thérèse, if I ever have to go there I'll just die!" "I've got half a mind to go and look." "Don't! If they catch you we'll never see you again, and I'll be all alone!" Pierrette huddled against her friend, who put an arm around her waist. "Cut it out, Pierrette, you know you shouldn't believe everything I say. You know I like to say scary things! We'll have to wait till noon, then we'll find out just what happened." That Monday morning the skipping ropes had really let loose in the school yard. You could hear skipping songs, loudly proclaimed, punctuated by the rhythmic ringing of heels with metal lifts or "One, two, button my shoe, three four, shut the door" so badly distorted that what came out of the little girls' mouths had no relation to the English language and sounded more or less like "One two, botte, émail, chou, tree fore, chat dehors." No one really knew where this English game came from or how it had reached the École des Saints-Anges, but it happened to be the most popular game at recess and the little girls threw themselves into it passionately, jumping on both feet or one at a time, arms crossed or raised above their heads, eyes open or shut, pigtails flapping against their backs and skirts flying in the wind. The teaching nuns would pass among the groups of skippers, distributing smiles and encouragement, or threatening detentions to pupils who seemed overtired or too out of breath. Thérèse leaned over toward Pierrette. "Sister Sainte-Catherine isn't out yet either." "I'm telling you, Mother Dragon Devil's going to eat them alive!" Despite their concern, they couldn't help bursting out laughing. Lucienne, utterly without pride, took

advantage of their outburst to try a comeback. She sat down
beside Pierrette, who scared her less, and foolishly joined in
their giggling, though she didn't have the faintest idea what
had brought it on. Her laughter rang false as she slapped her
thighs hard enough to redden the skin. Thérèse abruptly
stopped laughing and looked daggers at her. "Phony! You
don't even know what you're laughing at! Fat head! Spy!"
Lucienne recoiled at the insult. "Me a spy!" Thérèse got up,
walked around Pierrette and came and stood right in front
of Lucienne, who started to pout like a baby. "If you aren't a
spy you're just a tattle-tale! How come you waited till *after*
the bell to yell that Simone wasn't deformed any more, eh?
You wanted everybody to hear you, didn't you? You spy on
everybody and then you tell on them, you double-crosser!"
She suddenly started to hit Lucienne, pulling her braids so
hard that even Pierrette, who knew her well, was amazed.
Lucienne immediately started to scream like a stuck pig
when they heard the bell ring. All the skipping-ropes
stopped. The little girls began to group themselves by class.
But Thérèse went on hitting Lucienne, screaming, "There!
Get out! More! You like it when everybody can hear you?
Well then, yell your head off, fatso, go on!" Pierrette tried
hard to calm Thérèse down but, carried away by her fury,
her friend pushed her away, calling her a scaredy-cat. It was
a fine free-for-all. A few nuns joined the fray to halt the
battle, and it took four of them to separate the two little
girls. Lucienne was crying her heart out. Thérèse was so
furious she seemed possessed. Sister Sainte-Philomène,
Thérèse and Lucienne's teacher, an immense red-faced
woman, who had a lot of trouble hiding her enormous
breasts under her habit, was pale with rage. She picked
Thérèse up by the scruff of the neck and started to shake
her the way you shake a tree to bring down fruit. "To the
Principal's office! This minute! And you, Lucienne, pull
down your skirt, you're indecent!" Before Thérèse went in-

side the school, she turned to Pierrette, who hadn't budged, and said, "We're still going to find out .... If I don't come back, you'll know she had me for dessert!" Thérèse's anger had suddenly evaporated and she went off to the Principal's office, hopping.

Sister Sainte-Catherine had found her Principal in a deplorable state. She'd never seen her like that and thought at first that Mother Benoîte had had an attack. The older woman was prostrate in her chair, staring vacantly, white hands flat on her ink-stained blotter. She seemed broken, or in shock from some dreadful revelation or divine apparition. At first the Principal didn't seem to remember why she had called Sister Sainte-Catherine; she hemmed and hawed, getting bogged down in generalities and obscure remarks, then finally shook off her lethargy and emerged from her catalepsy more furious than ever (first for being caught out in her weak state, or rather on the defensive instead of on the attack, as her image required, and then, most of all, for getting flustered at the crass ignorance and stupidity of a poor little girl who, after all, had only been trying to answer her questions). Mother Benoîte des Anges was even more enraged because Sister Sainte-Catherine was wearing a smile – half-mocking and half-docile – that she found disconcerting. Never had a nun dared to show her a lack of respect, but Mother Benoîte sensed that the Six A teacher was about to make some move that would take both of them very far, perhaps to the labyrinth of mortal hatred, where no low blow is forbidden and only the crushing of one of the two parties can settle their differences. Mother Benoîte wasn't prepared to put up with any aggression, no matter how benign, while Sister Sainte-Catherine, for her part, felt an irresistible urge to attack, for the sheer pleasure

27

of provocation, of setting off a crisis that would push them both in the direction of out-and-out war. The laws of communal life were such that the smallest squabble, the slightest misunderstanding or the most inane conflict quickly took on exaggerated proportions, demanding to be lanced like an overripe boil, to be brought to a conclusion as if the fate of the world depended on it, and even to be waved like a banner, dividing the community into enemy camps, giving rise to other crises and new hatreds, sometimes dragging on for years, then finally overcome by forgetfulness – but never indifference, the effect always ready to burgeon and reproduce, but the cause buried in some hidden corner of memory. (For instance, if anyone had asked Sister Saint-Georges, who had served as portress at the École des Saints-Anges for nearly thirty years, why she hated Sister Sainte-Philomène, the Six B teacher, so much, she wouldn't have been able to say. Yet it was Sister Sainte-Philomène who, one day when the portress had refused to open the front door for her and made her walk around to the back like everyone else, had given her the nickname "Sister Clump Foot," which had stuck and made her the laughing-stock of the parish. Sister Clump Foot suffered daily from this gibe that described her so well, she whose work consisted, despite her severely disabled left leg, of emerging from a sort of dark cell pompously baptized "the portress's lodge" whenever a visitor appeared at the door of the École des Saints-Anges, then limp down thirteen steps (those damn thirteen steps she'd gladly have smashed with an axe, so much had she always hated her task) to pick up the caller's calling-card, the piece of information or the magic paper that would turn her all smiles or cold as ice, unctuous and servile or wild and intractable, with the intruder. When Sister Saint-Georges and Sister Sainte-Philomène met in the hall, they avoided each other's eyes, turned their heads and sometimes even sighed extravagantly, but neither one could have said why. They had forgotten. And Sister Saint-Georges continued to limp down her stairs, shoulders sagging under the insult concocted by her one-time cherished friend who had become her *bête noire*, her torturer.) So keen were the rivalries and so vicious, at times, the vengeance within the École des Saints-Anges, that when Sister Sainte-Catherine first arrived they had scared her. At the Mother House, where she had been trained to become a useful tool, dedicated and willing, life had seemed like Paradise to the pious, delicate girl who had entered the community a little because she thought she'd heard the call of her God and a lot because she was afraid of the world. She and the other girls had been protected, loved, nourished physically and intellectually as they probably never had been at home, and communal life had seemed to them the ideal refuge for broken hearts, fragile, troubled dispositions or the walking wounded who formed the majority of them. They had been warned, though, that life in the schools where their order worked would be very different, much harder, in any case, than the sort of warm, comfortable cocoon of the Mother House, but Sister Sainte-Catherine, who at the time was still called Catherine Valiquette, was so anxious to dedicate herself body and soul to teaching, she'd thought that the gratitude and affection of the little girls on whom she would bestow all her knowledge, with love and even with passion, would be enough to make up for the snags and hitches of everyday life, no matter how they might hurt or smart. But she hadn't counted on the shrewish dispositions, the intrusive lack of consideration, the belligerence of certain nuns who, having left the Mother House years before and to a degree lost any illusions they might have had about the firmness or relevance of their vocations, had become greatly hardened, forming in every school a nucleus of ambitious, squabbling women whose first task was theoretically to teach, in spite of everything, the often indifferent and always aggressive little girls who filled their class-rooms all year long, never complaining and humbly thanking God, but whose chief concern had soon become winning over the influential nuns by any means they could – flattery as much as false affection, hypocritical submission as much as denunciation or outright lies – in order to supplant them later, crush them mercilessly like ciphers they could simply ignore. Sister Sainte-Catherine had never wanted to use these ridiculous and childish means to climb the ladder of her community's hierarchy and she often found herself alone, confronting the jealousy, envy and dishonesty of her fellow nuns, who sensed that they had no hold on her, no way to destroy her, because she kept herself, in a way, outside their circle of pitiful plotting and laughable conspiracies. She was there to teach and she passionately loved her pupils, who returned her love, for they were aware of the openness and rectitude of their teacher's dedication. But that morning, in the office of the Principal, whose every gesture and nearly every breath she had been condemning for eight years, enduring without a sigh of impatience her cold rages, flagrant unfairness and insulting pettiness, for the first time Sister Sainte-Catherine felt like lashing out or resisting to the end the attack that the Principal had been preparing for some time (it was very clear from the understanding smiles she had spotted on the lips of Mother Benoîte's favourites). "Simone Côté hasn't come back to class, Mother ...." "Simone Côté fainted and went home, Sister Sainte-Catherine. Sister Saint-Georges was kind enough to take her right to her door." "Simone is a delicate child ...." "Simone is an impertinent child, who laughs in our faces behind those saintly airs of hers." "You don't know her." "That's enough! I'm the one who chooses the topics to be discussed in this office, Sister Sainte-Catherine, and don't you forget it!" Sister Sainte-Catherine held back an impatient sigh. The Principal was absent-mindedly drumming her desk blotter with her fingertips. "My word, you'd almost think you were taking me for a liar!" "I don't take you for a liar, Mother Benoîte, but you have an enormous task here and it's natural that you don't know *all* the pupils in the school." "I may not know *all* the pupils in the school well, but I know Simone Côté well enough to be aware of what to do with her. I've been watching her walk around with her deformity for several years now and I reached my verdict about her a long time ago, the little demon: it's obvious that she's carrying around a huge inferiority complex, which has turned her into a difficult student, undisciplined, almost undesirable ...." "Your psychology is very rudimentary, Mother Benoîte. The truth about Simone Côté is a little more complicated." Mother Benoîte pounded her blotter with her fist, so hard that Sister Sainte-Catherine jumped, surprised that the Principal was so quick to anger. "Rudimentary!" Two big blue veins, almost obscene, which Sister Sainte-Catherine had never seen before, appeared on Mother Benoîte's forehead and her face turned a rather disturbing brick-red colour. "You, a grade-six teacher, come and tell me that my psychology is rudimentary!" "What I meant was ...." "Be quiet! You'll only make matters worse! You will answer when I ask you a question!" Mother Benoîte was standing now, leaning over her blotter so that Sister Sainte-Catherine could smell her suspect breath, a very disagreeable mixture of decayed teeth and cheap toothpaste. "Mother Benoîte, you're very upset ...." Sister Sainte-Catherine had spoken in an even tone that sounded strangely like Mother Benoîte herself when she wanted to put off a particularly formidable opponent. Sister Sainte-Catherine's imitation didn't escape the Principal, who was stunned for a moment, breathing hard and sweating under the layered fabric of her habit. "Are you trying to tell me what to do?" Mother Benoîte had spoken in an almost normal voice, in which a bit of the white rage that had shaken her entire being still peeked through. "Far be it for me to tell you what to do, Mother Benoîte, but you've often told us that it's useless, perhaps even dangerous, for those responsible for souls, like us, to get upset." "You *are* telling me what to do! This is the limit!" Mother Benoîte des Anges sat down slowly and forced herself to breathe deeply, to calm the storm that was shaking her from the solar plexus to the brain, literally making her spinal column shudder and her limbs tremble. It was the first time she had let her anger show like this and the second time in an hour that she'd lost control in front of someone. Her humiliation was so bitter that two big tears, which she couldn't control, came to her eyes. Sister Sainte-Catherine was so amazed she recoiled. Mother Benoîte des Anges was crying! So this insensitive woman had managed to collect enough moisture at the bottom of her withered heart to produce the two droplets running down her neck, soon to disappear inside her collar! Or was it, rather, a new tactic? Emotional blackmail? A trick to make her give in, so the Principal would have time to get a grip on herself, then pounce and knock her out with one well-aimed punch? Sister Sainte-Catherine decided to launch her attack right away, before it was too late, to make the most of her advantage, consolidate her position and thereby ensure herself of victory – a little quick and much too easy, perhaps, but delightful all the same! She pressed her thighs against the edge of the desk and continued to speak in the tone she had borrowed from her Principal, the sweetness of which she was beginning to taste. "When we have problems with our pupils, Mother Benoîte, we often settle them ourselves without calling on you, and you should realize that it's natural for us not to want you to get involved. You've never been a teacher and you don't know what the atmosphere in a classroom is like, the laws and the sorrows, the affection and joy and intimacy. You're an excellent administrator, Mother Benoîte, you've spent your whole life at work in the community's offices because of the great gift the Lord has granted you, and our school is tremendously grateful for everything you've done over the past eight years to consolidate its financial situation. But you don't know anything about child psychology and you should have enough humility to admit it, and leave it to us, whose duty it is to look after the children for whom we're responsible." The explosion was so violent and sudden that Sister Sainte-Catherine winced as if she'd received an electric shock. In less than half a second Mother Benoîte's face was close to hers and the Principal, leaning across her desk once more, was clutching the nun's shoulders as if to nail her to the wall, her finger-nails digging right through the fabric of her habit and into her skin. The smell of decayed teeth and useless toothpaste now filled Sister Sainte-Catherine's entire body, and she wanted to vomit in disgust. "Sister Sainte-Catherine! Not only have you been disregarding my recommendations and even my orders for almost eight years, not only do you turn up your nose at every new regulation I introduce into the life of this school, and not only do you try to turn the new nuns who arrive at the beginning of each school year against me, now you dare to stand there and preach to me! I've put up with your sighs and your sarcasm long enough, my girl, it's time for harsh measures! I banish you – and the word 'banish' is none too strong – I banish you from this school for as long as I myself am here. And this very day I'm going to write a report about you that will close the doors of the easy, peaceful schools in this part of town to you forever! I promise you that next year you'll be in one of the most difficult schools in this city, where you'll learn to your cost the joys of discipline and obedience! Never has anyone put me in the state I'm in right now, and I want you out of my sight so I can forget this temper – forever! Pack your bag immediately. I want you on the bus to the Mother House on the stroke of noon, with the letter I'm going to write for you to take in person to Mother Notre-Dame du Rosaire!" She sat down again as abruptly as she'd got up, and Sister Sainte-Catherine lost her balance somewhat and stumbled forward, catching herself just in time to keep from falling on her face right on the Principal's desk. Despite her nausea, Sister Sainte-Catherine decided to bring out her last shred of argument – flimsy, no doubt, but virtually unassailable. She slowly straightened her coif, which had slid onto her forehead, and smoothed her veil over her shoulders. She managed to gather enough courage to assume the same tone she had used earlier. "You're forgetting, Mother Benoîte, that Corpus Christi is this Thursday, and that I'm responsible for the repository." Mother Benoîte des Anges, flabbergasted, stood rooted to the spot, for two long minutes, mouth agape, eyes locked with Sister Sainte-Catherine's, who saw a whole range of emotions – surprise, indignation, contempt and, most of all, hatred – cross the Principal's face. Then Mother Benoîte noisily cleared her throat, picking up a piece of paper to her right, on which she began to scrawl furiously. She spoke to Sister Sainte-Catherine without looking up. "Very well, I'll give you until Friday morning. And I don't care how you do it, but I want that repository to be the most beautiful you can manage – because it's certainly going to be your last!" She had spoken, this time, in her usual fine voice. Sister Sainte-Catherine snickered as she left the office.

When Sister Sainte-Catherine had been invited to take charge of the repository five years earlier, she refused at first, not wanting to draw attention to herself or, even more, to incur Mother Benoîte's wrath. Besides, for a long time the repository had been the preserve of Sister Saint-Jean-Chrysostome, who had just perished in an absurd streetcar accident (with their usual tact the newspapers had headlined the event "Nun sliced in half" and "Saint crushed to death") and was still being mourned. Sister Saint-Jean-Chrysostome had turned the Saint-Stanislas parish repository into an object of curiosity and admiration that people came from every corner of Montreal to gaze at – alone, with the family, in groups, by bus. As the school was located right across the street from the church, Sister Saint-Jean-Chrysostome got the idea of moving the repository, which had always been set up on the steps of the sanctuary, to the huge cement staircase leading to Sister Clump Foot's door. That way, the repository would face the church instead of turning its back on it and, as Sister Saint-Jean-Chrysostome, in her exaltation, had put it so well, "The Blessed Virgin will be able to wave to Saint Stanislas instead of just showing him her halo." The idea was judged to be excellent, and Sister Saint-Jean-Chrysostome had set to work with the energy that would soon be legendary. Her first repository had cost the parish dearly and Monsignor Bernier had raised his hands in horror, but its naïve splendour, and its excesses, which came perilously close to vulgarity, had been so popular that even the newspapers talked about it, vindicating this parish that wasn't afraid to glorify its great love for God right on boulevard Saint-Joseph and allow its joy in celebrating Him to shine forth in a way that was original and colourful, but still respectful. The *curé* had kept silent, then, and accepted with a humble smile the compliments that rained down on him from the four corners of the province. He had even declared to a reporter from *Le Canada*: "This parish is rich only in its love of God," which quickly became a favourite quotation of every *curé* in Montreal when it was time to beg for money to reconstruct some corner of a church or add a third marble fireplace to an already outrageously lavish presbytery. In two or three years, then, Sister Saint-Jean-Chrysostome's repository had become the star attraction of the Corpus Christi celebrations on the Island of Montreal. As a result, the École des Saints-Anges, during the first week of June – from Monday morning till Thursday night, the night of the famous procession at the end of which the *curé* would place the monstrance in the heart of the garish, flashy repository after he had criss-crossed the streets of the parish amid prayers, songs and papal banners – every year became a humming hive, of which the queen bee, Sister Saint-Jean-Chrysostome, huge, glowing, puffing and sputtering, directed its fate with an unsystematic and rather uncontrolled hand. Anarchy raced through the corridors and classrooms full of little girls making silver paper chains and nuns concocting new make-up for the statue of the Blessed Virgin or cutting and sewing dresses of taffeta and *point-d'esprit* for ten-year-old future angels who, for nearly four hours, would pretend to be blowing into papier-mâché trumpets coated with silver dust or coloured sequins. Forgotten were the fast-approaching final exams that until then had made hearts pound, and the absurd recitations that exhausted their brains, the five-hundred-odd bits of nonsense in the catechism of which they were supposed to know by heart all the answers and all the questions, by number ("Simone Côté, number 302!" "Uhhh." "You will write it out twelve times in capital letters and twelve times in small letters! And try and understand it, if you're capable of that!"), put off till next week the arduous and ridiculous compositions ("Imagine that you're in Heaven and your Father is speaking to you." "My father? What father? The good Lord? Poppa? If it's poppa it's the first time I saw it with a capital; and if it's the good Lord, it's the first time he ever lowered himself to talk to me. You usually have to go through the Blessed Virgin or Saint Jean-Baptiste or Saint Stanislas de Kostka even though nobody knows him, but they say he's nice anyway. Holy cow! Well, I guess I'll write about both of them.") and, most of all, consigned to oblivion were all laws, rules, reprimands and reproaches: this was a holiday and everyone was to make the most of it! Which they did, and then some. On the great day itself, the free-for-all reached its peak. As the repository went up, ever bigger, ever brighter, the inside of the École des Saints-Anges became a sort of battlefield where still-unfinished statues lay in the corridor, representing the dead, and where partly costumed children, dying of stage fright, acted as exhausted soldiers, dreaming that the assault is over and their mothers are tucking them in, saying softly, "It was lovely, but it wore me out!" And when the time came to take their places at the dazzling repository, the painted saints, the angels with their tin-foil haloes, the girl who came first in catechism dressed up as the Virgin Mary and the flower-girls already red with exhaustion all had to pee and the bathroom was filled with agitated youngsters trying not to soil their lovely costumes or break their wooden wings that were too wide for the cubicles and had to be taken off at top speed and leaned against the porcelain sinks. There was something profoundly pagan about Sister Saint-Jean-Chrysostome's much-admired repository that no one seemed to notice, but which nonetheless gave this very religious celebration a faint after-taste of latent orgy or of painted children for sale. Only Dr. Sanregret had remarked one day to Ti-Lou, the she-wolf of Ottawa, whom he'd brought to watch the procession and the ceremony that followed it, "There's something sexual about this masquerade that amazes me every year. Look at those children standing there, available, forced to pose and be admired for hours, on the verge of a trance. Really, the unconscious is the mother of all religious ceremonies." To which Ti-Lou replied, in her fine affected English accent: "At my place on rue Roberts in Ottawa, it was a repository all year long!" Sister Sainte-Catherine had hesitated for a long time, then, before taking on the back-breaking inheritance of Sister Saint-Jean-Chrysostome. Especially because Mother Benoîte des Anges, who already wasn't particularly fond of her, preferring the pale and indolent Sister

37

Sainte-Thérèse de l'Enfant-Jésus, who would certainly never take any initiative, but would be content with a faithful reproduction, year after year, an exact replica of Sister Saint-Jean-Chrysostome's festivities. But Sister Sainte-Thérèse had, in a way, withdrawn her own candidacy by falling sick (malicious gossip maintained it was a diplomatic illness: Sister Sainte-Thérèse was certainly too timorous to come right out and tell the Principal that she didn't want the responsibility and had probably preferred to "take sick," bouncing back as soon as Sister Saint-Jean-Chrysostome's successor was named) and Sister Sainte-Catherine was the only one left in the running. But she wasn't interested either in turning the school upside-down for the first week of June every year, or offering the parish a spectacle she considered somewhat disturbing and questionable. But Mother Benoîte, seeing that Sister Sainte-Catherine was definitely going to refuse out of sheer pigheadedness, decided one morning to impose this task on the Six A teacher, and took great pleasure in announcing the news herself, mirthful behind her cold mask. So then Sister Sainte-Catherine had thrown herself with all the energy of her despair into what she called "the Santa-Claus-on-High parade," but to her great surprise she found she quite enjoyed it, enjoyed sticking her hands into the naïveté of Catholic beliefs and their undeniably good-natured charm, juggling with these simple, almost violent images that were thrown to the populace to keep it on the "straight and narrow," discovering without really admitting it the delights of power as she played to perfection her role of little parish dictator. But under her rule, Corpus Christi had nonetheless become somewhat more civilized: where Sister Saint-Jean-Chrysostome had always been rather muddle-headed, turning the repository into a shambles of anarchic disorganization, Sister Sainte-Catherine, using exactly the same elements, had built on the steps of the École des Saints-Anges a moderate and controlled sort of picture-book that had first surprised the parishioners, then captivated them with its clearer, more polished appearance. Sister Sainte-Catherine was also far calmer than her predecessor, and under her command the preparatory week for Corpus Christi passed joyously rather than in a state of nerves. The preparations were about to begin this Monday, June first, 1942, and Sister Sainte-Catherine, entirely absorbed in her own preoccupations, went back into her class, forgetting almost immediately what had just taken place in the Principal's office.

"I got in a fight in the school yard." Thérèse, hands behind her back, was shuffling from one foot to the other. Sister Clump Foot looked her up and down, as if searching for the vestiges of the squabble that she had missed. "You couldn't have fought very hard, you aren't even dirty." "I beat up Lucienne Boileau. She didn't put up much of a fight." Sister Saint-Georges frowned. "What grade are you in?" "Six B, Sister." "Grade six is giving us plenty of headaches this morning! Who sent you, Sister Sainte-Philomène?" "Yes." "She's big enough to punish you herself!" Sister Clump Foot was the only nun in the community who called the children "tu." Her superiors had tried hard to break her of this unfortunate habit, but in vain. (They'd told her it wasn't polite, to which she replied, "Those girls aren't polite to me so I don't see why I should bend over backwards to call them 'vous'"; then she'd been given to understand that it gave the community a bad image and she laughed. "I'd rather call them tu and have some respect for them than say vous and beat them up – like some people I know! Don't blame me if the community's got a bad image!") Besides, Sister Saint-Georges had never shed her east-end Montreal accent, which had the good fortune of exasperating Mother Benoîte des Anges, who often told her, "By disfiguring our language, Sister Saint-Georges, you also disfigure our habit!" But Sister Clump Foot was stubborn and merely smiled, shrugging. She was the eldest of the nuns at the École des Saints-Anges and, though she had never taught (she had been a cook's helper in the Mother House before becoming a portress), she enjoyed the affection of the students, who heard from her alone the slang that was their familiar language. The little girls loved it when Sister Clump Foot called them "*tu*," thinking of her as an auntie who had turned out badly. Thérèse couldn't hold back a smile as she listened to Sister Saint-Georges talk about Sister Sainte-Philomène. Everyone at the school knew about the war that had been raging between the two nuns for so long, and they had a lot of fun with it. "You're going to be chewed out by the Principal and you've still got the heart to smile?" "That's 'cause I'm nervous." "I wouldn't want to be in your shoes, little girl! Mother Benoîte's had enough trouble already today, she won't be thrilled to have you turn up out of the blue." At that moment the Principal's door opened and Mother Benoîte des Anges strode across the lobby that separated her office from Sister Saint-Georges's. With one arm she pushed aside Thérèse, who was still standing in the doorway, rooted to the spot, and held out an envelope to the portress. "This letter must leave for the Mother House immediately, Sister Saint-Georges. If you can't find anyone else to deliver it, go yourself. It's urgent." She was about to go back into her office when she seemed to become aware of Thérèse's presence. "And what do you think you're doing there?" Thérèse, her eyes like saucers, lips pursed until they were white, didn't move. Mother Benoîte turned toward Sister Saint-Georges. "Take her back to her class before she makes a mess like her

friend." "She was coming to see you, Mother Benoîte." "Very
well, she's seen me, that's quite enough!" Mother Benoîte
rushed across the landing, which reeked of wax and disin-
fectant and shut her office door behind her. Thérèse swallowed, making a rather disagreeable gulping sound that
made Sister Saint-Georges smile. "You're a lucky girl! It isn't
often a girl gets to keep her hands behind her back like you
just did!" Sister Clump Foot's cell also served as an antechamber to the Principal's office. Anyone intending to call
on Mother Benoîte had to speak first to Sister Saint-Georges,
who knew all her comings and goings, her moods and her
tastes, and so was able to judge if such-and-such a problem
or such-and-such a person was worth disturbing her for, or if
it wouldn't be better to put it off till later. Sister Saint-
Georges was an excellent watch-dog and she screened the
Principal's callers very effectively. In fact, that was why
Mother Benoîte preferred to keep her where she was, rather
than get rid of her, as she had originally intended. Sister
Clump Foot took from a pigeon-hole a small green slip already stamped with the Principal's initials and signed it.
"You tell Sister Sainte-Philomène you saw the Principal and
she hit the roof ...." "That'd be a lie." "You saw her, didn't
you?" "I guess so." "Well, that's the main thing .... She hit the
roof before she saw you, but she did it!" She held out the
note to Thérèse, who took it, fearfully. "Did she hit the roof
on account of Simone?" Sister Clump Foot looked at Thérèse
for a long time before answering. "Shut the door behind
you." Thérèse obeyed. "Worried about your friend, eh?"
Thérèse nodded. "You can stop worrying, she went home.
She'll be back after lunch." "Was she sick?" "Well – nervous.
But she'll be okay. I took her home to her mother myself."
The gratitude she could read in Thérèse's eyes made Sister
Saint-Georges's heart turn over. "That operation helped her,
eh?" "Yes, she's going to be pretty now." "That's right, she's

going to be pretty." Thérèse left, at a run. Sister Saint-Georges picked up the envelope the Principal had left for her and limped out of her office.

Simone was shaking like a frightened rabbit. Her mother was bending over her, applying cold compresses to her forehead, changing them as soon as they were no longer cool. "Tell momma what happened. Momma won't get mad, honest!" But Simone was choking so much that nothing could come out of her throat except plaintive little growls that reminded Charlotte Côté of a dog she'd had as a child, which had died in her arms. "Tell me, sweetheart ... did somebody hurt you? Did you do anything you weren't supposed to?" When Sister Saint-Georges rang the bell, Charlotte Côté, spotting her through the lace curtains, thought at first that the nuns were canvassing yet again to raise money for one of their too numerous works of charity. (Nearly every month Simone would come home with a little tin box that had to be filled with coins to buy and baptize little Chinese children, or a blue or green envelope in which you were supposed to slip a banknote to buy and baptize little Africans, or some insignificant little thing made, knit or crocheted by the nuns to buy and baptize little Malaysians or little Japanese or little Indochinese. Inevitably, Ulric Côté would get on his high horse and scream, "How come those old maids never ask anybody to fill up empty pork-and-beans cans to baptize little French Canadians and give them a meal of pigs' feet stew, *tabarnac*! We haven't got two cents to rub together, but they expect us to give what we've got to people we'll never set eyes on! We'll fatten them like pigs, and twenty-five or thirty years from now they'll shit in our face! Not on your life! You tell that old maid your father hasn't got one red cent for people with faces as yellow as lemons

42

or black as the devil! Do I go begging from them?" Simone always returned to school with her little box empty, her little envelope empty, or her small objects unsold, and there was always someone who'd say spitefully, "The Côté's are always poor! If the father didn't drink so much beer his family might have enough to eat and a few cents left over for charity." Simone, too embarrassed to cite her father's reasons, would put up with it, swallowing her tears.) But when Charlotte saw Simone trembling, her nose running, by the side of the crippled nun, she rushed to the stairs and opened the door, shouting, "What happened?" Sister Clump Foot said nothing, merely pushed Simone toward her mother, and turned her back. Charlotte then came out on the balcony. "You could at least tell me what's wrong with my child! You bring her to me in little bits and then you take off as if you couldn't care less!" Sister Clump Foot stopped half-way down the outside stairs and turned to Charlotte. "Call the Principal. I don't know a thing. Excuse me." Charlotte took Simone in her arms, and ran up the inside staircase and into the house, cursing. Simone's dress was still wet, and Charlotte thought the poor child must have wet her pants, unable to hold it back, which had happened before and the nuns had sent her home to change. But when she realized that Simone couldn't even talk, as if she was over-whelmed by some strong emotion, she understood that something more serious had happened. She undressed her daughter, washed her in a big basin of warm water, singing the lullaby she'd loved so much as a baby, then laid her in her own bed, a rare treat that the little girl didn't even seem to appreciate. "Your throat must feel better now, Simone, you've been home for nearly an hour now. Try and talk, quietly .... At least try, or I'll have to call the Principal." Every time her mother mentioned the Principal Simone would clutch her arm and shake her head. Suddenly, Char-lotte thought she understood and she bent over her daughter. "Did somebody laugh at you on account of your operation?" Simone turned her head to the wall. Charlotte sighed and lightly kissed her daughter's moist hand. "Okay, momma understands. You'll tell me when you're ready. Now try and sleep. Momma's going to make dinner, your brother'll be back from school soon." She went out of the bedroom, leaving the door ajar. She had always felt that Simone's operation would lead to serious and complicated problems; she knew her daughter well, her excessive sensitivity and her unhealthy vulnerability, and she knew that the shock of the transformation would be hard on her. It wasn't until her first year at school that Simone became aware of her infirmity. At first she hadn't understood why the little girls in her class laughed at her, but after a few days she realized she was the only one with a twisted lip. Nobody at home ever mentioned it (not even her brother Maurice, though he liked to tease her), and in the end she'd finally forgotten it. The discovery was a disaster and for weeks Simone had refused to go back to school, screaming twenty times a day, "Why didn't anybody tell me I was ugly?" hitting, scratching and insulting anyone who tried to approach her. Then, with the help of Pierrette and Thérèse, who protected her and showered affection on her, and some of the nuns, who explained to their pupils that a harelip is a terrible thing to live with and that they must have respect and pity for anyone afflicted with one, she finally seemed to accept her difference and stopped talking about it. She still suffered deeply, though, because regularly some mean youngster would laugh or make faces at her, shouting, "Shut your mouth, Harelip, I can see your dirty teeth!" She would merely shrug and turn her back on her tormentor. But a few months earlier, when Maurice, who was three years older than Simone, had a heart-breaking cough and a temperature of 102, Dr. Sanregret, whom the entire neighbourhood adored because he was so gentle and understanding, came to the house and examined Simone's upper lip at length, frowning as he took notes. Ulric Côté took the doctor aside and told him, very aggressively, "Don't let that kid get it into her head that she's going to have an operation, Doctor! I could *never* afford it; you know that as well as me. Maurice is the oldest, and if I'm going to bleed, I'll bleed for him – if I've still got any blood! No, the best thing for her is to never talk about it. Never! She'll forget about it and so will we." The doctor didn't reply, but he returned a week later saying that one of his colleagues, a surgeon, was prepared to operate on Simone's harelip free, as a surgical experiment, on condition that the Côté family never mention his name so the news wouldn't get around. In fact it was a terrible lie: Dr. Sanregret was fond of Simone, whom he'd brought into the world under particularly difficult circumstances, and he paid for the operation himself, hoping to see her transformed from an ugly duckling into a normal, noisy, clinging, interfering pain in the neck like other little girls. At first Charlotte Côté had refused the old doctor's offer, claiming that it might be dangerous for an eleven-year-old growing girl to undergo such a drastic change overnight. "I know that child, Doctor, and I know that deep down inside her there's a fire that could burn forever if it escaped too fast. Please, ask your friend to wait another few years .... Wait, until she's able to understand what's happening." The doctor had put his hand gently on the woman's arm. "It's now or never, Madame Côté. It might even be a little too late. It's usually done when they're very young .... If we wait any longer, we won't be able to do anything. Don't think about the problems you'll have if we operate, think about how her life will be ruined if we don't." So Charlotte yielded, but not without warning Dr. Sanregret that she'd hold him responsible for the psychological after-effects that were sure to follow the operation. When Simone learned she was going to have an operation and that her harelip would almost completely disappear, she ran straight to the bathroom, stood on tiptoe to look in the mirror over the sink, looked herself straight in the eye and repeated at least a hundred times; "I won't be ugly! I won't be ugly! I won't be ugly!" Charlotte Côté opened the bottom of the icebox where a brand-new twenty-five pound block of ice sat imposingly, and broke off a small piece, using the pick she always kept handy. She came back into the dining-room sucking her ice cube. She sat in her favourite chair and turned on the radio, which after a few moments started producing very unpleasant noises. "Hey, who's been fooling around with my radio!" She turned the dial, stopped it at 70, and immediately the nasal voice of Nicole Germain spread through the house. For once, though, Charlotte Côté, who was crazy about the serials broadcast on Radio-Canada, wasn't listening to the melodramatic developments in "Francine Louvain: The Dramatic Story of a Fashion Illustrator and Her Daughter." She sucked her piece of ice, which was melting deliciously in her mouth, her eyes riveted on the little yellow light on the radio dial as they were every day between eleven and eleven fifteen; but this morning, even if Francine Louvain had announced she'd turned lesbian or that her daughter had been hacked into little pieces by a madman since the last episode (the previous Friday), she wouldn't have shuddered, lost as she was in her own uneasiness and fears. "I knew this would happen! I knew it! As if we didn't have enough problems already!" Suddenly, while Francine Louvain, on the telephone as usual, was giving her daughter advice in a tone of glib understanding ("Do as you like, child, but I'm your mother, don't forget. I've suffered and I know more about life than you do! Nothing can shock me, except vulgarity! Come now, tell me everything ....)" Charlotte leaped up and with a firm stride walked to the telephone, which hung on the wall (out of the children's reach) in the hall. "Now I'll get to the bottom of things!" She looked up the number in the phone book, then dialled the École des Saints-Anges.

Her hands were covered with blood and her mouth was full of vomit, but still she kept rummaging in Mother Benoîte's entrails. She burst the liver, the intestines, the bladder with a sadistic pleasure that disgusted, exhausted and delighted her all at once. She'd finally found a use for Sister Sainte-Catherine's last anatomy lesson: she could give a name to the parts she was tearing from the fat nun's body, she knew their functions and she could almost feel the pain she was inflicting as she tore them out. The Principal's mouth was open in a cry beyond pain or despair, but no sound came out. She was like a mask, fixed in an expression of horror. Her hands brushed the little girl's in useless gestures of supplication; she thrust them deep in her own entrails, trying to hold them back from her torturer, but the little girl pushed them aside, sniggering. Suddenly, with no transition, she lost all interest in Mother Benoîte's burst belly and picked up a huge pair of scissors that she'd brought with her. They were tailor's shears like her father's, heavy and unwieldy, with jagged edges that made a pretty but rather disturbing design when you used them. She could still hear her father's voice, "Don't you dare use those scissors for your goddamn homework! I use them to make my living and don't you forget it! The only reason you've got enough to eat is because those bloody scissors are on the go all day long, so don't break them!" She pounced on the scissors, shouting, "Don't try and take them away, poppa, or I'll cut you with them!" They were cold. She began to tremble as she moved – slowly, very slowly, too slowly for her liking – toward her victim, who had raised her arms to Heaven, her

47

red hands like flags in the still air, useless and dead. She came and sat next to Mother Benoîte and ran her fingers over the nun's forehead, her nose, her mouth, murmuring softly, "A pretty little jagged lip! A pretty little jagged mouth! A pretty little jagged Principal!" She took the nun's upper lip between her thumb and forefinger and pulled. She opened the scissors, brought them close to the lip. "Say you love me, Mother Benoîte, or I'll kill you!" The Principal was immediately transformed into a tiny grasshopper. It was very hot, and Thérèse and Pierrette were asking riddles. She had caught a green grasshopper and was saying to it, "Give me some honey or I'll kill you!" Mother Benoîte left a brownish mark on Simone's hand when the little girl crushed her, smiling her brand-new smile.

"You know, Madame, your daughter is a difficult child. She's inattentive, lazy, unstable and very undisciplined .... I have before me the report we keep on all our pupils and believe me, hers isn't brilliant. It's quite obvious, I think, that it will be hard for your child to complete her education – even primary school. Now I don't mean you should take her out of school, far be it from me to suggest such a thing, but you should be aware what a job it would be – for you as well as for us – to turn Simone into a decent, presentable young lady. Not to mention that we take her in free of charge! School itself is free, of course, but as you are doubtless aware, the pupils must assume some of the costs for supplies, for the edifying literature we provide them through our weekly newspaper *L'Estudiante*, and the materials required for certain special courses such as sewing and knitting. Throughout Simone's time at the École des Saints-Anges, four years now, everything has been provided free

because you said you were too poor to make the extra pay-
ments. I don't mind that you're poor, in fact you have all my
sympathy, but your daughter came back to school this morning after a month's absence, with her face transformed by an
operation that must have cost the earth! Put yourself in my
place, Madame Côté: if you have enough money to pay for
such an operation for your daughter (who needed it, I agree,
but if she'd gone on with her old mouth she'd have forgotten
it eventually), you might have the decency to send me the
two dollars for a subscription to *L'Estudiante* .... Mind you,
Madame Côté, that's all I'm asking for .... I could ask for the
arrears – eight dollars for a four-year subscription – but
what's past is past, and we'll say no more about it .... Show
your good will by sending me the two dollars with your
daughter, and we'll forget about this little ... unnecessary
squabble. Consider it a slight punishment for the nasty lie
you've been spreading, through Simone, all these years ....
Goodbye, Madame, and take good care of our little patient."
Charlotte Côté hadn't been able to get a single word in.
Mother Benoîte's flood of words, her peremptory tone, her
exotic expressions and the speed at which she uttered them
had rendered Charlotte powerless and left her speechless,
mouth agape, eyes wide in disbelief. As she put down the
receiver she imagined poor Simone before this word-mach-
ine, powerless and terrified in the face of such dishonesty
and adult cruelty, and she felt the rage rising up her spine,
colder and more powerful than before. "They always like to
humiliate us, the sisters. Why do we put up with it? Why?"
She went back to her bedroom, gently set the door ajar and
glanced at Simone, who had turned on to her side in her
sleep and was now dreaming, mouth open, brow furrowed.
She tiptoed in and sat on the edge of the bed, devastated by
anxiety and rage. "Nobody's going to hurt my children! Nobody!" Maurice and Simone were the two consolations in

her life as an irremediably poor woman who had always put up as good a fight as she could against utter failure, but never really succeeded, married to a man she adored and who adored her, but whose work as a tailor brought him little pay, less respect and even some ridicule. Despite all his flaws, drink being not the least, Ulric Côté worked relentlessly to feed his family properly, but now, with the war on, with shortages of everything, his craft had become nearly useless, as most people kept their savings to buy necessities on the black market rather than spending on clothes. Simone moaned slightly and opened her eyes. "I was dreaming hard!" She stood up on the bed, and threw herself in her mother's arms. "Can you talk all right now, sweetheart?" Simone drew back, frowning, as if under the shock of a particularly unpleasant memory. "I'm never going back to school! Never!" "Now Simone, I called the Principal ... and she told me everything was okay." "It is not! Everything isn't okay, momma, it's rotten! She wanted me to stay ugly 'cause we're poor!" Charlotte held her daughter tight and ran her hand through her hair, stroking, smiling, tender. "Don't think about that. Everything's going to work out." Simone, obstinate, got under the sheets, ensconcing herself in the pillows. "I'm staying right here and I'm keeping my new mouth!" Charlotte couldn't help laughing. "We'd have quite a job giving you back the old one!" It was Simone's turn to laugh. "That's true, it'd cost too much." Charlotte lifted the sheet and took her daughter's hand. "Don't think about money now, Simone, that's not your problem. It's something for your father and me to think about. You just go back to school, try to be a good girl, work hard and pass your exams, that's all we ask of you." "What about the Principal? She wants two dollars this afternoon, or else I can't ever go back to school!" "I'll take care of your Principal! Now you try and sleep a little more. You won't go back to school till tomorrow. Rest now, stay in my bed and leave everything to me." Simone pulled the sheet up to her chin. "I hardly even got a chance to see Thérèse and Pierrette!"

The refectory rang with bright laughter and happy whispering. The foul smells drifting in the air, though, were very depressing: the aroma of the eternal soup made from yesterday's leftovers mingled with another – more pronounced because it was always the same, omnipresent, embedded in the very caps of the cooks – the smell of boiled leeks that invariably accompanied the main dish. The younger nuns, in fact, had baptized Sister Sainte-Jeanne au Bûcher – who watched over the kitchen like a cat with its kittens, ruling it like the bossy woman she was – "Sister Saint Leek," which had the happy effect of irritating the poor cook, who could often be heard screaming, "I cook what they give me to cook! I'm not the one who decides! If there was anything cheaper than leeks you'd be eating that, so don't complain!" But right after grace, piously said by Mother Benoîte des Anges with downcast eyes, hand held out over her round roll, the nuns would forget what was on their plates and recount their mornings or their afternoons. Spoons clinked in the bottoms of soup-bowls but no one tasted the lukewarm liquid, in which a piece of meat embarrassed to find itself there or a flaccid noodle swallowed almost unconsciously, might be floating. No one except Sister Sainte-Philomène, Thérèse and Lucienne's teacher, one of whose great passions was eating (the other being arithmetic), who at every meal wolfed down a double or even triple portion of everything, never looking around, eyes riveted to the table, happy when her mouth was so full it was hard to chew and seeming lost or disconcerted when she'd finished eating and her plate stared up at her, empty, ready to put in the cupboard without being washed, so thoroughly had the nun wiped, cleaned and polished it with her bread. It was said that she'd "caught" her pale, protruding eyes, the colour of skimmed milk, from hunting for scraps of food at the bottom of her plate, and some particularly naïve nuns believed it. Throughout the meal, while her companions were telling of the latest escapades or the newest manoeuvres of their scapegoats or their pets, amid acerbic comments and appreciative clucking, Sister Sainte-Philomène chewed noisily, swallowed noisily, drank noisily, belched without excusing herself and sometimes even .... "Sister Sainte-Philomène! Really! Luckily it's spring and the windows are open or we'd have to evacuate the refectory!" "You can't help nature, Sister! Have to let out the bad to make room for the good!" Mother Benoîte des Anges often felt like knocking senseless this fat vulgar woman, who had probably been accepted by the community without their knowing of this serious flaw, or perhaps because of her huge dowry ("You know, Godin Cement ...."), but who had to be hidden away in the kitchen whenever a visitor came to eat with the nuns. Sister Sainte-Philomène didn't take offence at this disgrace, which should have made her burn with humiliation; on the contrary, whenever she was forced to eat in the kitchen she made the most of it, rummaging around and scraping the bottoms of saucepans with iron ladles, which she manipulated with surprising dexterity. One day, out of sheer exasperation, Mother Benoîte des Anges tried to fob off Sister Sainte-Philomène on Sister Sainte-Jeanne au Bûcher, but the cook was so upset that the Principal, despite her strength, was absolutely bowled over and finally gave in. After the tears, the gnashing of teeth, the threats and supplications, Sister Sainte-Jeanne au Bûcher concluded with a resounding, "Let her fart and burp somewhere else! I run a clean kitchen and it's going to stay that way! Keep her in the refectory so the flies stay out of my kitchen!" But Sister Sainte-Philomène was an astonishing arithmetic teacher, perhaps the best in the community, and strangely enough Mother Benoîte had to do battle every year to keep her at the École des Saints-Anges. She was beside herself over this contradictory situation, for every summer she would be forced into wheeling and dealing and sly acts of flattery to hold on to this peerless teacher whom she loathed and despised, because all the elementary schools under the supervision of her community fought over her, so great was her reputation. No one really knew how she did it, but Sister Sainte-Philomène worked wonders with the dullest students and those most hopeless in arithmetic, taking them aside after school, locking herself up with them and explaining figures, sums and operations with the patience of an angel and the passion of a bashful lover. That noon the leeks were giving off their excess water and tooth-crunching sand next to a greasy midget meatball, its colour indefinable yet quite precise: that of meat cooked at too low a temperature, so that it turned grey instead of brown. Sister Sainte-Philomène, however, was already meticulously wiping her empty plate with her bread, while Sister Clump Foot, who was seated next to her (as punishment,she maintained), had scarcely attacked the tough meat ball that was crumbling under her fork. Sister Sainte-Philomène was on the right of the portress, who had got in the habit of pushing her own plate slightly to the left so that she had to turn in the opposite direction to eat. The huge table was set smack in the middle of the room and the twenty nuns were distributed along the two sides, the ends being reserved for the Principal and any visitor who might turn up. No more than one person was ever invited at a time, and it was usually a man (the parish priest, who would have preferred to be elsewhere, the bishop of the diocese, who offered up this sacrifice for his sins, Dr. Sanregret, called to the bedside of a sick nun who, really, could have waited till the middle of the night to take sick and spare him a revolting meal). And so when Sister Sainte-

Philomène spoke, all heads turned her way as one, it was such a surprise. Never, could the nuns remember, had Sister Sainte-Philomène done anything at the table but eat and eructate! After releasing a deep, throaty belch that no one noticed except Sister Clump Foot, who thought, so she's been into the onions again!", Sister Sainte-Philomène raised her head, looked across to the two empty places that everyone had noticed but no one had dared to mention and said facetiously, "Isn't that strange – Sister Sainte-Catherine and Sister Sainte-Thérèse aren't eating." But the nuns' incredulity ended when the Six B teacher added with a covetous look that gave Mother Benoîte des Anges a bilious attack, "That means there'll be extra meat balls!" A few of the nuns bowed their heads and laughed, while others raised their eyes; Mother Benoîte took a deep breath to keep from exploding. That was when Sister Clump Foot did something so astonishing it would be the talk of the community for years to come and assure her a place in legend: she jumped to her feet, picked up her plate, dumped the contents on Sister Sainte-Philomène's with the help of her fork and screamed, exasperated, "Go ahead, you fat sow, eat! And when you're done we'll bring you the scraps from the garbage!" Then she stormed out of the refectory, slamming the door behind her. Sister Sainte-Philomène seemed quite unaffected by the outburst of her former close friend, and dug into the scarcely touched meat ball with an agile, well-aimed fork. Mother Benoîte decided that her week had got off to a very bad start.

Thérèse and Pierrette were standing on the doorstep on the second floor, eyes lowered, feet toed in. Thérèse was shuffling from one foot to the other, as usual, and Pierrette was twisting the hem of her skirt. These children, who could

laugh uproariously, explode with joy, fulminate when anyone annoyed them, fly into insane rages at the drop of a hat,
pound each other with their school-books and tear each
other's clothes when they decided to disagree, became ridic-
ulously awkward and clumsy when it was time to come and
inquire about their sick friend. They had stood in front of
the Côté's door, petrified, for a good five minutes before
deciding to ring the bell. In the end it was their hunger
pangs that made them press the button. "If we linger there
won't be anything left. My mother always has a fit when I'm
late, 'cause Marcel won't eat unless I'm there. Go on, ring
the bell!" Instead of complying, Pierrette asked one of those
questions Thérèse hated, because usually she didn't know
the answer. "Thérèse, what does 'linger' mean?" Thérèse
briskly pulled up her stocking, which was starting to droop.
"Gee, you're a pain in the neck! I think it means spend
forever in the toilet, but I figured maybe it worked for staying somewhere a long time .... The other day my cousin
Richard, the creep, was in the toilet for nearly half an hour,
but you couldn't hear a thing and my mother yelled at him,
'Richard, don't linger in there, you're too young!' That's where
I first heard it. Go on, ring the bell." When the door was
open and Madame Côté had shouted "Come in!" from the
third floor, the two girls still stood there, motionless. They
weren't looking at each other, they didn't dare look up at
their friend's mother, though she was a nice woman whom
they liked very much, although they knew her only through
Simone and had never been alone with her. "You came to ask
about Simone?" Silence. "Well, don't just stand there like a
bump on a log!" Silence. Thérèse fastened her garter which,
for once, hadn't come undone, Pierrette twisted the hem of
her skirt, which was getting wrinkled. Charlotte Côté shook
her head. "Okay, if you aren't coming up, I'll shut the door.
I've got better things to do than stand around waiting for
the pair of you!" Thérèse and Pierrette finally looked at each

other, but they didn't raise their heads in Charlotte's direction. "Do I have to come down and get you?" Thérèse made up her mind first. Cautiously she started climbing the stairs she had run up so many times before, feet pounding and yelling her head off, her gaze lowered now as if she'd lost something valuable. Pierrette followed her. Two convicts mounting the scaffold. They walked past Charlotte, staring at the toes of their shoes and stopped short as soon as they were through the door. "You aren't behaving like the little pests you usually are .... Let me tell you, there've been times I wished you were this quiet!" Charlotte often let her daughter's two friends come in, particularly in the winter, when Simone's room would become a playground in which cutouts, colouring books, crayons and wet paintbrushes would litter the floor amid endless laughter and childish squabbling that had to be stopped with a shouted threat from the kitchen or living-room. Thérèse and Pierrette instinctively headed for Simone's room, but Charlotte stopped them. "She isn't there, she's in my room." The two girls looked at each other, horrified. All they'd seen in this apartment was their friend's room and the living-room. Monsieur and Madame Côté's room – they knew because Simone had told them – was the one off the dining-room. So they had to walk through a good part of the house to get to their friend. "Aren't you going to ask after her?" Charlotte gave them a push to make them move faster. "How's Simone?" Once again Thérèse had taken the initiative. Despite the seriousness of the situation, Pierrette sniggered. Thérèse turned to her. "What are you laughing at, nitwit?" "'Cause you asked a dumb question, that's what! Why ask? We know she's sick, 'cause she went home from school the minute she was back." "You're such a genius, Pierrette Guérin! What'd you want me to ask? 'Is she dead?' We came to find out how she is, so I asked how she is!" In the dining-room, at the end of the table his mother had set for him, Maurice was stoically eating his bologna sandwich. At the sight of Pierrette he turned pale, then bright red; his mouthful of sandwich went down the wrong way and he started to cough, pounding the table with his fist. "Oh boy, I'd forgot all about him!" Pierrette puffed out her cheeks to let the air out of her lungs, making an unpleasant sound like a horse snorting. Maurice, from the height of his fourteen years, with his pimples and – too often – with circles under his eyes, had been pestering her for months now, sighing when she passed, slipping notes ablaze with passion in her mail-box, blushing to the roots of his hair when she deigned to look his way, turning white with suppressed rage when she walked past him with her nose in the air. At first, Pierrette had been very flattered by these signs of interest, but Maurice soon got on her nerves, with his cow's eyes filled with dumb, even dim-witted adoration. The day he'd worked up the courage to ask her for a kiss (it was one Saturday in May when it was raining cats and dogs and the two little girls had retreated to Simone's room), she had put him in his place by shouting loud enough for his mother to hear, "Leave me alone, drip! And keep your dirty kisses to yourself! I'm not interested in grade-nine boys!" Maurice had been punished (no dessert at supper time) and still held a grudge against Pierrette for having spurned him. He went on adoring her, however, but from afar, wishing her as much bad as good. Charlotte opened the bedroom door and glanced inside. Simone was fast asleep this time, calm and almost smiling. Charlotte opened the door completely, but held back her daughter's friends, who were, she sensed, ready to throw themselves on Simone, uttering cries of victory. "Don't wake her up. She had a heck of a time getting to sleep." She crouched down between the two girls, her hands on their shoulders. She spoke very softly, tenderly, the way you talk when you're explaining a particularly delicate problem to someone you love. "Girls, this was really hard on Simone. It was a shock, you see, to

57

see herself ... pretty like that, overnight, practically, and ... somebody at school wasn't very nice to her .... She's going back tomorrow, but I'd like you to take good care of her, if you can. Even better than before. See, her whole life's going to change now, and it has to be for the better .... But I'm not worried about you two!" Maurice, who had recovered from his choking fit, burst out laughing just then. "Thérèse, there's a run in your stocking; you'll be an old maid!" His mother turned toward him so abruptly that he started. "And you, you simple-minded little twerp, shut up and eat your bologna!"

Sister Sainte-Thérèse de l'Enfant-Jésus would have mortgaged part of her soul to see Sister Sainte-Catherine's face light up with a smile, even the saddest smile in the world. Sister Sainte-Catherine had taught her classes until half-past eleven without giving too much thought to her scene with the Principal, but as soon as she walked out of her classroom and the little girls were rushing down the stairs, whispering – for shouting would have been a serious infraction of school discipline – she had fallen into Sister Sainte-Thérèse's arms, no longer able to hold back the tears that were bathing her face, making it shine as if waxed, declaring to her friend in a husky voice, "I don't want to leave the school! I don't want to leave you, Sainte-Thérèse!" Both had gone into the big shed behind the nuns' house, the storage place for the sets, costumes and props that would once again enable the people in the parish of Saint Stanislas-de-Kostka to make their great love of God shine in the eyes of the entire province of Quebec. The nuns' house, located on rue Garnier, was a severe red-brick structure that rested against the École des Saints-Anges as if to retain it or hold it up. Some twenty women lived there in supposedly perfect harmony. No one who entered the cenacle would have guessed from the order that reigned there, from the smell of cleanliness that permeated everything, the shamelessly healthy succulents that flaunted their almost too perfect green in your face, or from the silence that haunted the corridors, at the pacts that were the cement in this fine house where everything seemed so simple and so pleasant. Behind every too well varnished door with its too highly polished handle, there lurked a shadowy recess, a grey corner, sometimes even a blank wall of despair, that the nuns must hide beneath a uniform mask imposed by the community, a face on which a faint smile might flicker but which was never openly hilarious or totally despondent. The saddest nuns found it hard to compose this mask that was so unlike them, while the happiest ones, those with the overly red cheeks and the scandalously shining eyes, were even more to be pitied. How, in fact, were they to hide the happiness that they had coveted, attained and now were required to deny, under that common face that might well have been the face of each of their companions as much as their own—and above all, why? Those who had truly searched for God and found Him were often among the gayest, but the rules of their community required them to hide their true joy beneath a uniformly impersonal varnish that made them uncomfortable because it forced them constantly to cheat. Sister Sainte-Thérèse de l'Enfant-Jésus was one of those who had to struggle constantly against her deepest nature, for the communal personality didn't suit her at all; deep down she was nothing but a joyous child, carefree but brilliant, who had learned to play the made-up role of typical nun so well, who had succeeded at camouflaging her true personality so well, that she was judged to be pale and silly, when in fact she was just the opposite. Only Sister Sainte-Catherine knew her laughter, like wind chimes, and her face, so easily lit up with happiness or gratitude. After getting out of the chore of directing the Corpus Christi procession, Sister Sainte-Thérèse de l'Enfant-Jésus had mischievously come to offer her assistance and Sister Sainte-Catherine had seen in the depths of her eyes a mockery that delighted her. Since then they had become the closest friends in the École des Saints-Anges, a situation that infuriated Mother Benoîte des Anges, who had for a long time wanted to take Sister Sainte-Thérèse under her own wing but had been politely turned down, the nun declaring herself unworthy of the protection of so exalted an authority. It was not uncommon to see pairs of friends taking their evening walk together or strolling arm in arm during recreation periods; it could even be said that every nun in the community dreamed of one day meeting the kindred soul who would share her joys and tribulations, while helping her to maintain the neutral outward appearance that was required of her. (Sister Sainte-Philomène and Sister Saint-Georges had formed one of those inevitable couples for years before the incident at the front door, and their break had come as a shock and a surprise, for the other nuns had followed their relationship with emotion and even with envy.) When someone really wanted to punish a nun she would be moved to another school and her special friend left behind: that sentence was the cruellest and the hardest to endure, and it was what Mother Benoîte des Anges was trying to do by banishing Sister Sainte-Catherine before the school year was over, without saying where she intended to send her. Sister Sainte-Catherine had, of course, told her friend everything; surprisingly, Sister Sainte-Thérèse hadn't seemed too upset at the news. The sorrow that could be seen on Sister Sainte-Catherine's face was too heart-rending for her friend to stop and consider the reasons for it; first she must ease the pain, cleanse the wounds and cover them with balm before she asked questions and tried to wipe out the sickness altogether. "If the situation wasn't so serious,

Sainte-Catherine, I think I'd tease you .... You look funny up there sitting on the Blessed Virgin's throne .... You don't look much like a queen, let me tell you!" Sister Sainte-Catherine had taken a seat on the sturdy, inelegant wooden bench covered with peeling gilt that had served as a throne for the little girl who, the year before, had been chosen to represent the Virgin in the repository and who had categorically refused to remain standing for hours. "The Blessed Virgin will forgive me for being so sad on her throne, you know .... What are we going to do, Sainte-Thérèse?" Sister Sainte-Catherine put her hand on the shoulder of the other nun, who was sitting at her feet, on a little stool that had once been used for milking cows, but which now served as a prie-dieu for one of the kneeling archangels in the repository. "First of all, we're going to forget about it for this week; afterwards, we'll see. The week ahead is too important for us to make a big fuss about it on top of everything else! Let's organize a beautiful Corpus Christi celebration, the very best we can, conscientiously, lovingly, and I'm sure there'll be a reward for us at the end!" Sister Sainte-Catherine envied her naïve friend, who saw life in terms of rewards, indulgences, the Great Bank of the Catholic Church that promised happiness in exchange for every good deed; she wished she could believe that every good deed is rewarded, that every prayer is entered as a credit in your bank account, that every sacrifice is admired, appreciated for its true value by the All High Himself, in person, who hears all, sees all, sorts, compiles, resolves and settles everything. Not that Sister Sainte-Catherine was a sceptic: she believed in God, worshipped Him and devoted her life to Him, but the Church's way of dispensing his Word and causing his Goodness to shine forth often embarrassed her and always irritated her. And so this ceremony for which she was once again about to feign enthusiasm, even though she had changed it appreciably over the years, still made her uneasy, so much did it take advantage of the parishioners' credulity. "If you only knew how little I feel like getting involved in it this year ...." "Think of the girls, Sainte-Catherine, how excited they'll be, how ecstatic when the Blessed Virgin is placed on her pedestal .... Think of the fervour of those children who usually have so much trouble concentrating, whom we keep nagging till they get annoyed with us – but who, on that one night, are radiant with joy because of us!" The door of the shed opened abruptly and Sister Clump Foot came hobbling in. She was so agitated she didn't even cross herself as she passed under the huge gilded canopy that would shelter the *curé* and his monstrance during the procession through the streets, partly hiding them from the sight of parishioners on their balconies, who would complain, as usual, because they hadn't had a good look at the good Lord. "Your absence was noticed .... If you ask me, you're both going to get it." She was red and out of breath, embarrassed at the sight of Sister Sainte-Catherine stroking her friend's shoulder, not daring to confront them openly, letting her gaze wander instead over the heavy objects that once more would have to be dusted, moved, transported, freshened up and thrown to the lions: the overexcited students who would mistreat them in their eagerness to see the repository completed. "I think we've been punished enough, Sister Saint-Georges .... We've had enough ...." Sister Clump Foot untied the white apron she had been holding at arm's length. "I brought you some fruit and tomatoes and a piece of cake that was going to get stale in the pantry ...." Sister Sainte-Thérèse exploded with laughter that rang for a long time through the dry and musty shed. "What a nice thing to do, Sister Saint-Georges! I was thinking I'd have a hard time holding out till supper." The portress placed the fruit and cake on another milking stool, painted corset pink, while Sister Sainte-Catherine sat by her friend. "Aren't you going to eat with us, Sister Saint-Georges?" "I don't know if I ought to .... I don't want to bother you when you're getting ready for the Corpus Christi ...." Sister Sainte-Thérèse patted the floor beside her. "Come on, Sister Saint-Georges, you never bother us." Pink with pleasure, the portress managed, despite the club-foot, which complicated her task somewhat, to sit on the floor with the others. "You should have sat on the throne." "No, no, it's been a long time since I've sat on the floor like this. A long time .... More than a long time, it feels like an eternity .... The last time, I think was when I was a little girl." They ate happily in the midst of sad costumes stiffened by the damp, laughing with their mouths full, and immediately assuming contrite expressions that provoked more giggling and gleeful tears. In the middle of a particularly joyous burst of laughter, Sister Saint-Georges brought her hand to her mouth as if she'd just committed some great misdemeanour. "I might feel guilty later on, but right now, let me tell you, I'm having the time of my life!" When the frugal repast had ended and Sister Sainte-Catherine had said grace, her sorrow suddenly returned and she sighed. "I don't think I have the courage to deal with all that today. Let's wait till tomorrow .... After all, three days is more than enough to get ready." "But tomorrow's confession, Sainte-Cathe ... I mean, Sister Sainte-Catherine." Sister Sainte-Georges pretended she hadn't heard and swallowed her last apple quarter, which she'd been chewing for a good minute to extract all the juice. "We'll take our pupils to confession first thing tomorrow, Sister Sainte-Thérèse .... As far as today's concerned, I think I'll take this afternoon off. I'm really too upset." Sister Sainte-Catherine turned toward Sister Saint-Georges, who saw the question coming and blushed furiously, so great was her joy. "Sister Saint-Georges, would you take my place in class this afternoon? I'm going to rest for a few hours." The portress sprang to her feet with no help from the others and headed for the door of the shed. "I'll go right now, I've got to ring the bell pretty soon .... What're we teaching this afternoon?" Sister Sainte-Catherine couldn't help smiling. Sister Saint-Georges wasn't authorized to teach, but still – it was the least she could do – her self-esteem had to be flattered. "Have them write a composition ... on whatever subject you want." Sister Sainte- Georges didn't limp when she left the shed. She was flying.

"I can't do everything, Mother Benoîte! You asked me to take the little Côté girl home and I took her. Then you gave me an errand to do but I didn't have time and I couldn't find anybody else .... Mail your letter, it'll get there just the same!" Because of the din from the laughter and shouting of six hundred little girls starting to burn up their lunch-time calories, Sister Saint-Georges had to talk very loud, enunciating with a grimace. She had never used this tone of voice with her superior, who was wondering what could have happened to the poor old cripple to make her so nervous, impatient, anxious to be off – she was usually too clinging for her taste. (Mother Benoîte des Anges valued highly the subaltern's chores that Sister Saint-Georges performed so well, but the portress's flaws were beginning to get her down. The Principal thought of Sister Saint-Georges as one of those beings who walk straight as long as you keep them on a tight rein, but who start to prance about as soon as they are given a little freedom, while, in fact, the portress was an emotional woman who operated on affection and thoughtfulness under her eternally grumpy mask.) "But I told you it was urgent!" Mother Benoîte des Anges had caught Sister Saint-Georges, radiant, as she was leaving the shed, which encroached somewhat on the school yard. Sister Saint-Georges had seemed very embarrassed at this accidental meeting and immediately assumed a half-sly, half-guilty expression that shocked the Principal. "Sister Saint-Georges, this is the second time I've caught you out in three-quarters of an hour!" The portress lowered her gaze. Sighed. "Come to my office, we'll get to the bottom of this in private!" Mother Benoîte was some distance from the shed when she realized that Sister Clump Foot wasn't following her. "Sister Saint-Georges!" A few little girls turned around and the Principal had to come back to her assistant so she wouldn't have to raise her voice. "My word, Sister Saint-Georges, you're disobeying me again!" The nun cleared her throat, and swallowed noisily before replying, "It's just that ... you see ... Sister Sainte-Catherine asked me to fill in for her after lunch." Mother Benoîte received the blow without flinching. She knew how passionately Sister Saint-Georges loved those blessed half-days when the portress could think of herself as a teacher, reigning like a queen on her dais, chin up, coif pointed, her tone peremptory and ridiculous. Asking Sister Saint-Georges to replace a sick teacher meant handing her a priceless gift and the Principal didn't have the heart to take it away; things were going badly enough without turning her assistant against her! The Principal even wondered if Sister Sainte-Catherine hadn't deliberately asked Sister Saint-Georges to replace her, thereby preventing the letter from reaching its destination. "Sister Sainte-Catherine doesn't even know that the letter exists .... If I turn paranoid on top of everything else we'll never get to the end of this." Her position was a very delicate one: she didn't want to punish Sister Saint-Georges by depriving her of an afternoon's supervision (in fact she'd already decided not to punish her for leaving the table without permission, understanding her anger at Sister Sainte-Philomène and even approving of her gesture), but she wanted the letter to reach the Mother House that very day; she had to be ruthless against the too intelligent Sister Sainte-Catherine, without causing a blow-up before the Corpus Christi procession. "Still, my authority's at stake! I'm getting soft .... Where is my fine self-assurance of yesteryear!" Her self-confidence returned like the crack of a whip; she made her decision in less than three seconds. "Sister Saint-Georges, that letter must be delivered immediately! Ring your bell and get moving!" She turned on her heel as soon as the words were out of her mouth. She was scarcely inside the school when the shed door opened behind Sister Saint-Georges, who hadn't moved an inch. Sister Sainte-Catherine glided over to the portress and placed a hand on her arm. "Give me the letter, Sister Saint-Georges."

Every afternoon between two o'clock and half-past two, Sister Sainte-Philomène felt dog-tired. She ate too much too fast and had poor digestion, so that an hour after every meal heartburn would torment her and she could be seen taking out her little white pills and gulping them down, waiting for the salutary effect with eyes shut, concentrating on the pain she wanted to bring under control, following its decline minute by minute. A short time later, the urge to sleep – a pressing, uncontrollable need that shut her eyes and made her drop off right in the middle of her first class – would catch her while her class took advantage of the situation to whisper, laugh, talk out loud, get up and change places, make a commotion, pass notes, sing in chorus and even get into the odd fight (the two tallest girls in Six B, Claudette and Ginette Latour, identical twins who enjoyed passing for each other, were inveterate skirmishers, who would take any opportunity to pull each other's braids and slap and scratch and clobber with obvious pleasure, hurling the worst sort of invective with vigour and a vocabulary that would make your hair stand on end). Lucienne Boileau often took advantage of the commotion to come up to Thérèse, attempting to lure her with topics of conversation that were fascinating to her but bored Thérèse to tears, offering her the finest apples or a sheet of bubble gum she'd kept just for her, even offering to correct her essays (while Thérèse, who was much better at composition, was infuriated at this insulting proposal), botching her attempt every time because Thérèse didn't have the slightest interest in her, but bravely renewing her advances and compliments, so desperately did she want to become part of "Thérèse-'n'-Pierrette." Cringing at her classmate's rebuffs, she would go back to her seat every time, pitiful, sticking her nose in a book while she waited for Sister Sainte-Philomène to wake up or for Louise Bérubé to start singing O Canada to warn the class of danger. Louise Bérubé, a good-natured, fat, ruddy-faced girl whom everybody liked, who saw everything as a joke, something to laugh at, sat at the desk closest to the door, the one called "the little portress's" because the girl who inherited it had to open the door for any visitor who showed up. When the hullabaloo became too overpowering, then, she would go and stand on guard and the girls knew she'd start to bellow O Canada if some passer-by, the Principal, some other teacher or even an overly zealous pupil (everyone knew, for instance, that all the grade nines were tattletales and squealers) came a bit too near the classroom door. Once the signal was given, the wildest free-for-all could calm down in seconds and a studious silence – suspect, because it was humanly impossible for any classroom to be so peaceful – would settle over the room. The little girls wouldn't necessarily be in their own seats, but they would be seated; they weren't always bent over their own books and perhaps weren't scribbling at their own notes, but they were serious and concentrating. That day, Sister Sainte-Philomène was felled by fatigue so abruptly, falling asleep so rapidly that Louise Bérubé couldn't help exclaiming, "Now we've had it, she's dead! Send chocolates, not flowers." The nun's nose was hidden in the hollow of her shoulder, as if she were a huge bird, and her gentle snores rose in the class-room, even and bland. Lucienne Boileau immediately left her place and headed for Thérèse, who was still laughing at Louise Bérubé's joke. "Did you see Harelip?" Thérèse and Pierrette had got back to school very late and Lucienne, frustrated, hadn't been able to question them about their friend's mysterious disappearance. Thérèse slowly turned her head toward Lucienne, who was sucking a clear candy and spoke in a neutral tone, as though the fat girl had asked her for information. "Harelip? Who's that? I don't know any Harelip .... You must have got the wrong number." Then she plunged back into her arithmetic problem, which had to do with two trains, one of which left Montreal, the other Quebec city, at half-past seven a.m., travelling at seventy-five miles an hour, and the question was at what time would the two meet, given that the length of the journey was one hundred and ninety miles. Lucienne swallowed the insult, hesitated for a moment, then decided to rephrase her question. "Have you heard anything about Simone?" This time Thérèse didn't even bother to look up from her work. "Simone?" The din around them grew louder and louder, and Lucienne raised her voice a little. "Don't try and tell me you don't know Simone!" "Depends which one you mean. There's Simone Guérard and Simone Côté ...." "You know very well I mean Simone Côté! Don't play games with me! Are you sick?" "Is she your sister?" "My sister? What are you talking about, dumb-bell!" "Your cousin?" "Thérèse, quit pulling my leg and answer!" "I asked if she was your cousin." "No, she isn't my cousin!" "Is she your friend?" Lucienne hesitated for a scant quarter of a second before answering, but Thérèse greatly enjoyed the slight hesitation that spoke volumes. "Yes, she's my friend! And I want to know how she is!" Thérèse slowly put down her pen, slipped out of her seat, got up and finally looked Lucienne in the eye. "Simone isn't your friend. She's mine. Simone couldn't care less about you, and me neither. As far as you're concerned Simone's dead, so what difference does it make to you if she's sick or if she's well?" Thérèse leaned over Lucienne, who was turning beet red. "I didn't get you this morning, Lucienne Boileau, because I didn't have time, but if you don't go back to your seat this minute you'll be going home with blood running down your fat face and two inches cut off your braids – from the top! I guess you're still playing policeman for Mother Dragon Devil, you tattle-tale creep!" This time the affront was really too much for Lucienne, who started to cry. Thérèse sat down, ignoring her. "I try as hard as I can to be nice, but you always say I tell on you and it isn't fair!" As she received no reply, Lucienne turned and staggered back to her desk, cheeks wet, her heart like a potato. As Louise Bérubé had launched into O Canada in a nasal voice that made some of the girls laugh but still produced results, the class started running back to their places or usurped someone else's, so that a few had to sit wherever they could and the inevitable game of musical chairs began, ending with a frantic race by Claudette Latour, one of the twins, who had to circle the classroom completely before she found a seat. Louise Bérubé remained by the door. "There wasn't anybody. I just wanted to know if my regiment of skinny cows was still in shape." Of all the crumpled paper that landed on her head, only one piece contained the right answer to the problem about the two trains between Montreal and Quebec. It came from Thérèse.

Sister Sainte-Catherine had a long way to go. She had boarded the number 27 bus at the corner of boulevard Saint-Joseph and rue de Laroche to avoid any indiscreet gazes. There she waited, the letter pressed against her bosom, throat tight with anguish and heart pounding, for the rules of her community did not allow her to venture into the outside world alone. Another nun should have accompanied her, but who would have consented to travel with a renegade who leaves school right in the middle of the afternoon, without permission, to deliver a letter containing her own condemnation? Sister Sainte-Thérèse de l'Enfant-Jésus would have gone, but Sister Sainte-Catherine didn't want to involve her any more than was necessary in this sordid business that she'd decided to settle herself, at the risk of losing everything. But now that she was sitting in the rattan seat that pricked her back in the places where the fibres had given way, part of her was congratulating herself on this bus and streetcar ride on which she'd just set out, on this near freedom that would enable her to escape the inevitable rosary by speaking only to her companion about this fantastic adventure that seemed to belong in a serialized novel rather than the life of a self-respecting nun. She was afraid of what was waiting for her at the other end, but very grateful for this break in her monotonous life that allowed her to look out the window she'd flung open at the opulent houses of boulevard Saint-Joseph, the lovely grassy medians with flowers that divided the pavement in two, making a sort of garden down the middle of the street, at the few passers-by going about their business, unaware that they were being watched, the new leaves, tender green and motionless in the late spring calm, through which you could judge the mood of the sun. A small breath of freedom blew across her soul and Sister Sainte-Catherine caught herself smiling despite the seriousness of the situation. She had made up her mind very quickly, without thinking it over, trusting her intuition: she would go herself and place Mother Benoîte's letter on Mother Superior's desk; she would get on her knees before that wise, respected old woman and tell her version of the facts; she would accept rebukes, threats, even punishment, but she would beg not to be taken away from the school she had learned to love so much, from the parish where she was happy, and finally, from Sister Sainte-Thérèse, for whom she felt so much tenderness and trust. Yes, she would even mention Sister Sainte-Thérèse, if she was pressed, talk about what united them and what she didn't want to lose, for any reason. She was well aware that it wouldn't be hard to choose between a school principal and a grade six teacher, but she insisted on stating her interpretation of the facts, on discussing her rights, on cleansing her honour of the mud with which Mother Benoîte had certainly splattered her. She hoped that Mother Superior would appreciate her candour, that she would deign to hear her out, that she would understand, in the end, that the younger nun was not as black as the Principal had painted her and that the truth was to be found somewhere between the humiliating missive and her own version, which would also not be free – she was well aware of it – from exaggeration tinged with bad faith. Sister Sainte-Catherine got off the bus at the corner of avenue du Parc, crossed boulevard Saint-Joseph and stood waiting for the number 80 streetcar, which would take her to the north end of town. She was alone. Once again she was struck by a thought: She was free! The taste of freedom she'd begun to savour on the bus was going to her head, and she felt light, almost drunk. She wanted to dance, to try out a few awkward steps on the pavement, to say hello to passers-by and bring a smile to their taciturn lips. Perhaps she was on the road to perdition, but she was travelling with a light heart! The streetcar clattered to a stop with a sound of rusty metal, spitting a shower of sparks. "Are you an orphan today, sister?" The ticket-collector took her transfer, examined it at length, a sardonic smile lifting the corners of his mouth. "I don't trust you nuns! Wouldn't put it past you to try and get away with a week-old transfer!" Sister Sainte-Catherine laughed heartily and remained standing beside him. An old gentleman offered her his seat, tipping his hat, but she refused with a smile, saying she preferred to stay where she was. Insulted, the old gentleman sat down again, grumbling. The ticket-puncher leaned over toward Sister Sainte-Catherine.

"Are you really a nun?" "Why do you ask?" "I never saw a nun turn down a seat on the streetcar! Usually they stand right in front of a man so he has to get up." "I'm not tired." The ticket-puncher gestured to the letter Sister Sainte-Catherine was still holding close to her. "You wouldn't be a mail nun?" Sister Sainte-Catherine burst out laughing. "That's right – I deliver urgent letters." "So that's why you're by yourself." "Yes." Sister Sainte-Catherine caught herself listening to the sound of the motor, when the streetcar stopped for passengers. The two notes, close together and endlessly repeated, reawakened in her whole slices of her childhood, clear, vivid memories of nearly every summer afternoon. When her mother's work was done and she had a few idle hours, she would take little Catherine by the hand and say, "Come, we're going for a nice streetcar ride." In fact, Sister Sainte-Catherine's mother had been what her father called "nuts about streetcars." For years she had travelled the thoroughfares of Montreal, from Saint-Henri to Repentigny, from boulevard Gouin to rue Notre-Dame, haunting the yellow streetcars that had just one conductor with an enormous task: to collect fares, punch transfers, point lost passengers in the right direction, and drive his vehicle, getting out at corners to shunt the rails with a long metal pole; the larger olive-green cars that you entered through the back door, where a ticket-puncher, imposing in his little wooden cage, would intone: "Don't push, there's room for everybody" or: "Stand clear of the door: somebody wants out!"; and even the gilded streetcar that toured the city for fifty cents, that people always waved at as it passed the churches, clean and shiny, its little bell tinkling gaily. Often when the streetcar stopped at a corner, her mother would say: "Listen ... listen to the motor .... Do you know what it's saying? Listen carefully, you'll hear it .... It's saying: 'A pocket, a pocket, a pocket.' Can you hear it? When he's running he doesn't say it, but when he stops he sounds like a tailor!"

Sister Sainte-Catherine leaned against the big black window. "A pocket, a pocket ...." The ticket-puncher looked at her suspiciously. "Were you talking to me?" Sister Sainte-Catherine brought her hand to her mouth. "Was I talking out loud?" "You're no ordinary nun!" At the corner of Bernard, Sister Sainte-Catherine said goodbye to the ticket-puncher and got out of the car. She was almost at her destination and she felt a pang of anguish. But the memory of her mother, whom she had revered, restored her self-confidence and she headed briskly for the Mother House.

Charlotte Côté arrived at the school on the arm of Dr. San-regret, who had left his patients in his waiting-room to accompany her. He was a stooped man who had once been handsome, but the miseries of the world had worn him out prematurely, making his cheeks hollow, lining his forehead with indelible wrinkles and filling his gaze with an indefinable light that bore witness to the horrors to which long years of practice had subjected him. Dr. Sanregret had often told his neighbour, Ti-Lou, in the days when, out of sheer pity, he would deliver "happiness pills" to her home: "Poor people's diseases are the diseases of poverty; poor people's diseases are ugly diseases that sneak up on the weak and ignorant and defenseless; poor people's diseases just make you want to go and hide, because neglect and ignorance and backwardness unfortunately can't be cured with medicine." When Charlotte burst into his office without knocking, out of breath, tears pouring down her neck, he realized immediately that it had to do with Simone, that something had happened at school. He never would have guessed, though, that Mother Benoîte des Anges—whom he mistrusted so much because he sensed that behind her unctuous civilities and false airs of a fat, generous woman, she could be dan-

73

gerous – could be the very root of the problem. He knew that Simone's class-mates wouldn't let such a chance pass without a few remarks of their own, flattering or devastating, but he never would have thought that the Principal would stoop to question the need for a minor operation because of money. So he had reacted very belligerently to Charlotte's account. He sprang to his feet, took down his hat, which he always wore when he went out, even on the most humid summer days, took Charlotte's arm, and said, "We'll settle this right now. That old goat won't get off so easily, believe me!" Dr. Sanregret's office was quite near the school, only a hundred yards away. They crossed rue de Lanaudière, almost running, Charlotte repeating over and over, "Get her, Doctor, she can't get away with this!", the old man merely grunting as he chewed on his dead cigarette. But the doctor slowed down and even stopped at the cement steps. "Catch your breath, Madame Côté, you don't want her to see that you're nervous. With people like that, you can't show your emotions." Charlotte took several deep breaths, hoping to control the beating of her heart, which she could hear pounding against her chest. Before he started up the stairs, Dr. Sanregret had made a remark that astonished Charlotte. "From what I can see the farce hasn't started yet." "The farce? What farce?" "The repository, Madame Côté. They usually start putting it up on Monday afternoon." As she placed her foot on the bottom step Charlotte saw once more the angels that delighted her every year; the robes of pink, green or blue cotton, the gilded throne, the Virgin whose face changed every year, now pimply and obese, now dry and nervous, sometimes – but rarely – lovely as a summer day, like the real Virgin, and she thought it was a pity such a fine repository should conceal the true face of a school where injustice had always reigned. They rang several times before the doctor realized that, surprisingly, the door wasn't locked. "Sister Saint-Georges isn't here today! But she's healthy as a horse!" They went up the few steps inside the portico, which led up to the portress's and the Principal's offices. Sister Saint-Georges's was empty. "We'll have to go straight to the Principal." "That's fine with me. Better, in fact. Not so complicated." At that moment Charlotte felt hostility climbing up her spine, an almost pleasant prickling along her back, and when she looked toward Mother Benoîte's office door her heart, instead of calming down, beat even faster – in a way she didn't mind at all. She felt like rushing the door, going inside the office without knocking, as she'd done at the doctor's, and throwing herself at the fat nun, covering her with insults and spit. But the doctor put his hand on Charlotte's arm and she realized she must be sedate, calm, cold and articulate – the exact opposite of her true nature. The doctor rapped three times and a curt "Come in!" followed almost immediately. The old man walked slowly into the office. Charlotte stayed on the threshhold. And the wave of words that followed came almost without her being aware of it. She hadn't even put one foot inside the Principal's office, as if she was afraid of getting it dirty, but all her frustrations, her fears, her memories of sleepless nights spent turning over reproaches made by overly strict nuns with no thought for the pain they might cause; all those years of detentions, of memory work, of supposed impurities flushed out where they didn't even exist, of suspicions, accusations, tears of helplessness, of contained rage, poured out of her mouth in a single breath like lace worked of sick words, a ribbon of endless phrases, green as rancour and wet with bile. This haemorrhage of reproaches, this sentence with no right of appeal, was handed down from the doorstep in a nearly toneless voice and an even, dispassionate tone. And Mother Benoîte des Anges took it open-mouthed, as one receives an unexpected *coup de grâce* from an unforeseen direction. "Aren't you ashamed! Doesn't it ever get to you, being so mean! When you go to bed at night

and think over what you've done that day, the way you nuns
always taught us to do, don't you blush with shame? Don't
you turn *blue* with shame? All the punishments you've
handed out and all the times you humiliated us, don't they
choke you? Nothing's changed here. You still take out your
frustrations on poor defenceless kids who trust you to show
them how to live their lives! You've always got a crucifix in
one hand and a wooden ruler in the other! As long as we're
on that subject, why don't you just light out at the kids with
the crucifix in both hands – it'd hurt them more! Is it because you just haven't got that far yet, or is your hypocrisy
holding you back? I spent seven years here, not all that long
ago, and what I remember about it isn't very happy. Childhood ought to be a happy time, but my memories of the
time I spent here are rotten and dirty and twisted because
of crazy women like you who don't know the first thing
about children. You try and turn them into puppets instead
of women! Oh, I knew a few Sisters that were all right,
smart, gentle nuns who loved us, but nuns like you always
make me forget them and when I think about this school
what I see is a blackboard with my name on it at the top of
the list of detentions! When you've had the bad luck not to
be at the top of your class or a brown-noser, your memories
of school will be bad, because you nuns couldn't care less
about anybody except the brown-nosers and the teachers'
pets! It was no joke when my child, my daughter, who I love
more than anything else in this world and who I want to see
grow up like a normal human being, was old enough to start
school here: I was even scared to send her! But I couldn't
afford to put her in private school and I heard that the École
des Saints-Anges had changed a lot since I was here fifteen
years ago, that it wasn't as strict and they showed more
respect for the girls than they did back then. But nobody
told me about you, Mother Benoîte! A mental case like you
can ruin the reputation of a whole community of nuns, you
know. You're responsible for your school's reputation, god-

damn it, so you better keep your eyes open! How dare you talk about money to a child who doesn't even know what money is! How dare you ask a little girl for two dollars when that little girl's never seen anything bigger than a dime or a quarter? My daughter just had a shock, Mother Benoîte, a big shock. She just found out she can be beautiful. Yes, beautiful! and I couldn't care less if you don't like that word, I'm going to say it again! Beautiful! My daughter's going to be a beautiful woman and I hope she'll find herself a handsome husband and they'll make beautiful babies too! And let me tell you, you old sow, I don't want you ruining her happiness by upsetting her like you did this morning! I don't ever want you to say another word to my daughter, understand? She's none of your business, you're just the Principal of this school and she's got a teacher that understands her! So don't talk to her, don't have anything to do with her, and don't even look at her if it bothers you that she's going to be beautiful! And you're not getting the two dollars I owe you! You're not getting that money because I haven't got it! Simone'll be here tomorrow morning and she won't have any two dollars, but you're still going to let her go to her class, otherwise I'll be back here myself and next time you'll get more than insults! Maybe the other parents are too chicken to do anything, but I'm not, so hold onto your hat! I always wondered if nuns had any hair on their heads and I sure would like to check for myself! And if you ever have to talk about money again, phone me. I'll be glad to tell you straight out that I haven't got any! It doesn't humiliate me any more, I'm used to it, but Simone still doesn't realize how poor we are and I hope it'll be a good long time before she does find out. That child has everything she needs because my husband and me, we don't care if we have to do without so she won't have to know right away that we're poor; but we sure as hell aren't going to do without things we need to subscribe to *L'Estudiante*! I know two dollars isn't much for rich people like you, that hang around with priests and lawyers, but to us it means a lot of quarts of milk and a lot of slices of bread! If you can hide your Christian charity under your hanky you can get along without our two dollars! It's women like you that make our childhoods miserable! Even though you're supposed to be there to show us the way! And how come you always point us down the road of humiliation? How come you don't teach us self-confidence instead of always putting us down? Well don't put my daughter down, it's hard enough for her to stand up straight! Her teacher and I, we're going to do everything we can to see that she finishes this school year like everybody else. I'm certainly not going to give you the pleasure of making her repeat grade six! Now shut your mouth, you're slobbering all over your chin!" When Dr. Sanregret heard Charlotte Côté's footsteps on the stairs, he opened his eyes, for he had closed them to keep from bursting out laughing at the comical expression on Mother Benoîte's face. Then he walked out of her office without a word, closing the door softly behind him. Charlotte was sitting at the bottom of the cement steps, and at first the doctor thought she was crying, for her shoulders were shaking convulsively, but as he approached her, he realized she was laughing, openly and happily, laughter that bubbled like a fountain, spreading over boulevard Saint-Joseph, clear notes that tinkled in the still air. "This is the happiest day of my life! I don't know why I waited so long; I really needed that!" Then, thinking of what had brought her this far, of the pain that still lay at the heart of her enormous relief, she became silent, wiping the tears that ran down her cheeks. Then she got up, sighing. "But I'd rather have it locked up inside me than see Simone in the state she's in!"

Mother Superior was playing with the wood and metal cross

that hung on her bosom. She had the most famous hands in the entire community: people talked about their elegance, their delicacy, and their whiteness, and maintained that they could heal or, at the very least, console, and Mother Notre-Dame du Rosaire knew how to use this to advantage. Not that she was hypocritical or deceitful, but when she found herself in a delicate situation like the present one, the fascination her hands exerted over other nuns could prove highly useful. Strangely enough, however, Sister Sainte-Catherine didn't seem to notice her Superior's gesture and Mother Notre-Dame was somewhat disconcerted. Sister Sainte-Catherine was staring at her without blinking, waiting with obvious anxiety for the reply that was so long in coming. Mother Notre-Dame had always been very fond of Sister Sainte-Catherine. She even felt a maternal affection for the young nun, and the letter she had just read, of nearly Dantesque excesses, in which the word "witch" appeared no less than four times, left her deeply perplexed: either the person standing before her, who had refused to take a seat while she was reading, was an angel of patience and indulgence and the letter she held in her hands a tissue of lies, the work of a paranoid lunatic, or Mother Benoîte des Anges was right and Sister Sainte-Catherine was, as she put it so vividly, "a vile creature who is doing her utmost to ruin us, whom we must thwart in her desire to serve the works and ceremonies of her Master, the Devil." Mother Notre-Dame felt that Mother Benoîte had gone too far, that her missive was very melodramatic, but she respected the usually cool, calm Principal and didn't like to think that she'd suddenly, out of the blue, become passionately unfair because of some prank played by one of the grade six teachers; no, as Sister Sainte-Catherine had said before handing her the letter, the truth must lie somewhere between the two versions. But where? It would have been much easier for her to sentence Sister Sainte-Catherine with no appeal, to send her back to her school with a reprimand, but when a nun travels across a good part of the city to deliver, in person, the letter that repudiates her, she can't be completely in the wrong unless she's very crafty indeed .... Her hand gesture was caused as much by nervousness, then, as by the wish that Sister Sainte-Catherine would stop staring at her. But the younger nun hadn't moved a muscle and Mother Notre-Dame du Rosaire sensed that she must say something, that Sister Sainte-Catherine wouldn't stop looking at her face until the verdict had been given. Mother Superior started slowly, changing course, hemming and hawing, reproaching Sister Sainte-Catherine for travelling by herself and for not wearing gloves, though that wasn't really the issue; then she asked about the repository, which she intended to visit herself this year, as Mother Benoîte des Anges and Monsignor Bernier had invited her to join the Corpus Christi procession, and then she stopped in mid-sentence and simply admitted to Sister Sainte-Catherine how ill at ease she was. "I respect you both, for different reasons, and I am bitterly grieved by this conflict." "But you're the one who must decide, Mother Notre-Dame." "You ask me to choose, Sister Sainte-Catherine ...." "I'm asking you to be fair." Mother Notre-Dame bowed her head. "Then you're condemning yourself. The only justice I know, Sister Sainte-Catherine, is the justice of the hierarchy. And so I must ask you to sacrifice yourself, to accept this ... inconvenience in all Christian humility. Understand me ... I can't impose you on Mother Benoîte des Anges and I can't transfer your Principal. She's doing an excellent job where she is. You know all she's done for the school, and moving her now would raise questions I couldn't answer. Leave the École des Saints-Anges with your head high, Sister, and I promise to send you somewhere less difficult, where the people are better off and the children more disciplined and more receptive .... I know you adore the Saint-Stanislas parish, but remember – the pain you will feel when you leave there will subside in time, and the years

80

to come will be more ... gratifying for you in a parish that isn't so rough. Offer up the next few months in atonement for the sins of the world: that's the very reason for our existence and too often we forget it .... Above everything, above your own pain and troubles, above all wickedness and desires and accusations, Sister Sainte-Catherine, our Heavenly Father judges, and He judges fairly. God has already made His choice, Sister; beside it, my own choice would be laughable." An unbearable silence settled over Mother Superior's office after this last remark. Mother Notre-Dame knew very well that this sermon on the Creator's judgement had been only for show, a smoke-screen, and she felt bitterly ashamed. She wished she could leap up and run out of her office screaming, or throw herself at the feet of Sister Sainte Catherine, whose life she had just destroyed, and beg her pardon, holding her to her heart, but she couldn't move. She maintained that she was unable to choose, and yet she was making a choice: the hierarchy over justice, demanding sacrifice and submission instead of showing signs of humanity. She could still feel Sister Sainte-Catherine's gaze on her, heavy, burning, disconcerting. And it was the younger nun who finally broke the long, uncomfortable silence. "You're abandoning me, Mother." She said this without passion, almost affectionately, and Mother Notre-Dame thought she would die of humiliation. Sister Sainte-Catherine walked to the door and opened it. Before she went out she paused briefly, but didn't turn around to speak. "I'm not asking what you intend to do about Sister Sainte-Thérèse de l'Enfant-Jésus, Mother. I'm too afraid of what you might tell me." After Sister Sainte-Catherine left her office, Mother Notre-Dame tore Mother Benoîte's letter into four pieces, dropped them on her blotter and stared at them for several long minutes.

The Six A class greeted Sister Sainte-Catherine's replacement with disappointment, sensing that their afternoon in the shed – taking out the props, sets and costumes for the repository, spreading them out in the main yard under their teacher's supervision and choosing the ones still in good condition and those that would have to be replaced as quickly as possible, during the next two feverish days – had been put off till tomorrow or, according to Pierrette, the top-ranking defeatist in all three grade-six classes, that the procession had simply been cancelled and that the week they'd been talking about for so long was going to be totally ruined. But immediately after prayers, Sister Saint-Georges reassured them, explaining that nothing was wrong, that Sister Sainte-Catherine had decided to postpone getting started until the next day and take half a day to rest before plunging into what would be, for her, a very busy week. The little girls were swallowing these explanations without batting an eye until Pierrette expressed her doubt in a tone that made several heads turn. "Don't you believe me, Pierrette Guérin?" "The week's got off to such a bad start I can't really believe what you just told us." "You're very rude, you know!" "I wish I could believe you, Sister Saint-Georges, but listen: Simone took sick this morning the minute we got to school, then Sister Sainte-Catherine disappeared as if somebody'd put her under a spell and now you turn up out of the blue and act as if nothing was wrong. But whenever you come into a class, Sister Saint-Georges, it's because there's something wrong somewhere! We all like you – but we like you out in the hall!" "How do you expect to get through life with an attitude like that? Do you know that thoughts like that can hurt you for the rest of your life? If you'd think about tomorrow's pleasures instead of whining about today's little problems, your life would be a lot happier!" Affectionate mockery greeted this awkward little sermon and Sister Saint-Georges was silent for a moment. "Okay, girls, I'll tell you why I'm here." Silence was restored. But Pierrette said, loud enough for everyone to hear, "We're too old for fairy-tales!" Sister Saint-Georges climbed up on the platform, limping slightly. "You've all got to behave yourselves this afternoon. Sister Principal doesn't know I'm filling in for your teacher ...." The little girls looked at each other, frowning. "I had an errand to do for Mother Benoîte, but Sister Sainte-Catherine wanted the afternoon off, like I told you, so she asked me if she could do it instead .... Now don't ask me any more because I don't know any more .... All I know is, right now Sister Sainte-Catherine's probably already on the bus, on her way to the Mother House." The silence was broken by a few little girls giving everyone else the benefit of their conjectures on their teacher's disappearance. "She doesn't want to do the repository!" "She just found out she's got a fatal disease." "Mother Dragon Devil kicked her out 'cause she's too nice!" The most preposterous suggestions began to rain down, punctuated by laughter from the little girls; then one of their classmates came out with a particularly good one. "She's allergic to her nun's clothes!" "She fell in love with Monsignor Bernier and Sister Principal's jealous!" "She's Simone Côté's real mother and she took her baptismal certificate to prove it to Mother Superior!" Pierrette Guérin didn't appreciate this last remark by Diane Beausoleil, and she turned to the other girl, who was sitting just behind her. "You're a drip, Diane Beausoleil! If my best friend's mother was a nun it'd mean her father was a priest, and Simone's father's a tailor, stupid!" Diane Beausoleil, who didn't like the "Thérèse-'n'-Pierrette" trio one bit, made a face, and replied, "You're stupid yourself, Pierrette Guérin, how come you're first in class?" "Maybe I'm not a genius, but I work. Not like you, going steady and you're only eleven!" Diane Beausoleil had got to her feet, and now she was leaning over Pierrette. "I'm going steady 'cause the guys like me! I haven't got a mouth full of crooked teeth and I don't smell like I need a bath!" A full-blown ovation followed this exchange. The little girls loved a no-holds-barred battle in which the most far-fetched arguments came together, blended, got tangled almost without let-up, so voluble and imaginative were they, until the subject (often very ordinary, even utterly harmless) was completely forgotten and the argument turned into unrestrained fantasy. "Point for Diane!" Pierrette turned away from her adversary. "Maybe my teeth are crooked, but after school they stay in my mouth. You have to take yours home to your mother in your lunch-bag!" "One for Pierrette!" Sister Saint-Georges slammed the ruler on the desk. "Cut it out, this minute!" The class's attention returned to her. She cleared her throat. "Now that you're letting your imaginations run wild, do something useful with them! Sister Sainte-Catherine told me to have you write a composition." There was some applause. A few little shouts of protest, too. And even a "Nuts!" from Diane Beausoleil, who hated writing compositions. Pierrette smiled. "Diane's going to make another hundred and fourteen mistakes, just like last week!" Sister Saint-Georges got up, hobbled to the edge of the platform, but decided not to step down and went back to Sister Sainte-Catherine's desk. "Hold on, girls, I'm not done yet .... She said I could pick whatever subject I wanted ... and I think I've got it. You're going to write me twenty-five lines on why Sister Sainte-Catherine went away. Make up stories, give your little brains some exercise, do whatever you want – but I want thirty compositions on my desk at five to four!" At first the class looked at each other dubiously, then Sister Saint-Georges's assignment sank in until finally even Diane Beausoleil took some pleasure in sounding this mystery that was making them all feel uncomfortable. "Now be quiet! No copying! I don't want to see two stories the same!" A few minutes later Sister Saint-Georges was gloating. She had good reason to be proud: the girls were quiet, the afternoon would pass without incident and that very evening she'd show the thirty compositions to Sister Sainte-Catherine and Sister Sainte-Thérèse, and they'd certainly congratulate her for her intelligent initiative. Pierrette had seen Thérèse in the school yard at recess and told her all about it. "Hey, that's fun! What'd you put in your story?" "Well, I said Sister Sainte-Catherine was a German spy working for the Germans and she had a really important message to pass on to her superior who's the head of all the German spies in Canada working for the Germans." "That doesn't make sense." "Listen, you'll see, it's good .... Anyway, I said that Mother Superior isn't the real Mother Superior, that Sister Clump Foot's the real Mother Superior and she's disguised as Sister Clump Foot but she isn't really .... See?" "No." "So anyway, Sister Sainte-Catherine gave a *real* message to Sister Clump Foot, who's the real head spy, and then she took the bus so the French spies'd follow her to the phony Mother Superior ...." Thérèse suddenly let out a little cry, and turned pale. Pierrette started. Both girls were leaning against the big wooden fence that went around the school yard and Thérèse, tired by her friend's overly complicated story, had glanced between the grey-painted slats. "What is it, Thérèse?" "Look! There he is again!" Pierrette stuck her nose against the fence. A young man in his early twenties, handsome as a god but visibly anxious about something, tormented even, was sitting on some steps on the other side of rue Garnier. He was looking toward the little girls. "He sure is! And he's looking at you!" Thérèse stepped back a few paces. She was trembling slightly. "That makes four or five times he's done that." "I told you to tell your mother." "No, I know him, I met him in Parc Lafontaine last month .... He isn't dangerous... And he's so handsome." "How come you're shaking like that?" Thérèse looked her friend square in the eye. "'Cause I like it."

SECOND
MOVEMENT

Andante moderato

He was lying on his back, eyes wide open, hands flat on top of the sheet, on either side of his body. He hadn't slept all night. So tormented had been his waking hours, so painful the long period of trying unsuccessfully to analyse his situation, because his intelligence was hardly enough to fill a thimble, as his mother used to say when he was young, that at times he felt like screaming, like bashing his head against the walls, like running out of the Gariépy house and throwing himself under a car. He knew the desire that had been racking him for a month now was forbidden, dirty. He was even afraid to admit his true intentions, and tried to persuade himself that the image he was pursuing was suffused with purity or real emotion, something like the admiration one might feel before a precocious child, the fascination of a developing personality that is breaking its constraints and seems about to blossom. Sometimes at night he even imagined himself a little boy, chastely kissing on the cheek, with no ulterior motive, the little girl who didn't yet know how to use her beauty; but when he was before her, when he caught a glimpse of her through the wooden slats of the fence around her school, all his illusions took flight. This blow to his heart that made his knees quake, the desire that coursed through his body, suddenly, beyond his control, the dizziness he felt when she surreptitiously watched him, while she feigned interest in her skipping-rope ("One potato, two potato, three potato, four ....") or in what her friend with the crooked teeth was saying, overwhelmed him every time, and every time he told himself, "What the hell am I doing here? I can have all the women I want, what am I doing spying through a fence, scaring the wits out of some little school-kid?" That was what he'd been trying all night to analyse, but he couldn't even untangle the contradictory feelings that had him so perturbed. He always persuaded himself in the end that he had no intention of throwing himself at her, that would be contemptible; but what was the meaning of those erections that overwhelmed him, the sudden desire every time he laid eyes on her? Would the time come when he'd no longer have any control over himself, when .... Old lady Gariépy's alarm clock began ringing at the other end of the house and Gérard started. Cold sweat was pouring down his face. Yet at eight o'clock in the morning it was already so hot .... He heard old man Gariépy belch, clear his throat, spit. Old lady Gariépy's voice was raised for the first time that day, hoarse and choked from all the shouting she'd done in her life. "I hope that one landed in the spittoon, you pig!" Gérard Bleau's room was at the back of the house, in a sort of cubby-hole between the kitchen and the back shed. This put him rather near the garbage, which could be inconvenient during summer heat waves but, as he put it so well whenever his landlord asked why he didn't try to find a bigger, brighter, airier room, "I'm used to your smells and I'm used to your voices and I'm used to my room .... If I was in another one I'd never get to sleep!" And now for more than a month he hadn't been able to sleep, even among these familiar things that used to give him such a feeling of security .... He heard old lady Gariépy go into the kitchen, fill the kettle with hot water and put it on the stove. "You awake, Gérard?" He didn't answer. It was better if she thought he was still asleep. "You going to work today?" He'd said he was sick two weeks earlier, and he'd been killing endless days walking all over Montreal, head buzzing, sobs catching in his throat, invariably ending up – in the morning when he had no control over himself or in the afternoon when he managed to control, somewhat, his desire to see her – near the École des Saints-Anges, his nose pressed against the wooden fence, heart palpitating. The day before, however, he had plucked up his courage, got up, washed, shaved, taken the lunch old lady Gariépy made for him every morning (it was included in the cost of his room and board) and gone to work. He had been greeted with laughter, applause and slaps on the back, but once he was in front of the bus that had to be cleaned up and repaired, the emptiness of his life hit him in the face and he got a flash of the endless line of buses he'd have to clean up and repair till the end of his days, and the image of Thérèse pulling up her stocking, fastening her garter, frowning, so seriously did she tackle everything she did, and the other people in his life as an underpaid worker everyone looked down on, added to all that, increased his feeling of helplessness, making him reel under the shock. He threw down his huge grease-stained gloves and streaked out of Provincial Transport, colliding with his stupefied employer, who shouted, "That's right, go back to bed if you're still sick, you son of a bitch! But don't show your face around here again! I don't need weaklings like you!" A weakling .... He saw his mother again, on her deathbed, two years earlier, cheeks blazing, breath foetid, eyes feverish. "You're such a handsome boy! You'll never have any trouble. Use your looks! The way I used mine. They'll all say you're too handsome, that you look like a girl, that you're a weakling – but really they'll just be pissed off! And you just let them be, Gérard – they've got it coming to them!" But Gérard, so popular with the women that certain jealous husbands sometimes showed up at the Gariépys' door carrying a baseball bat or a broken beer bottle as he took off down the lane like a scared rabbit – a pitiful Don Juan whose ridiculous escapades were the laughing-stock of the Côte Sherbrooke – had wanted to prove to himself that he could get along without women after his mother died. He was nineteen at the time and the list of his conquests was already fairly respectable. So he'd tracked down a job he thought was well paid at first, but it soon proved to be mind destroying and so dirty he could spend hours cleaning himself without completely getting rid of the oil stains on his hands and, worst of all, that brought him no gratification aside from the questionably good pay. When one of his new conquests asked where he worked, he'd answer evasively or quiet her with a hastily executed kiss. "It's ten after eight, Gérard, you'll be late." "I lost my job, Madame Gariépy!" Brief silence. "I got all the time in the world!" Five seconds later, old lady Gariépy was standing in his doorway, a slice of bread in one hand, a knife in the other. "Lost your job?" "Yeah." "What'll you do?" He tried his finest smile, but then remembered that old lady Gariépy was too old or too foolish to appreciate it, and thus was immune to his charms. "It's spring, Madame Gariépy. I'm taking a rest." "And who'll pay for your room? Your women?" "I got some money put aside, Madame Gariépy .... I never gave you any trouble with that, so don't get your shirt in a knot .... And if I ever run out of money, I'll leave." Reassured, Madame Gariépy went away. Gérard sighed. "That's right, don't ask if it matters to me or if it's changed my life or how I feel .... Just make sure you'll get your five bucks." Two minutes later the aroma of fresh coffee drifted through the house. "I'll get up anyway." The fears that had obsessed him the night before vanished as soon as he was at the table with a big cup of coffee and four golden slices of toast.

"If she's that pretty, tell her to come over and see us." Albertine put the quart of milk on the table. Immediately Marcel, a broad white moustache under his nose, held out his glass, smiling. "What do you say, Marcel?" "Please, momma!" "Put your glass on the table, I don't want a mess like last time." At the thought of the spilt milk, the broken glass and the fight that had ensued, Philippe burst out laughing. His brother Richard shrugged. "Gee you're mean this morning,

Flip. Is it only other people's trouble that makes you laugh?" Albertine, who had just sat down between Thérèse and Richard, slapped his hand, which had just grabbed a piece of toast without asking permission. "You haven't even swallowed what's in your mouth and now you want another piece! Maybe your mother hasn't brought you up right, but I will!" Richard immediately crooned, "Please, *ma tante!*" "All right, but just one. There's a war on, remember! Think about the little kids in France with nothing to eat and offer it up to the good Lord." Thérèse sighed loudly. "Oh momma, come on, stop talking about the war every time we put any food in our mouths." "You've got a short memory, my girl! There's rationing on and you know what that means. We explained it to you and you aren't morons! You need coupons to get sugar and meat and butter ...." The children, who'd known her refrain by heart for two years now and who, in any case, had never been deprived of anything, had already stopped listening. Albertine spread a generous layer of butter on her toast, her eyes gleaming with greed, then she chewed slowly, seriously, washing down every mouthful with a sip of tea, which she drank so hot everyone expected to hear her scream with pain whenever she brought her cup to her lips. Ever since the fat woman, Richard and Philippe's mother, had left for the hospital two weeks earlier, Albertine had been transformed, as if her new responsibilities had made her human: she was as grouchy as ever, but now behind the insults and slaps she still distributed left and right, you could sense a sort of crude love, unformed and ill controlled but present nonetheless, which made her a very efficient if not terribly likable head of the household. Albertine wasn't cut out for communal life. She'd always thought there were too many women in the house on rue Fabre, that the tasks weren't properly shared and most of all, that she and her sister-in-law did each other more harm than good. But now that her mother, old Victoire, hardly left her room any more and her brother's wife was in the hospital, Albertine was responsible for taking care of everybody's needs and problems and she was secretly proud of herself. Now there was nobody to get in her way and criticize her, and she could do everything according to her own tastes, rhythm and personality. For instance, she liked to eat breakfast and lunch with the four children. She rarely smiled and showed no more affection than in the past, but the children sensed the difference in her nature and indeed, Richard and Philippe, who had always hated her because she was constantly giving their mother hell, were slowly learning to love her despite her considerable flaws, which, as it happens, were turning out to be very funny when you learned to make use of them as Thérèse had always done. Philippe was already a past master of the art of checking her fits of rage: he had discovered that a well-placed kiss or a lavish, unexpected caress would make her splutter, blocking her completely, leaving her disarmed and at the mercy of the person at whom she'd been hurling abuse a minute earlier. They both took great advantage of it. It had become a sort of game between them: Albertine knew now that when she got angry at Philippe, something would happen to make her lay down her arms before she knew it and she didn't struggle any more as she would have done just a few short weeks before. She was learning, almost in spite of herself, how sweet a child's caresses can be, and she was developing a liking for them, without admitting it even to herself. "Getting back to your friend Simone, Thérèse, ask her to come for lunch today. I'd like to see that operation of hers." Four heads turned in her direction at once. "Why are you gawking at me like that? I'm not a monster! Can't I even ask one of your friends to come and eat with us?" It was the first time she'd done so, and the children were flabbergasted. There were always too many people at the table to allow the children to invite their friends for a meal. In any case, Albertine had always been a little ashamed of their daily fare, which was quite respectable and far more varied and abundant than what most families on rue Fabre had to eat. ("I don't want the neighbours to know we eat bologna twice a week, even if they eat it every day!") Thérèse said nothing. She merely smiled at her mother, who turned very red and went back to her cup of tea. That, too, was a first. "Can I ask Bernard Morrier? I ate at his place last Tuesday." Albertine looked up. "Look, Richard, ask Bernard Morrier some other time. We don't have to feed the whole neighbourhood just because Simone Côté had an operation on her face, goddamn it! I said one guest for lunch and that's enough for today!" Richard wrinkled his nose and mouth as he played with the rest of his unfinished toast. "And get a move on: it's a quarter after eight, you're going to be late again!" She had already started clearing the table. The three oldest children ran from the table. Marcel finished his milk in peace, then asked innocently, "What about me, momma, can I ask Duplessis?" Albertine nearly dropped her teapot. She swung around toward her son. "Marcel, momma's told you not to talk about Duplessis. He's been gone for a month now and Marie-Sylvia's eating her heart out. There's no more Duplessis: he likely got hit by a streetcar or clawed to bits by one of his cat friends. Momma's tried to tell you twenty times now." Marcel smiled very condescendingly, not looking at his mother. "The lady that lives downstairs from Bernard Morrier said she'd show him to me today. He's getting better!" Albertine sat down beside Marcel and ran her hand through his hair, which was short and bristly. "And momma told you not to tell stories, Marcel. It isn't nice. Momma's glad you've got an imagination, but cripes, you're only four now, what'll you be like when you're twenty?" Marcel frowned, obstinately. "Liars always get punished, Marcel, because they always get

95

caught." Marcel looked up at her. His voice shook a little when he spoke. "How come you don't believe me, momma? How come nobody believes me?"

Simone and Pierrette were waiting for Thérèse at the bottom of the stairs. Simone was in a very pitiful state. Pierrette had her arm around her friend's waist, as if she was afraid Simone might collapse on the sidewalk or vanish into dust in the morning sun. Simone looked stubbornly at the toes of her shoes, frowning, her expression obstinate. Pierrette gestured helplessly to Thérèse, who decided to use good humour rather than pity. "If it isn't the lovely Simone Côté herself in person! How's every little thing? Are you cold? You're as stiff as if you'd been waiting for two hours on the skating rink .... Look what a nice day it is, Simone! The sun's telling you hello." Pierrette rolled her eyes, and gestured to Thérèse that she was laying it on a bit thick. Thérèse made a face and went on in the same vein. "The little birdies are going chirp-chirp, your little friends are going to walk you to school, the sky's blue, you've got the prettiest face in the world, what more do you want?" Still Simone didn't answer. Thérèse, whose patience was always short-lived, turned her back on her two friends and walked away, muttering be-tween her teeth, "You're so pigheaded you're a pain in the ass, Simone Côté, but you're not going to make me late for school!" Simone dropped Pierrette's arm and ran after Thérèse, who was swinging her school-bag at arm's length. "Wait, Thérèse, I don't want to be late either!" Pierrette, her feelings hurt, grumpily caught up with them. And the trio, "Thérèse-'n'-Pierrette" turned the corner of Fabre and Gilford as usual, arm in arm, but their hearts weren't in it that morning; no song rose up, no laughter either. Three silent little creatures were walking gravely toward rue Garnier, keeping in step far more out of habit than conviction. Simone seemed smaller, more fragile than ever, and her two guardian angels, whose good moods had vanished – the one out of sheer impatience, the other out of simple jealousy – didn't support and flank her quite as well as usual, as if a spell had been broken. Pierrette broke the silence first. She looked over Simone's head at Thérèse and spoke as if the third girl wasn't there. "If I knew we'd have to take this crap from her, I'd've pushed her face in when I saw her this morning; that would've been a lot simpler than spoiling her like a baby!" Thérèse couldn't hold back the hint of a smile. "You aren't jealous because she followed me, are you?" "Me, jealous!" Pierrette turned suddenly scarlet, humiliated that her jealousy was so easily discovered. "Jealous of a little drip who'd rather have insults than kisses and cuddles! Are you nuts? Keep Simone Côté if you want her that bad! There's lots of other girls that'll be glad to make friends with me!" Simone abruptly broke free of their embrace. They had just reached the corner of Gilford and Garnier. "Quit talking about me as if I wasn't there. I can hear you and I can understand you, you know, I'm not a three-month-old baby! You didn't even come and see how I was after school yesterday and now you expect me to throw myself in your arms as if nothing happened!" Thérèse and Pierrette looked at each other, dumbfounded. "We went yesterday afternoon ...." "I was asleep, that doesn't count!" "Hey, come on, we thought you were supposed to be resting ... that's what your mother said." "Anyway, I'm big enough to go to school by myself!" And for the first time in years, Simone ran off alone, leaving Thérèse and Pierrette high and dry, mouths agape, arms empty. A few moments later Simone heard her friends running after her. "Wait for us, Simone! Wait!" But instead of slowing down she doubled her speed, crossed boulevard

Saint-Joseph without even looking for cars and rushed into the school yard like a suicide into the river.

The day before, when she came back from the Mother House, Sister Sainte-Catherine hadn't seen either Sister Sainte-Thérèse or Mother Benoîte. She had gone immediately to her little room, bolted the door and knelt at her prie-dieu. All evening she tried to find a course of action, a plan that would release her from the Principal's yoke, that would rid the school of Mother Benoîte; the most harebrained schemes, the wildest plots were hatching in her mind, ridiculous and impossible to carry out, the childish outpourings of a soul in need of revenge, but knowing there was no recourse, because obedience and submission were inscribed forever, in letters of fire, on her life. She gave in to the wildest dreams because they were her last resort. In the few days she had left she could, to keep from exploding with rage, going mad with anger, imagine herself in control of the situation, and let loose from the darkest corners of her soul the reproaches, cries, tears, laments and accusations stored up and bound there since she'd first met Mother Benoîte, that were only waiting for an occasion like this to burst like pomegranates in the sun, letting their poisonous juice gush out. The injustice was so flagrant, so caustic, that she was surprised to catch herself trembling at times as she stared at the great crucifix, her mind elsewhere, seeking a form of humiliation that would reduce Mother Benoîte to silence, fell her like a rifle-shot, or embarrass her, consume her, devour her down to the smallest bone, evaporating even her densest fluids. Around eight o'clock, just before the bell for evening prayers, she heard a scurrying, like mice, in the corridor, and then someone scratched at her door. She knew it was Sister Sainte-Thérèse, but she didn't want her friend to see her in such a state, so she didn't answer. Then the beloved voice came through the wooden door, pleading, "I know you're there, Sainte-Catherine .... You've hardly eaten all day .... I brought you some fruit ...." But Sister Sainte-Catherine held firm, hardly breathing so there'd be no sound for Sister Sainte-Thérèse to hear. Again, the scurrying sound like mice. A door quietly closing. Silence. Then she let go and wept; the tears welled up, then poured down her hands, spread over her face. She was bent double, like someone in pain, and moaning softly, desperately, alone. Her small bedside light was still burning very late that night. But Sister Sainte-Catherine wasn't reading *The Imitation of Christ* or the *Journal* of Sainte Thérèse of Lisieux: she was dreaming of sweet violence and splendid hecatombs. And her insomniac dreams weren't very different from those spun by Simone as she slept: in just one night Mother Benoîte was murdered seventeen times, in seventeen different ways, several of them utterly original and hitherto unknown.

Mother Benoîte saw Simone come running into the school yard and throw herself into the arms of Lucienne Boileau, who seemed very surprised but absolutely overjoyed. It was eight twenty-nine and the principal had been hoping that Charlotte Côté would keep her daughter at home to avoid the anathema of the nun she had dared to insult so generously the day before. "If that child doesn't have her two dollars I don't know what I'll do to her." Mother Benoîte walked up the few cement steps and gestured to Sister Sainte-Georges to ring the bell. Just then Thérèse and Pierrette rushed into the yard, obviously looking for their friend. When they saw her in conversation with poor Lucienne, who seemed pitifully happy, they stopped short and looked at each other, incredulous. The bell rang through the school yard as though to freeze this moment for all eternity: Simone's betrayal would remain forever engraved in the hearts of Thérèse and Pierrette, who would still be reproaching her for it twenty years later, in the bar of the Coconut Inn or in Betty Bird's little cream-and-pink salon. ("Remember that time you came back to school alone because you were pissed off at us and threw yourself at that fat pig Lucienne Boileau just to get our backs up?" "Me? I never did such a thing!" "C'mon, Harelip, I remember like it was yesterday! And believe me, kiddo, if I hadn't held myself back that morning ....") Six hundred pairs of little feet flitted across the asphalt yard. They got in line quickly. A grade-nine girl sneezed three times in a row and her whole class burst out laughing. Their teacher rolled her eyes. Sneezing powder, which hadn't wreaked its havoc for several months now, had reappeared in her class the day before, and something had to be done right away to nip these troubles in the bud, otherwise the week would be a trying one, filled with giggles and sneezing. Sister Sainte-Angèle turned her head toward the Principal, who understood the alarm signal and with all her might blew the little whistle she always wore around her neck but rarely used. "Nine C, I'm warning you: If I hear one more sneeze the whole class is going to be searched like you were last February! And this time I'll search you all myself, and the guilty party will be sent packing like a beggar!" The thirty pupils of Nine C were terror-stricken. Just the thought of being searched by Mother Benoîte was enough to curb the most effervescent spirits. The Principal, irritated by this diversion that had forced her to turn her attention away from Simone Côté for several seconds, brought her gaze back to Six A, looking for the little girl, who had hidden behind a class-mate, to make herself unnoticeable. Mother Benoîte was about to descend the steps again, heading for Simone, when Sister Sainte-Catherine's voice rose in the school-yard, sweet, clear, even playful. "Will everyone in grade three please stay in the school yard: We must start getting the repository ready today if we want it to be done by Thursday night. But we mustn't forget that Friday is first Friday .... So all grade-six pupils will go to confession now, without returning to class first; that way we can start to work as soon as we get back." Smiles appeared on the faces of the grade-six pupils. Holidays were starting! No classes! No homework or lessons till Friday! Two whole days laughing and shouting amid the decorations to be mended, the costumes to be cleaned, scaffolding to be repainted, statues to be dusted .... Ever since Sister Sainte-Catherine had agreed to look after the repository, the organization of the Corpus Christi celebrations and part of the procession fell to her pupils and those of Sister Sainte-Thérèse and Sister Sainte-Philomène. They started thinking about it right after Christmas holidays and they'd talk about it till the end of the year. All the girls at the École des Saints-Anges went through "Sister Sainte-Catherine's year." The youngest ones would say, "I can't wait for the repository!" while for the older ones it was, "Hey, wasn't it fun!" The classes started to file past Mother Benoîte as usual – the smallest girls first, then the bigger ones – but that morning the Principal didn't rush off to her position in front of the staircase on the second floor as usual. She stayed outside on the steps, staring foolishly at the grade sixes. You could see the fury in her eyes and Sister Sainte-Catherine's pupils were starting to fear that their lovely holiday would be ruined before it even began. Sister Sainte-Catherine, too, could feel the Principal's gaze on her back. An ironic smile had formed on her lips and the little girls were somewhat reassured. Simone, however, was still hiding behind her taller classmate Claire Morency, school-bag clutched to her chest, eyes lowered. Pierrette had come and stood beside her in line because that was her place, but Simone could feel a sort of chill emanating from her friend, and her face reddened and her heart thumped with shame. She realized it had been stupid to throw herself into the arms of Lucienne Boileau, whom nobody liked, especially herself, but how could she make amends now? The offence had been committed and Thérèse or Pierrette would never forgive her. "Boy, this is awful! And I thought everything'd be so simple when I was pretty!" When all the other classes were inside the school, Sister Sainte-Catherine spoke again. "Now we're going to the church, in silence please .... I said silently .... Once we're there, Sister Sainte-Philomène will have you examine your consciences while Sister Sainte-Thérèse and I let the priests know we're there. Don't forget that the first Friday in June is a very special first Friday: it's the last one you'll be spending in school before summer holidays, so your Communion on Friday morning has to be one of the best of the year." Just as she was giving the signal to start, Mother Benoîte walked past her, heading toward her pupils. The Principal stopped beside Simone, who shrank down without raising her eyes. Pierrette, despite her anger, couldn't help gesturing to her friend, but she was stopped dead by a furious look from the Principal. When Mother Benoîte spoke, her voice filled the school yard and resounded off the walls, producing an un-pleasant sort of echo that bounced back, hard, like an India-rubber ball. "Simone Côté, have you got something for me?" Simone was paralysed. She suddenly turned pale, her head hunched down between her shoulders. "I'm speaking to you, Simone Côté, and I want you to look at me. Now look up!" Simone painfully raised her head. Tears of sheer terror were running down her cheeks. "I asked you: Do you have some-thing for me?" Simone seemed to get her wits back and murmured, "Yes, my mother gave me something for you." It was almost inaudible, but still brought a smile to Mother Benoîte. "So! The die-hards are giving in! This will be a good lesson for the whole school!" Simone took a long white envelope from her school-bag and held it out to the Principal, who snatched it from her. But she didn't find the two-dollar-bill she'd been expecting. All the envelope contained was a short letter, which she read with growing fury.

Mother Benoîte des Anges
École des Saints-Anges

Madame,
Your pupil Simone Côté is presently going through a very difficult period in her life. I know the child very well, having brought her into the world, taken care of her and watched her grow. I have also grown very fond of her, to the point of taking it upon myself to have an operation performed to correct the slight deformity with which she was afflicted at birth, as her parents are too poor to provide what I consider to be an essential need. It is as Simone Côté's personal physician as well as the physician appointed to the École des Saints-Anges that I am taking this pupil under my protection and humbly request that you do not concern yourself with her case. If Simone were to be upset in any way during her period of recovery, I would be forced to report it to the School Board and to your Community.

Thanking you in advance for your co-operation.
Edmond Sanregret, M.D.

Mother Benoîte turned on her heels abruptly, startling Simone, who was more or less expecting to be beaten or covered with insults because she knew she didn't have the two dollars the nun wanted. The Principal walked away from the grade sixes with a great swishing of skirts and veils, and went inside the school, slamming the door behind her. Sister Sainte-Catherine craned her neck to see Simone's face. "Simone, do you feel strong enough to come and work with the rest of us, or would you rather I gave you the day off?" Her reply came so promptly that the three nuns present couldn't hold back a smile.

Sister Sainte-Catherine awakened that morning feeling fresh as a daisy, as if spending the night murdering her Principal had put out the fire that was blazing in her soul when she'd gone to bed. And so she decided to wait until Friday morning to deal with her conflict with Mother Benoîte des Anges, and to devote the next three days exclusively to the repository, for which her feelings now were quite mixed. Sister Sainte-Catherine regretted very much that she hadn't opened her door to Sister Sainte-Thérèse the night before, but she told herself it was better that way, that she'd spared her friend, as much as herself, a painful scene that would likely have ended in tears, recriminations against the Principal and even, perhaps, in some hazy, useless scheme for revolt or flight. After this crisis, which had shaken the very foundation of her life, casting her for long hours into the Hell of despondency, she suddenly felt regenerated, as if some power she had only a hint of, that was gestating deep inside her, was about to burst out now and smooth over, cauterize, heal and gradually transform this painful period into just one memory among so many others, more beautiful or worse. Was this strength the state of grace she'd been trying for years to explain to her pupils, never succeeding because she didn't really believe in it herself? Or was it that particle of God Himself, that minute part of her God to which she was entitled, according to the laws of her religion, and which was now revealing itself? No. She wished she could believe it, but her soul – the soul of a believer but not a stupidly naïve one – refused once more to settle for the easy answer that God would always turn up, like the hero of a popular novel, to come and save a soul in distress or a community of poor Catholics in peril. She believed far more in the human being's capacity to heal himself through the force of will, reflection and wisdom, than in the superficial outward trappings of a religion that preached inner peace, grace and happiness through ready-made formulas and ready-made beliefs, leaving no initiatives to its flock, which the Church crammed with promises for fear the faithful might see through its tricks and abandon it, leaving it destitute; for despite its preaching and sermons about the vanity of the things of this world, it was so accustomed to indulgence and silks. Of course Sister Sainte-Catherine had never mentioned these doubts to anyone, especially her confessor, Father Langevin, an easy-going *bon vivant* for whom a plate heaped with spaghetti was a direct reward from God, and going without a meal, a punishment. She had found shelter in the life of her community and lived a parallel inner life that no one suspected, still teaching her pupils the catechism, but with a slight, imperceptible difference that turned her lessons into short, fascinating hours, whereas the other nuns succeeded only in boring their pupils or putting them to sleep. She gave her pupils the freedom to express, in the presence of their class-mates and herself, whatever doubts were troubling them, trying always to answer them clearly and simply, but, unlike the other nuns, never falling back on the formula that had been suggested to them for difficult cases: "That's one of the Catholic mysteries and you just have to believe, even if you don't understand it." It often caused her cold sweats and rough times, and when she couldn't come up with the right answer to certain questions (often so naïve they made her dizzy, and rarely clear or well-structured) she would simply admit her ignorance, saying, "You'll have to ask someone more intelligent or competent than I am .... Our brains have limits, you know ... they can't understand everything ... but that's no reason not to ask questions .... Questions air the brains, keep them from getting clogged up .... I'll find out; I'll try and get the answer for you." The children preferred this simplicity to a peremptory order to believe unquestioningly, even if the road suggested by Sister Sainte-Catherine was more arduous. When she came into the refectory after morning mass, all heads turned in her direction. She greeted the Principal as the etiquette of her community required, then took her place, smiling. The smile slapped Mother Benoîte in the face: she'd been expecting to see Sister Sainte-Catherine burst in, stricken with remorse, hollow-eyed, exhausted, even repentant, yes, repentant; instead she saw a fresh-looking, joyous nun who greeted her insolently and then tucked into her breakfast, chattering with her neighbours, especially her friend Sister Sainte-Thérèse de l'Enfant-Jésus. She, too, was quite astonished to see Sister Sainte-Catherine in such dazzling form, but her delight swept away any dark ideas at one stroke, the way a good gust of wind can sweep the morning clear of a lingering fog. Sister Sainte-Catherine murmured, "I'm better now, I'll tell you later ...." and that made up for the sleepless night her friend had passed. They laughed as they ate, while Sister Saint-Georges looked on longingly and Sister Sainte-Philomène slurped her porridge.

"I just wanted to be sure you'd done the errand I sent you on yesterday afternoon." Sister Saint-Georges was briefly taken aback; she looked down, then up at the Principal, cleared her throat and swallowed. "If you didn't go, Sister Saint-Georges, you must tell me ... and give me back the letter. I'll

106

deliver it myself if I have to." Sister Saint-Georges shuffled from one foot to the other as she did when her club-foot hurt her at night, after she'd spent the day going up and down those damn stairs in the school. "I promise I won't scold you, Sister Saint-Georges .... I suspect you didn't go for some reason or other, and I can accept that quite calmly. As you can see, I'm not at all angry. When you admit you've done something wrong, you know, you're already half forgiven." Sister Clump Foot stepped back toward the door of the office. Her lips were quivering and Mother Benoîte could tell she was on the verge of cracking. "Sit down, Sister Saint-Georges. You seem upset. Come now, sit down." Sister Saint-Georges sat on the edge of the straight-backed chair, hands flat on her knees, head lowered. Mother Benoîte leaned forward slightly, elbows on her desk, and tried hard to smile. "Sister Saint-Georges, you're a great help to me here at the school, you're a valuable assistant and I'd be very sorry to lose you .... But a portress must never, under any circumstances, hide anything whatsoever from her Principal, you've known that as long as you've occupied your position of trust .... You're my right arm, and a right arm must be faithful, efficient and loyal!" She leaned back in her chair suddenly, and her smile disappeared. "I don't doubt for a moment that you have all those qualities – but you must prove it to me." Sister Saint-Georges's intelligence wasn't very highly developed, but her instinct for survival was, and it had often warned her about the maliciousness, bad faith and hypocrisy of community life; thus she had developed a sort of sixth sense that sometimes helped her sniff out self-seeking flattery or suspicious good grace, without her really being aware of it. She had walked into the Principal's office with her mind made up – like the well-trained servant that she was – to tell everything that had happened the previous day if Mother Benoîte should ask her. It would be very painful to sell out Sister Sainte-Catherine, but she was so convinced – it was one of the first rules of the community – that the truth, any truth, is always rewarded, was its own reward, redeeming itself when it was ugly and trumpeting the glory of God when it was beautiful, but unleashing all the fires of Hell when it was hidden by that work of Satan, that insult to the Lord in His infinite goodness (who, in any case, sees everything), that filth that splatters the entire community when it is perpetrated by one of its members – a lie – that denunciation had become second nature, almost an asset, to her. But when she saw Mother Benoîte set to work with her low, vile flattery, calling her her right arm when she'd always despised her, and trying so hard to smile so that she'd talk, a little alarm sounded in Sister Saint-Georges's head and her imagination (mediocre though it was) had gone to work; words came to her, phrases, ideas that she let flow without trying to hold them back or channel them: with casual bad faith she recounted her trip on the bus and streetcar, her meeting with Mother Superior, how nice she was, how angelically beautiful; she described their fascinating conversation and even the cup of tea and the cookie she'd been served on white china, so delicate it was almost transparent. She told it all looking Mother Benoîte straight in the eye, unable to believe she was telling these lies, so well and clearly, and with utter hypocrisy, taking such pleasure in the defeat she could read on her Principal's face, and controlling with violent joy the urge to laugh that was making her whole body shake. When her spring had run dry she got up without asking permission, on the pretext of some task or other to be done in some corridor or other, and headed for the office door, which she opened with a hand trembling with excitement. Before she crossed the threshhold she turned one last time, the final provocation, an ambiguous smile on her lips: "Mother Notre-Dame hadn't read your letter yet when I left, but she likely has by now. She sure was nice to me."

The three grade-six classes had crossed boulevard Saint-Joseph in relative calm: you could sense a slight wind, a harbinger of freedom that promised all sorts of favours and special permissions, as well as allowing capering in the corridors and cries thrown out like challenges, rising above the ranks like a constant twittering that it would have been hopeless to try and silence, and even little laughs that tried to be discreet, but that Sister Sainte-Catherine and Sister Sainte-Thérèse could hear perfectly well, smiling in spite of the slight disruption, they too feeling a little nervous. The only one who didn't seem thrilled by the morning sun already beating down, bathing the skin like a warm, beneficial fluid, was Sister Sainte-Philomène. The fat nun had been hit hard when Sister Sainte-Catherine told the students that the Six B teacher was to guide them as they examined their consciences. This task, which was absolutely obligatory and came back like a sentence the first week of every month, had always been a torture for Sister Sainte-Philomène (her pupils knew it, and rejoiced for days in advance, murmuring among themselves: "I can't wait for Sister to examine our consciences! Is it today?" or "Maybe she'll burst this time!" or again, "I wonder what sin'll make her blush the most this month, impurity or gluttony!" as they nudged each other or hid their faces in their hands to laugh) and now she'd been given the responsibility for preparing three classes for confession! Three! Ninety pairs of eyes were going to peer at her, watch her breathing, the blinking of her eyes, the hoped-for sweat on her forehead and, most of all, her cheeks that wouldn't fail to turn red at the uttering of a few sins she wouldn't necessarily feel guilty of herself, but would still make her uncomfortable, because they represented either forbidden delights she could well imagine because it was hard not to fall into their traps, or shameful pleasures she didn't understand exactly but seemed to her (without her knowledge, against her will and contrary to her soul) interesting, despite their reputation as the antechamber of Hell or the complete and irreparable loss of one's soul, one's body, of the protection of God and the Church, of one's vocation and – first and foremost – (because you can hide them all your life and nobody will ever find out anything about them) the respect you owe yourself. It didn't bother her to talk to eleven-year-olds about pride or avarice or envy; she knew their little souls were utterly free of these sins that would come only with adulthood, sins of a society in which competition, success seeking and the inevitable struggle to keep what you've got while taking from others, are breeding grounds for the development of all sorts of infectious diseases from which children are, luckily, spared; but talking about gluttony (the easiest of the seven deadly sins, the first one to be tried out, so sweet and gratifying, and so accessible that you give in without thinking, without wanting to, the one you're always surprised to find among the seven big ones) and talking about impurity (or lust, depending on which word was harder to say on certain mornings of certain months), this sin of all sins, this curse she renounced when she took the veil though she'd never come close to it (in the days when she and Sister Saint-Georges were a couple whom the other nuns took a cruel pleasure in maligning – another very ugly sin – if anyone had told her their relationship came within a hair's breadth of lust, she'd have been thunderstruck, she was that unaware of things) and especially having to *explain* impurity (or lust) was completely beyond her capacities. When the time came to utter one or the other of these words she abhorred, things would start to spin; she would blush, sweat, stammer and, without fail, she would wish herself in front of a plate of spaghetti or a whole roast chicken or a nice rare roast (still palpitating, as Sister Saint Leek would have said), alone with her own sin, responsible and consenting (but was the mere *desire* to eat part of gluttony, as the *desire* for impurity and the *desire* to steal were in the same category as lust and envy?), repentant even before the fall yet falling nonetheless because, really, gluttony didn't warrant such a sentence with no appeal! The coolness in the church surprised the little girls, who were suddenly silent, as much because they were afraid of being cold on such a nice day as because they must be silent in the presence of their God. A few old ladies or elderly damsels, neat as pins, discreet, excessively humble and prostrate so that all the world could see them, still decorated the huge nave of Saint-Stanislas-de-Kostka, small dark spots amid great swathes of sunlight that drifted in through the garish stained-glass windows. The three classes, led by their teachers, headed for the sanctuary and took over the first ten rows of pews, making a commotion that raised a few pious heads and wrinkled the brows of several candle-sniffers who felt taken in, robbed by these young souls who were going to divert all the Lord's attention from themselves, even though they'd been addressing to Him, for some minutes now, their confused and dissolute gossip. When all three classes were on their knees, Sister Sainte-Catherine took out her wooden clapper and struck it once. All heads bowed piously. "Sister Sainte-Thérèse and I are going to leave you in Sister Sainte-Philomène's good hands. Listen to her advice, think things over carefully, open your souls to the sacrament that's being prepared for you and, above all, think of the Holy Communion, which is your reward for all the trouble you're going to." The two young nuns moved toward the sacristy, leaving Sister Sainte-Philo-mène on the verge of apoplexy, eyes bulging, mouth dry, hands – hidden, luckily, in the broad hospitable sleeves of her habit – trembling and cold. Sister Sainte-Philomène had just realized, to her terror, that all the ladies present were going to take heed of her words so that they, too, could examine their consciences, and she felt as if she'd just been hit with a hockey stick or a baseball bat. She walked slowly to the back of the church, sat on the first empty pew behind the three classes and fell to her knees like a mighty sinner who had come to place herself in God's hands after a lifetime of folly, breaches, defiance and indulgence. "God, help me! Help me, God!" But all that came out of Sister Sainte-Philomène was a long, pitiful fart that she couldn't hold back, which stupefied the ladies present and even the little girls, who realized for the first time the extent of the torture that the Six B teacher had to undergo every month.

Simone bitterly regretted her thoughtless act. Exchanging just a few words with Lucienne Boileau was all it took to remind her that the fat little girl from rue Papineau was really a waste of time: no sooner had they thrown themselves in each other's arms than Lucienne was swearing fidelity, exclusivity and undying friendship, circling Simone's waist with moist hands that left marks on everything they touched, brushing against her shoulder with greasy pigtails that smelled of French fries. Simone felt as if she was just trading one trap for another smaller, more suffocating one. But what could she do now to dump Lucienne and show Thérèse and Pierrette that she was sorry about her outburst of independence and felt as if she was going to die without them? "Gee, I was a dope. I don't see them for weeks and weeks, then the second time we get together I ruin everything! That stupid Lucienne! It's all her fault anyway. I'll never talk to her again as long as I live! I'd rather have my tongue pulled out!" Simone sighed and Pierrette, who had managed to slip in beside her on the church pew, turned her head in Simone's direction, hoping her friend would cast a pleading glance her way; but Simone didn't budge and Pierrette thought she'd sighed at the thought of her sins. "They can't be very serious." She was having some trouble concentrating on the petty infractions that had filled her month. Pierrette had always found it humiliating to tell some old man hidden behind a grille that she'd lied to her mother (twice, no, three times, no twice; the third time she wasn't sure if it was a lie or not); that she'd stolen a piece of cake from the cupboard; that she'd been disobedient once (she'd worn her yellow dress one morning when her mother had just washed and ironed her brown one); that she'd been impatient (several times: with Simone, with Thérèse, with her mother, her father, her teacher); or that she'd succumbed to gluttony and eaten two slices of pie one night when she wasn't even hungry after her meat! After all, her private life was her own business! And anyway, as long as she didn't lapse into the real, serious sins, the ones that practically lead to damnation and need the help of a priest and strict penitence (at least one rosary) before they're forgiven, she'd be all right. She believed quite literally what she'd been told about sins ever since grade one: venial sins were inconsequential little marks she could wash away with a sincere prayer, while mortal sins left nearly indelible stains that required the help of an envoy of the Lord to wash them away forever. But as she had never, to her knowledge, committed a single mortal sin (one day she'd even taken a vow never to commit one as long as she lived, though she was already starting to think that it might be quite a long time), she'd always thought her brief visits to the confessional were as useless as they were unpleasant. Some priests accepted her small misdeeds, those of an innocent child, without batting an eyelash, and sent her away with three Hail Mary's to be recited at the Lord's table; others, though, like Father Bernier for instance, whom *all* the girls in school tried to avoid, he was such an inquisitor, never settled for what she said, as if they didn't trust her or doubted her intelligence; they would ask embarrassing questions she didn't always understand but that always made her uncomfortable. "Is that all?" "Uh huh." "Are you sure?" "Um ... yes." "Absolutely sure?" "Well ... I can't tell you anybody else's sins, I don't know what they are!" "Don't talk back! You seem like a strong-minded little girl. What's your name?" "Jeannine Trépanier, Five C." (That's right, a lie for next month already! And tough luck for Jeannine Trépanier, who'd pushed her in the school yard the day before!) "Well, Jeannine Trépanier, Grade Five C, are you sure you haven't committed any more serious sin this month?" "Yes!" "Don't you ever, sometimes at night ... when you're taking your bath or going to bed ... don't you ever touch yourself?" "Are you kidding? I'm not a boy!" Until then, she'd always got off with a penance of less than a rosary (while some of the grade nines would shout it from the roof-tops that they'd just joined the more-than-one-rosary league, which gave them a certain prestige but also surrounded them with a sort of smell of sulphur that terrified some of the younger girls), but for how much longer? Actually, the attentions of Simone's older brother, Maurice, had disturbed her a lot more than she'd admit. Maurice had lifted in her soul a corner of the thing, so ugly, apparently, it sometimes caused diseases that could kill you (yes, yes, yes, *kill* you). In fact that was one of the reasons Pierrette had so far resisted the charms – and he had a good many – of handsome Maurice Côté, who went limp as a rag whenever she deigned to approach him: she'd been properly warned that boys were not only a source of almost unpardonable sins, but also – and this was much more serious – the source of all sorts of diseases, each one worse than the last, "the family way" being not the worst, only the most obvious. Pierrette had absolutely no desire to end up with a big belly like her three sisters, Germaine, Rose and Gabrielle, after granting Maurice a long kiss that was the apparent cause of all evil and the beginning of damnation. It was her turn to sigh without realizing it, and she didn't see Simone turn a supplicating face in her direction. She was about to pluck up her courage then, and tell the priest, if he wasn't too curious, that she'd lied to her mother again, that she'd stolen another piece of cake .... "They're going to figure out who I am, I always say the same things!" As for Lucienne Boileau, she was so happy she couldn't keep from turning around every thirty seconds to look at her new friend, who was five rows back, hidden behind Charlotte Turgeon, who'd certainly put her big frizzy head in front of Simone on purpose. That morning she felt a violent, unhoped-for happiness that was very hard to contain, because it wanted to explode in bursts of joy and songs of victory, and she wanted to tell the priest who, in a short time, would be leaning forward to hear her sins that she didn't intend to ever commit a single sin in her whole life, not even a venial one, because she was finally experiencing a true state of grace. But something deep down inside warned her that her definition of the state of grace wasn't necessarily the same as the priest's, and there was a danger that she'd get in trouble if she talked about it; so she decided to keep her great happiness to herself and say whatever came into her head at confession. "I'll examine my conscience some other time, I'm too happy to worry about it this morning!" As for Thérèse, she was plunged in the first great dilemma of her life: was she going to confess everything that had happened since her last confession, at the end of April—her meeting with the attendant at Parc Lafontaine, the delicious confusion in which she'd been left by the kiss she stole from the young man, the warmth that spread through her every time Gérard Bleau looked at her, which happened fairly often because he'd started following her, the excitement, in fact, of knowing that a man, *a man*, not some little creep like Maurice Côté, who melted at the sight of Pierrette, was already following her, even though she was only eleven and not completely developed? Or wouldn't it be smarter to keep it all inside her, admitting only the most benign sins, as usual, to give the priest a clear conscience, because really, as far as she was concerned, all that business about venial sins and mortal sins was pretty hard to swallow? Thérèse was a lot more practical-minded than most of the other girls in her school, even the older ones: it was harder for her to accept the legends, often so naïve and even downright stupid, and the primitive, simple-minded theories about Good and Evil with which the Catholic religion was imbued, but she was prudent enough not to mention it to anybody, foreseeing the scandal she'd set off if she were to ask Sister Sainte-Philomène why the robe of Our Lord Jesus Christ had no seams, and why it mattered and, above all, what use it all was; or how come the baby Jesus had a purely spiritual father before he had a real mother like everybody else; or how he'd managed to ascend to Heaven like a plucked pigeon; or how come the Holy Family wasn't any richer after the visit of the Magi, with their gold and incense and myrrh, which must be very precious metals; or how come you could cleanse your soul so easily after you'd committed sins as serious and ugly and bad for your health as lust, concupiscence, impurity and sensuality? Some of her class-mates were overjoyed by these "mysteries," which set them dreaming and overwhelmed their narrow little souls, but Thérèse remained impervious to the charm of the Lord multiplying fish (Fish! Now, I ask you – Why not porridge while you're at it?) or of Jonah surviving for three days in the belly of a whale (Yikes!) or of Jesus Christ (it always came back to him) walking on the water of Lake Memphremagog! Confession, for her, had quickly become a game of hide-and-seek, in which she'd tell

116

the priest part of the truth but never completely open up to him. That morning, though, she felt like shocking and provoking, for Simone's burst of independence had put her in a terrible mood. Despite her high intelligence and her very precocious insights into certain things she normally wouldn't understand until much later, there was still a childish side to Thérèse, which made her tend to confuse what was important and what wasn't, sometimes obsessively blowing inconsequential details out of all proportion and minimizing vital facts that would have a great influence on her life. She often enjoyed what was dangerous, and worried about harmless things. Once again, she fastened her stocking, which had started to slide down her leg. "That rotten Simone, she's going to pay for this!" When Sister Sainte-Catherine and Sister Sainte-Thérèse came back from the sacristy, followed by four priests, who seemed very annoyed to be there, Sister Sainte-Philomène suddenly straightened up and blurted out desperately, "Remember now: avarice, sloth, envy, wrath, pride ... gluttony and ... and ...impurity!"

To keep Marcel from leaving the house, Albertine had refused to dress him. He had cried, wept and pleaded, swearing that he'd play in the lane and not even go near "the lady downstairs's yard," but Albertine resisted his promises and went about her business (gravely insulting Marcel, who didn't understand that someone could do something else when *he* had problems). Finally, he took refuge on his sofa in the dining-room, hugging a huge doll that was all dirty and battered, from which he absolutely refused to be separated and which brought great shame to his mother whenever they had company. He didn't sleep, but just stared at the ceiling, sighing for several minutes, fixing his mother with a reproachful gaze whenever she walked past him as she did her dusting. "Come on, Marcel, try and get some sleep. You're over-excited." "No! I don't ever want to go to sleep again!" "You're a stubborn little mule; you're as bad as your sister! All I have to do is tell you once not to do something and you threaten to stop eating and drinking and sleeping! If I've told you once, I've told you a thousand times, carrying on like that won't change things a bit, I know very well you aren't going to quit eating or sleeping! Now, if you said you weren't going to give me any more hugs and kisses, then I'd understand and it'd hurt me ...." "Well, I'm not going to give you any more hugs and kisses then!" "Come on now, Marcel! Either you aren't very bright or you're too smart for your own good and you're trying to pull my leg!" She half opened the door of her brother Gabriel's bedroom, made sure he was asleep, then gently shut it. "You've made me raise my voice again and you know your Uncle Gabriel has to sleep till noon ...." Marcel considered running outside in his pyjamas, but he thought that maybe the lady downstairs wouldn't like to see him like that, because she was always so clean and tidy and her three daughters smelled of soap .... So he decided to bear his troubles with fortitude. His mother would dress him eventually. It never occurred to him to put on his clothes by himself. The family had always treated him somewhat like a doll .... The other members of the household took turns looking after him, dressing him, feeding him with a spoon, washing him and, sometimes, even helping him go to the bathroom (he still sometimes peed in his pants if he was worked up about something, but he'd learned to let them know of his other needs by squirming at the bathroom door), but oddly enough, their way of looking after him hadn't changed, while he, though he was very small for his age, had for some time been developing with strange rapidity. He always let them do as they pleased, but he was already starting to ask himself questions, while they still thought of him as a six-month-old baby. Around mid-morning, forgetting that he was mad at his mother, to pass the time he started humming a sentimental song that his grandmother often sang as she rocked in her big chair next to the radio. *"Jeunes fillettes, profitez de temps .... La violette se cueille au printemps ...."* Albertine, who was rubbing lemon oil on the radio cabinet, stopped suddenly, as if she'd just noticed something for the first time, turned to Marcel and stared at him for a long time while he went on singing. When he finished what he knew of the song, substituting "la la la" or "dum de dum" for words that he couldn't remember, Albertine walked around the dining-room table and came and sat at her son's feet. "Are you going to dress me now?" "In a minute ... Momma's got something to ask you first." Marcel hid his face behind his eviscerated doll. "I didn't go in my pyjamas, honest!" Albertine was so happy she couldn't keep from smiling. "No, no, no, that's not it .... Marcel, that song you were singing ...." "It's gramma's song." "I know that, I've been listening to it for thirty years .... But ... before ... you couldn't sing that song very well, remember?" "Yes ...." At the sound of that one word, a yes pronounced so well, so distinctly, instead of the usual irritatingly lisped "Yeth," Albertine started as if someone had jabbed her. She bent over her child. "Say what you just said, Marcel." "What ... what'd Marcel just say?" A broad smile lit up Albertine's face, and she took Marcel in her arms, laughing. "Marcel ... you aren't lisping any more!" "I stopped that a long time ago!" Albertine lifted Marcel off the sofa, ran through the house and burst into her mother's room without knocking. Old Victoire, who was reading last Saturday's *La Presse*, uttered a little cry like a frightened bird and brought her hand to her heart. "Momma, momma, Marcel stopped lisping!" Victoire didn't even look at her daughter and her grandson. She stuck her head back in her newspaper and said with a sigh, "That's just what we needed around here – a miracle!"

He was going to speak to her. It had to be today, but he couldn't have said why. Though he'd been satisfied until now to follow her, spy on her, sometimes letting her see him so he could watch the reaction on her face (perhaps he was looking for fear, but she was always impassive when she noticed him, and several times he'd even caught her with a smile in the depths of her eyes and it was he who was afraid), spending the rest of his time hidden under an outside staircase or behind a tree on rue Garnier. That morning, however, when he left old man Gariépy's, breathing the June air that smelled so clean, as if spring had done a big washing and spread its immaculate laundry over the city, where it was gently drying, standing on the balcony freshly painted a dazzling green, he thought, "Today's the day everything will be settled. This has been going on for a month now, and that's long enough! Either I get what I'm looking for and figure out just what's happening to me, or I don't, and then I'll go off my rocker altogether. But something's gotta happen!" He had come down the three steps from the balcony, whistling, but with his brow furrowed. He knew he couldn't see her before ten o'clock recess, so he decided to walk to the École des Saints-Anges instead of taking the Papineau streetcar to boulevard Saint-Joseph. He walked quickly up the Dorion hill and on to Sherbrooke, which was already very congested. He didn't like this street at all: it was too wide for his liking and made him feel small and insignificant. He took longer strides to hasten the moment when he would enter Parc Lafontaine, which he had to cross from south to north to get to rue Fabre. Parc Lafontaine was in splendid form, exploding with *joie de vivre*; the trees displayed every possible shade of green, from the tenderest (the new leaves that had just barely emerged from their envelopes) to the deepest (the first leaves that had come out a month ago, now fully grown, and bending on their stems as though to protect the little new ones), and including the transparent, almost jade colour of the gaily rustling, gleaming aspen leaves and the dark and restful shade of maple leaves, as broad as your hand and already weighty. The hydrangeas were in bloom, sprinkling the still virgin grass with white. All this life, the sun's rays making their way through the muscular branches of poplars and elms, the birds singing to their hearts' content, announcing to everyone that it was June and time to rejoice, the squirrels (especially a family of albino squirrels, grotesque but fascinating, that lived inside a maple tree, whose movements always delighted him), free spirited, recalcitrant, chattering, a nuisance, and most of all the pure, almost warm air that sometimes smelled of horse manure and sometimes of the flowers that were furiously trying to set free their scents, all this life went to Gérard's head and he felt his heart swell to twice its size, as if a few lungfuls of the air in Parc Lafontaine was enough to dissipate the fog that had kept him for too long in the dark. Rather than go along rue Papineau, he sprinted through the park, almost happy, forgetting his suffering and concerns, though he knew very well they'd be waiting for him at the corner of Rachel and Fabre, ready to jump on his back like vicious animals as soon as he'd left the salutary shelter of the trees. He stopped at a water fountain and took a long drink, conscientiously, eyes shut, an impalpable, intoxicating moment of grace before the brunt of the storm that was gathering somewhere in the corner of his eye. Just before he left the park he stopped dead in the middle of a dirt path, struck by the thought that God could see him. God knew! The revelation was so overwhelming that he started to tremble and had to seek refuge at the base of a tree. He hadn't thought about "the good Lord" since leaving school after a seventh grade that had been heavy going for him and worse for the teacher, who'd had to put up with Gérard's shocking inertia and crass ignorance; not once had he given a thought to the creator in a white robe and flowing beard who wandered around somewhere in the sky, on a big cloud, spying on every blink and heartbeat of the unfortunate monsters born out of his sick mind and wallowing in their suffering, at times handing out some laughable consolation, but most often lavishing pain and disgrace with maniacal generosity, this God of Goodness he'd been forced to believe in, who should have governed his life utterly, but whom he hastened to forget as soon as he'd left school for good. He'd never gone back to mass or even to church, and that (news travelled fast along rue Dorion) had given him, in the eyes of the women in his neighbourhood, a slight aura of Hell, to which they were far from averse. And here he was on a magnificent morning, when for once he'd left behind him the yoke that had imprisoned his heart for a month now, and the God of Vengeance had just ravaged him at one stroke, filling him with shame and guilt, though he had done nothing and, above all, wanted nothing. Beside a hydrangea bush where, a few weeks earlier, Richard had poured out his heart, a disproportionately painful confession for his fragile little body, to a prostitute who had happily granted him absolution, Gérard Bleau wept in the presence of his God who, he knew, would never forgive him for the sin he hadn't yet committed.

"Bless me Father, for I have sinned." "Never mind the formula, just tell me your sins." There was a brief silence in the confessional. Father Vaillancourt sighed. "What is it? Cat

122

got your tongue?" The little girl came a bit closer to the grille, almost sticking her nose against it. "Will it count just the same?" "Of course it'll count just the same! Now let's stop wasting time and tell me your sins." The child seemed to be hesitating still. "You got something hard to confess?" "No ... but this is the first time I didn't say the formula .... It's going to seem like it isn't a real confession." Father Vaillancourt cut her off so brusquely you could hear him as far as the altar, where a dozen pupils were doing their penance. All heads turned toward the confessional. "All right, all right, say your formula, but get cracking!" He listened to the long recitation, gazing at heaven. He ran his hand over his stomach, which was burning atrociously. He'd forgotten his little white pills and knew he'd have to survive another half-hour of timid and insignificant mumbling by little girls with questionable breath who came to him because they had to, and whom he could (perhaps even should) absolve with a wave of the hand, without even listening to them. He could feel gas rising up to his oesophagus and thought, "No, I don't want to burp! The pain afterwards will be so terrible!" But he had to let it out and a few moments later he was nearly bent double. The little girl had finished her formula. "Go on, what're you waiting for?" "You don't look very well." "Can you see me?" "Yes. The sun comes in through the door of the confessional and I can see you." In fact, a ray of sunlight was touching Father Vaillancourt's confessional like a long bluish finger, after passing through the robe of some saint or other (Saint Stanislas of Kostka himself, perhaps) who seemed to be blessing a flock of sheep in one of the pretentious stained-glass windows on the east. The priest turned to the little girl. "I can see you, too." She smiled shyly. "Hello, Father!" Father Vaillancourt moved back as if he'd just been stung by a vicious bee, resumed his original position, knit his brow. "Patience ... I must be patient ...." He spoke as calmly as he could, but his voice contained the hint of a threat, and the child was well aware of it. "If you don't mind, will you please tell me your sins so you can get the heck out of here and leave me in peace? There's another kid waiting on the other side, I can hear her squirming around like a devil in holy water …. Go on, I have to hear her confession, too!" The child stopped smiling. She piously lowered her eyes and seemed to reflect profoundly before speaking. "I just wanted to tell you I didn't commit any sins last month 'cause I was in the hospital!"

"I don't want to rape her! I never intended to rape her! So why should I feel guilty? Why do you have to feel guilty before you even get around to thinking about committing a sin, for Christ's sake! I just want … I just want to see her! I don't even want to talk to her!" Gérard Bleau had gone back to his observation post under the stairs of a house that faced the entrance to the school yard. It was a quarter to ten and the little girls would soon be pouring out of the school like water set joyously free after being kept prisoner for a long time, among them, Thérèse, with her obstinate air, her moods, the demands she made on her two friends that he often thought went too far, but that Pierrette and Simone seemed to consider quite normal. He had never again spoken to Thérèse after the incident at Parc Lafontaine, but by following her, watching for her, at school and on the sidewalk across from where she lived, by seeing how she lorded it over everyone in her entourage, and demanded (without really showing it, unlike Lucienne Boileau, who didn't know how to dissemble) that they do exactly what she wanted, directing the games of her little brother, who obeyed her conscientiously, with ingratiating sincerity, as well as those of her two boy-cousins, who seemed to feel boundless admiration for her, leading around her little court with supreme disdain, while hiding her great love for her subjects (a love she let loose from time to time, however, without realizing it, embracing one or pouncing on another, stifling her brother with untimely caresses, or Simone, by grabbing her around the neck until she cried for mercy) under a very flimsy layer of indifference, by watching her develop with that innate casualness that made her an undeniable gang leader, he had finally come up with a fairly accurate picture of her, despite his relative lack of intuition. For instance, he knew she'd never give him away, not to her parents or to the nuns at school, because a sort of pact had been made between them, through looks exchanged between the slats of the school fence or across rue Fabre; they were going to live out their silent, unsettled relationship until something happened that would make them talk to each other or not, depending on the choice they made at the time, when he'd explain himself once and for all, with broken words, with sobs and gulps, or choosing to remain silent, still quenching his thirst from afar, with mixed feelings of passion and fear. When the recess bell rang throughout the school, Gérard's temples began to throb; he stuck his hands in his pockets and pressed his forehead against one of the steps. The two doors that gave on to the school yard opened at the same time, and a wave of black uniforms, white arms and legs sheathed in beige poured in to the large asphalt square; skipping-ropes began to make circles in the sun, hair flew in the wind, monotonous, absurd laments rose into the air ("Tell me the name of the man I will marry ... A, B, C ...") Gérard emerged from his hiding place, crossed the street, as he did so often, to gaze between the fence slats. Thérèse's class was not outside yet. He was starting to recognize the pupils in Six B and when he didn't see Thérèse right away, he looked for the tall twins, Claudette and Ginette Latour, or fat Lucienne Boileau, who was always hanging around Thérèse .... But that morning Six B was absent. A detention? Were the thirty girls prisoners in their class-room because one of them had done something wrong? (There it was again: Fault. Sin. Guilt. God.) Gérard felt like screaming, "Leave me alone, you goddamn voyeur!" to that presence within that was always with him, weighing on his soul like a sentence, but he knew that the presence would reply, "You're the voyeur." Convinced that he wouldn't see Thérèse before school got out around half-past eleven, he was heading back to his post under the stairs when he saw the three grade-six classes coming back from church in pious rows, silent and calm. The first group was barely thirty feet from him, so flight was impossible; he decided to lean against the fence like a passer-by lingering innocently and watching the noisy children at play. Sister Sainte-Catherine's class filed past him first, disintegrating into squawking, excited children just as soon as they were outside the school yard. Pierrette turned pale when she noticed, so nearby, the man who had been following Thérèse for weeks now. She was almost transfixed, and Lucie Brodeur, who came just behind her in line, had to push her through the gate. When Sister Sainte-Philomène's class started walking right beside him, Gérard wanted to take off, to hide under the staircase and lick his sores like a wounded dog. Thérèse pretended not to see him. She walked past him, head high, haughty and disdainful. A sob rose in Gérard's throat, and he had to swallow several times to contain it. Sister Sainte-Thérèse de l'Enfant-Jésus walked past him next, murmuring *"Bonjour, monsieur,"* so happy and innocent that Gérard felt it like a slap. Thérèse had run over to Pierrette and the two friends were already engaged in a lively discussion. Pierrette pointed toward Gérard and Thérèse held her back by the arm, stamping her foot. Again Gérard was alone in the giddiness that, once

126

more, had him bent double. "I don't want to rape her, God; it isn't true! Help me!"

"He's practically inside the school yard! Pretty soon he'll want to play with us, at this rate!" "Mind your own business, Pierrette Guérin, I didn't ask for your opinion!" "Maybe not, but *he's* going to ask you for something!" "Come on, he isn't dangerous." "You never know. You've been saying for a month that he isn't dangerous, but one of these days he might attack you and next thing we know we'll find you underneath a gallery chopped up in little pieces." Thérèse gave a hollow laugh that surprised even her. "Little pieces! Why not put me through the meat grinder while you're at it!" "Anyhow, if this keeps up I'm telling Sister!" The sudden pressure of Thérèse's hand around her wrist made Pierrette grimace in pain. "Don't you dare!" "Let go, that hurts!" "If you tell Sister I'll never talk to you again. Understand? Never!" "Let go!" "Promise you won't tell Sister!" "I won't tell her; now let go." Thérèse released her grip and started to rub her friend's wrist, as though seeking forgiveness. Meanwhile, at the other end of the school yard, Simone was staring at her feet as Lucienne hurled abuse at her. "You come here this morning, you throw yourself in my arms and say you're never going to talk to them again, that you want to be my friend and now you've got the nerve to tell me you want to make up with them!" Simone, obstinate, made no reply. "Come on, answer me! Say something! I'm ready to be your friend, but I won't share you with them! I don't want you to have any other friends except me! They're crazy!" Simone didn't raise her head to speak. She even leaned forward a little more, to be quite certain that Lucienne couldn't see her face. "Why do you keep trying to talk your way into things, Lucienne? You know very well we don't like you .... Thérèse doesn't and Pierrette doesn't and I don't. I only talked to you this morning 'cause I wanted to bug them, you should've known that .... Maybe I told you I didn't want to talk to them again 'cause I was mad, but I sure as heck never said I wanted to be your friend! And quit hanging around us like a fly at a manure pile. It's your own fault if people make fun of you!" Simone turned her back on Lucienne and took a few steps toward her friends, who were still waving their arms. But Lucienne ran up behind her, grabbed her arms and spun her around. "Don't think you're going to get off that easy, Simone Côté! You deserve a good swat and you're going to get it! Maybe not today or even this week, 'cause I don't feel like getting punished and I want to work on the repository, too, but believe me, you've got it coming!" Lucienne, a fat, hypersensitive girl, gulped as she talked, her face wet with tears, her whole body shaken by spasms, her voice high and uncontrolled. "One of these days when you aren't expecting it, I'm going to really give it to you, and when I'm done you'll be so ugly you'll wish you still had that harelip!" Simone abruptly broke free. "Quit dreaming, Lucienne Boileau! You couldn't hurt a fly and you know it! I'm not scared of you 'cause you aren't dangerous!" She ran toward her two friends who, in the meantime, had calmed down somewhat. However, she stopped a few feet from them, without looking up. Thérèse saw her first and nudged Pierrette with her elbow. "Hey, look: the penitent returns ...." Pierrette immediately forgot Gérard and the threat he represented for Thérèse and turned all her attention to Simone, who still hadn't moved a muscle. "What do we do: talk to her or give her a hard time?" "She's just got over being sick, Thérèse, her mother asked us to look after her yesterday." "That's no reason to let her make fun of us!" "She wasn't making fun of us ...." "What do you call it when somebody drops her friends and throws herself at creepy fatso Lucienne Boileau? She

128

didn't just make fun of us – she betrayed us!" Thérèse raised her voice to be sure Simone could hear, and when she heard the word "betrayed" she raised her head. "Yes, you're right, I betrayed you. But ... I'm sorry .... Let me come back." Thérèse felt a surge of pity at her sorrowful manner, like a little bird that's fallen from its nest; she rushed toward Simone, took her in her arms, and hugged her so hard she nearly smothered her. "Don't ever do that again, Simone." "I won't ever!" "Did you at least go to confession?" Simone broke free of her friend's embrace. "Do I have to?" "Of course not! I'm just teasing!" Then all through the school yard you could hear three laughing voices, and heads turned to see three little girls, the famous trio "Thérèse-'n'-Pierrette," united once more, linking arms as their joy at being reunited rose to the sky.

On the other side of the street an exceedingly handsome young man was foundering in questions that were bigger than he was, railing against nature which had awakened in him a strength he'd never suspected and which he was afraid he wouldn't be able to subdue, hurling insults at his God, who had appeared to him for the first time in years, with the features of an inquisitor, finger pointing at him and eyes filled with reproach, instead of the merciful and understanding being you can trust. He just realized for the first time where the quest on which he'd embarked a month ago would take him, and the revelation crucified him. He hadn't seen the young nun crossing the street, heading his way with a smile, so he started when she spoke to him, though her voice was gentle. "Excuse me ... I noticed you just now ... you were looking in the school yard and ... I don't know how to put this but ... I was wondering if you were looking for work." Gérard heard himself answer "No," though he wasn't really aware that he had spoken. "You aren't looking for work?" This time he said nothing. "You look upset .... I know, it's awkward to talk about .... Look ... I need someone to give us a hand – my pupils and I – we're taking things out of a shed and some of them are fairly heavy .... I can't pay very much, but enough to buy yourself a good meal tonight .... The school doesn't give me a very big budget." The situation was so absurd – the innocent nun who was clearing the way for him at the very moment when he should have run away – that Gérard caught himself smiling, with the smile that was so effective, that he'd used so often in the past. He sensed the nun's pleasure at the handsome face, so pure and open, that he was showing to her, and the wolf in him chortled. "So that's the way it is! You want to make things easy for me? Okay, to hell with feeling guilty!" He didn't know if he was addressing this idea to the nun or to God, but it took a huge load off his mind, and a burst of joy went to his head. He straightened up on the staircase. The erection he'd been cursing just a few minutes ago had left him, and he could feel his strength returning. "I'll be right with you, Sister, I'm not scared of hard work!" When Sister Sainte-Catherine walked into the school yard followed by the splendid-looking young man, the grade six girls could feel their hearts flutter. "Gee he's handsome!" "Who is he?" "Sister's got a boy-friend!" But Thérèse, Pierrette and Simone, stupefied, stood there petrified, their arms around each other, heads turned in Gérard's direction, as he looked at them and smiled. As for Lucienne, it could be said that she was happy, in her fashion: she sat hunched on the cement steps, licking her wounds.

He insisted that his mother dress him in the short white pants she'd bought for Easter, which made him feel so handsome; he himself had chosen the powder blue sweater that he liked so much because Thérèse always said he looked good enough to eat when he wore it; as for his white boots, they were already old and worn, but a thick coat of polish did a fairly good job of concealing the scuff marks in the imitation leather and, anyway, Marcel had a theory that boots didn't really matter, that the rest of his person was quite sufficient to attain the goal he'd set himself: to seduce Rose, Violette, Mauve and, in particular, Florence their mother, into leading him to his great love, Duplessis. At first, his mother resisted, exclaiming, "What's the idea of getting all dolled up in your Sunday clothes when it's only Tuesday! Are you out of your mind? I don't even want you to go outside, and here you're talking about dressing up like the Prince of Wales to go and visit an empty house!" Three times in the past month Albertine has asked her brother, Gabriel, to go and check that the door to the house next door was bolted, and each time the fat woman's husband had come back and told her that Marcel's imagination was working overtime, and that one of these days it might backfire on him. But even though she'd never seen him go into the house next door, Albertine believed her son when he told her that's where he had been. She didn't believe the rest of his stories – the women who knit baby booties all day long while drinking tea certainly came from a picture Marcel had seen somewhere, or a story his grandmother had told him; but as he often disappeared for hours at a time and no one knew where to find him, yet always came home again clean as a penny, with freshly combed hair and a cherubic smile, she knew he really did go to that damn abandoned house, where he wandered through the rooms and fabricated a world where he took refuge, then brought to his horrified mother bits of inventions that scared her but that she found beautiful in spite of herself. Some nights she had trouble falling asleep, so preoccupied was she with

Marcel. "If I've produced a lunatic I'll do everything I can to cure him, but if he's a poet there's no cure and I'll never forgive myself!" One Wednesday morning, when her washing was soaking in the huge tin tub she used for laundry, she went down the outside stairs to see for herself if the door to the house next door was really closed. Marcel wasn't feeling well that day and he'd stayed in bed (Marcel loved being sick, because his mother would let him sleep in her bed, the vast black wooden ship with the smells that excited him, which he savoured with his eyes shut). She hesitated a long time before pushing the metal gate, considering this visit ridiculous, but nonetheless feeling the need to turn the door handle of that damned house, even ring the bell, so she could see, just take a look .... She tiptoed across the cement alley, like a thief in the night, walked up the steps with infinite care so the wood wouldn't creak, then stuck her nose against the glass in the door, her hands shielding her eyes from the light. The absurdity of her situation suddenly struck her like a slap in the face. She swivelled around to see if any of the neighbours were laughing at her, Madame Lemieux for instance, who spent her days on the balcony since quitting her job at Giroux et Deslauriers a few weeks earlier, because the baby she was expecting kept her from bending down to her customers' feet to help them try on shoes, or Marie-Louise Brassard behind her lace curtain, who always saw everything with her searching eyes and always seemed to be judging you, no matter what you were doing. But the street was quiet: only an old dog sprawled on a patch of dirt where a few stalks of devil's lettuce grew, looked at her curiously, as if he understood what she was doing and supported her, though with some concern. Then Albertine—who never laughed—started laughing hysterically, leaning against one of the columns of the balcony, resting her head against it, because it had started to swim, and holding back her tears with her hands so they wouldn't

run down her neck. She didn't see Marcel walk slowly out of
Florence's house; he sat on the stairs to wait for her, a smile
on his lips and eyes filled with wonder. While she had
thought he was asleep in her bed, fighting off a slight fever,
he had slipped out and gone to see his good friends, who
greeted him in their living-room that had so many pretty
things in it, both strange and useless, that transformed every
visit he paid them into a discovery of the world. When
Albertine saw him on the steps, she suddenly stopped laughing and sent him back to bed, threatening him with her
open hand, which used to terrify him but now only amused
him. This Tuesday morning, though, Albertine had no intention of letting Marcel go out. He had begged, cried, wept and
even made as if to kick, but thought better of it when he
saw the threat in his mother's eyes. "Lord Almighty, Marcel,
you've quit lisping but now you've got St. Vitus' dance! You're
running around like a tornado!" He ran and hid behind his
grandmother's rocking-chair, sniffling. Then he seemed to
forget about his plan to go out and fell into a mournful
silence that upset his mother more than his fits. Just before
eleven o'clock, time for "Francine Louvain" on the radio, old
Victoire limped out of her room and, taking small, cautious
steps, walked the length of the house. "Damn leg of mine! It
always was shorter than the other one, but I think it's got
even shorter as I've got older! Now I'm going to be late and
I'll miss the start!" Albertine came to help her, telling her
not to worry, that she'd turned the radio on five minutes ago
so the tubes had had time to warm up, and she wouldn't
miss a single word of her favourite soap opera. "I hope not! I
hate it when I can't follow what's going on." "Come on,
momma, you've been listening to that program for years!
You could stop listening for three months and you'd still
know what was going on! It's always the same rubbish!"
Victoire stopped right in the middle of the hall and grandly
pushed her daughter away. "I have a good cry every day

when I listen to 'Francine Louvain' and I don't intend to stop for three months!" "I didn't say you should, I just said it wouldn't make any difference if you did!" "It would so make a difference: it'd make a difference if I didn't cry for three whole months! Can you see yourself not crying for three months?" "I could live with it." "I'm not talking about your life; I'm talking about the radio!" "It isn't the radio that makes me cry!" "It does so! You cry just like anybody else, Bartine! I've seen you, and I've heard you too, blowing your nose in your apron!" "Momma! For Heaven's sake! I never blow my nose in my apron! Are you trying to say I'm a slut?" When Victoire saw Marcel prostrate behind her rocking-chair, she turned to her daughter. "Didn't he go out this morning? It's a nice day." Albertine hesitated for a moment before replying. "No .... He isn't feeling well ...." Victoire moved her chair a little closer to the radio. "Of course he isn't feeling well! If you're waiting till he's better to let him go outside, he'll still be in that corner on his wedding day!" Victoire had squarely turned her back on Marcel and settled into her chair with a contented sigh. "Quiet, now, it's start-ing." Marcel, of course, chose that very moment to come out of his lethargy. He plunked himself right beside his grand-mother – though he was so afraid of her he usually never came near her – and asked in a self-confident voice, "Gram-ma, can I go outside? Momma won't let me." Just then, Nicole Germain's voice came bursting out of the radio, shrill and affected: "Francine Louvain, *bonjour!*" Victoire, her eyes riveted on the luminous yellow screen, happily cried out *"Bonjour,* Francine," in answer to her old friend. Marcel frowned at his mother. Albertine had taken advantage of the moment to come up and push him toward the kitchen. "Gramma doesn't want you bothering her when she's listen-ing to the radio." "How come gramma talks to the radio? You always tell me not to! Can Tantine Louvain hear her?" "Her name isn't Tantine, Marcel, it's Francine." "How come gramma talks to Tantine Francine?" "Marcel, are you being a dingbat on purpose?" "What's a dingbat?" Victoire shouted so loud that Marcel and Albertine jumped. "Bartine! Get that brat out of here or lock him up somewhere, but do something or I'll whomp him!" Albertine picked up Marcel up in her arms, crossed the dining-room as fast as she could and went to her room. Marcel was smiling. His mother sat him on her big bed. "You win! I'd sooner let you go out to do your nonsense than put up with one of her fits." "I want my good clothes." "Don't worry. When you leave here you'll look like such a little prince everybody on the street'll laugh at you because it's only Tuesday! If the people around here think we're crazy, we'll give them good reason .... Go get your good clothes, sweetheart, so momma can dress you up!" At five past eleven, then, Marcel was out on the balcony, wearing his Sunday best but not terribly clean, because his mother hadn't bothered to wash him. After all, he just smelled of peepee a little bit. As soon as the door shut behind him, he went down the stairs humming. He could feel his heart beating and couldn't help laughing out loud. "I'm coming, Duplessis, I'm coming. Wait for me!" On the balcony of the house next door, Rose, Violette and Mauve were knitting.

Gérard hadn't looked at Thérèse once since he started working. He threw himself body and soul into the shed that was piled high with the most unbelievable collection of odds and ends he'd ever seen, and waded into the statues, canopies, altars and cheap brocades, telling Sister Sainte-Catherine, "Open the doors wide and tell your girls I don't want to see hide nor hair of them in this shed. I'll hand you things one at a time, that way you can see what shape they're in." Sister Sainte-Catherine was delighted that she didn't have to ask her students, who were too delicate and even more awkward, to empty the shed that she'd always considered dangerous, but that Mother Benoîte stubbornly refused to have repaired. As for Sister Sainte-Philomène, whose physical strength was legendary in the parish, her chronic awkwardness and lack of organization made her more of a nuisance than a help; once, she'd knocked down a little girl with the left hand of a statue of the Sacred Heart, then dropped the same statue on the foot of another child, who had come to the aid of the first. She had also torn the veil of the Blessed Virgin's costume when she shook it out, and stepped through a canopy she'd thought was a platform. She was very useful, though, once it was time to construct the repository (sawing wood and driving in nails seemed to be passions into which she threw herself with delight), but that wouldn't be done until the next day, so Sister Sainte-Catherine had assigned her the task of watching over the three classes without concerning herself about what went on in the shed, while she and Sister Sainte-Thérèse acted as a link between Gérard Bleau and the school yard. Gérard rolled up the sleeves of his checked shirt, thinking, "The weakling's going to have to move his ass this morning!" With disconcerting ease, he sorted the damp and dusty hodgepodge that had accumulated in the shed during the past year. His gestures were precise and sure: gently but confidently he moved the biggest statues, which he picked up bodily, labouring under the burden, and moved them in one go, then set them down with infinite care, despite the effort; he even managed, with no help, to take out the big hardwood platforms, dragging them behind him, and letting them fall on to the cement, after shouting, "Hold your ears, there's going to be a bang!" Sister Sainte-Catherine was beaming. In less than half an hour the shed was empty, and all the props for the repository were lying in the school yard. But it was such a mess and so uninteresting that Sister

Sainte-Thérèse briefly felt discouraged, though Sister Sainte-Catherine put an end to it by shouting, loud enough for everyone to hear, "It's always a little depressing when you see everything all jumbled up like this, but you'll see – when everything's in place, it'll be beautiful!" She didn't really believe it, but she'd seen her friend's long face and a few of the girls looking at each other with big questioning eyes, and she thought it wise to reassure them. While Gérard was labouring in the shed, Thérèse and Pierrette were silent under the astonished gaze of Simone, who was still thrilled at their reunion. Thérèse couldn't have said whether she was overcome by fear or some new delight she couldn't name, that numbed her so she couldn't do a thing, not even think. She was working like everyone else, straightening up the statues that Sister Sainte-Philomène refused to leave lying on the ground ("Nobody's ever seen the Blessed Virgin lying on her back and we're not going to start today."), or carrying the piles of cloth that Gérard tended to drop on the cement like a bunch of old rags; but she did it all mechanically, hardly aware of what she was doing. She carried out Sister Sainte-Philomène's orders as well as she could, but they didn't really register, and Pierrette, who was quite simply scared, followed her around like a puppy, perhaps to help, certainly to protect her if anything happened. And something was going to happen, Pierrette could feel it. Now that Gérard was among them, *inside* the school yard like a wolf in the sheep-fold, Pierrette was sorry she hadn't acted on her first impulse and told everything to her mother or Thérèse's mother, or even to Sister Sainte Catherine, who was so kind and understanding. Pierrette didn't even know what a man could do with a woman or to a woman, but she knew from her catechism lessons that such things were allowed only within marriage and even there, according to her sister Rose, who at twenty-two was unhappily married and already doomed, those things were pretty unpleasant and very dirty (it had something to do with your bum, apparently; just imagine, your bum!). But she'd never heard that a man could do those things to a little girl, and the mere thought that her best friend, Thérèse, who was more than a sister to her, so beautiful and changeable and, above all, so inconsistent, might be in danger (but in danger of what, for Heaven's sake, how and in what form!) terrified her. She wished she could run to Sister Sainte-Catherine and ask her if she could spare twenty minutes to talk about a serious problem, but a minute later she was following Thérèse like a shadow, telling herself she had no right to leave her friend alone for a minute. Thérèse kept looking toward the shed. "Is he spying on me? Is he watching me? Jeepers, he's actually here! He came across the street for the first time! He asked Sister if he could work for her! And he did it all just to be near me!" She was swinging between the two poles of fear and joy, savouring the one with a frown and diving into the other as she brought her hand to her chest, her heart was beating so fast. "Maybe he'll ask to give me back my kiss!" She'd dreamed almost every night about the kiss she'd stolen from Gérard a month earlier and she thought about it constantly: when she was doing her homework or brushing her teeth, reciting her lessons or skipping rope. And as long as her fantasy relationship with Gérard stayed at the level of that kiss, there was no problem: he was handsome, she'd felt like kissing him, she'd done it, everything was fine, she could dream and not run any risk; but when she caught a glimpse of him under her staircase or on the church steps on Sunday morning, pale and undone and still just as handsome, her innocent dreams burst like bubbles and Thérèse dived into the troubled waters of desires that she didn't understand because of her inadequate education, but which she could feel like a prickling all over her body that almost burned. "But if he asks me to give him back his kiss and I say yes, what else is he going to want? Will he want something else? Will he go away and not come back? If he's going to go away afterwards I'd tell him no, so he'll stay! But if he hangs around too long he'll get sick of waiting and maybe he'll go anyway! Lord, I hate it when I don't understand!" One day her mother had told her, "If a man ever offers you candy, run away as fast as you can and tell me, so I can call the police!" Needless to say, two days later, her harmless Uncle Edouard had offered her some Sen-Sen, and Thérèse took off through the house, looking for her mother, screaming, "Momma, momma, a man just offered me some candy!" The whole family, especially the fat woman, who always maintained that Albertine never expressed herself very clearly and leapt on this opportunity to have a good laugh at her sister-in-law, had chortled for weeks and Thérèse had been thoroughly humiliated; she'd even decided never again to turn down candy, but no one ever offered her any. She stood in the school yard, then, her head full of unanswered questions, and gradually she was filled with anxiety. Despite the exertion required, despite the fatigue that was knotting his muscles and the sweat running down his back, Gérard hadn't taken his mind off Thérèse for a moment; at first he thought the work would affect him like a cold shower, that the fire engulfing him would eventually go out as he – the weakling – struggled to move heavy objects, but every time he came out of the shed, carrying a statue that was too big for him or pushing a platform that gave him trouble, on which he scraped his hands, the sun struck him on the forehead, as if he was suddenly in the field of vision of God Himself, and the gravity of what he was preparing to do to this child, who was too beautiful, who had come to disturb his dull and silent life, appeared to him in all its horror. He avoided looking in Thérèse's direction, but his senses found her; he could feel her on his left or right, her adorable head turned his way, the half-cruel, half-innocent smile finely drawn on that mouth that had been able to lead him astray forever with a simple peck. Several times he nearly dropped everything, the ridiculous religious objects, the nuns with their aggressive coifs, the stupid children with their oh's and ah's whenever he took from the shed a painted Saint Joseph or a few yards of sky-blue velvet, yellow at the folds; but what existed outside this school yard, what was left of his life outside this too splendid day in June when God Himself had descended from His distant domain to touch him with His scorn, what would tomorrow be without Thérèse – or even with her? And when his task was done, when all the props for the repository were spread out, somewhat like corpses, and the school yard looked like a real battlefield, Gérard had a second revelation, which left him petrified on the doorstep of the empty shed: he understood that once he had achieved the abjection for which he'd been created, he would have to disappear; death awaited him at the end of this spring day, and the thought came as a relief.

He already knew the living-room very well, because he'd spent hours there listening to Florence talk about her family, humble or loutish generations, all descended from the ancestor who came from France because the Thirty Years War had so devastated his part of the world that his village was unrecognizable: weeds had overrun the forge, rats nested in the bread ovens and there were only ruins where once there had been farms, poor but proud and somtimes even clean, at a time – the seventeenth century – that was particularly dirty. They always sat Marcel down in the same spot, like a little man, beside a black coffee-table whose varnish smelled so good that sometimes, in the middle of a story or while waiting for his snack, the little boy would stick out his tongue to taste it, eyes closed. When his tongue touched the varnished wood he was overcome by a strange, warm,

melting sensation, and he felt as if he was floating through
the room; the sharp taste would make his mouth water and
he would suck the edge of the table until Florence or one of
her daughters brought his cookie and glass of milk, or said
in mid-sentence, "Don't do that, Marcel! Varnish isn't good
for you, it's poison!" But the milk, which tasted sweet after
the acid taste of varnished wood, sickened Marcel a little,
and he took only a sip. The living-room, which had surprised
him at first because of the huge pieces of furniture and the
large number of objects of all sorts that were strewn around
it – enormous old pictures with such elaborate frames you
wondered whether you should be looking at what was in
them or simply admire the carved flowers or the finely cut-
out leaves decorating them; the dolls with cracked faces,
under glass domes, that seemed terrified at the sight of
anyone walking into the room; boxes, dozens of boxes of
metal, wood or glass, that had once contained things whose
odours still lingered, things that Marcel knew only by name
because Florence had told them to him, or by smell because
he had stuck his nose into containers of all shapes that he
found everywhere, on the little tables, the floor, the window
sill – had gradually become familiar to him, and he now
moved freely and comfortably among them, daring to ask
questions, whereas at first he had simply stared at an object
when he wanted to know what it was, picking things up as
if they belonged to him, moving them around and playing
with them, even if he'd been told they weren't toys; above
all, he was happy, because all along he knew that a reward,
in the form of a great mass of tiger-striped fur, was waiting
for him in the kitchen on the apron of the stove. Florence
had told him, "We'll give Duplessis back to you when he's
feeling better. In the meantime, come and see us as often as
you like. We can tell you all sorts of nice stories." And so
he'd been immersed in legends about the *chasse-galerie*, in
stories about Pharamine, the creature that bites your feet if

they stick out of the covers and your fingers if they stick out of your mitts in the winter; he had learned that a big fight was going on in a far-off country and his father had gone there to defend the mother country; and even more important, he'd learned to stop lisping. It happened gradually, and with surprising ease. By saying over and over the sentences he was asked to repeat ("I thee the cloudth in the thky .... I see the clouds in the thky ....") he finally shed this slight flaw that his family had never bothered about. But Marcel still had seen only the living-room in Florence's house. He'd never been invited to visit the other rooms; in fact, he'd never wanted to. Once he had asked, "Where do you sleep?" and Mauve had answered, "In our bed." Marcel had imagined a big bed with the four women lying on their backs, side by side, fully dressed, and he laughéd at the thought. He knew, though, that the kitchen was very busy, because it gave off aromas that made him reel: there was always a golden-crusted pie in the oven or a fragrant stew or some sort of roast that crackled as its fat ran out. That morning, however, Florence's house seemed strangely quiet. As soon as Marcel opened the gate, he sensed that the three knitting women were looking at him differently, and when Florence came to get him on the doorstep, he felt a tremor of fear at the bottom of his heart: wasn't Florence a little older, a little paler than usual? Almost transparent? She put her hand on the little boy's head. "Duplessis's waiting for you, Marcel." Oh joy! Marcel threw up his arms and placed his hands on those of Florence, which were stroking his head. He couldn't speak, but his expression, infinitely tender and filled with joy, made Florence shudder, and she cleared her throat before she spoke. "Duplessis's all right now. You can have him back. But you'll have to keep him for yourself. You mustn't talk about him, to anybody. It'll be our secret, okay? If you talk about him nobody will believe you, and they might even hurt you without meaning to." She looked at him so intensely that Marcel realized that what she was saying must be very important, but he couldn't concentrate, so delighted was he at being with Duplessis again. "You have to promise you won't tell anybody you've got Duplessis back." Marcel's lower lip started to tremble just a little, and Florence realized that it was cruel to further delay the reunion between the child and his cat. "Go get him. He's on the apron of the stove. But I want to talk to you before you leave." Marcel rushed into the hallway with a happiness that was near to despair; he passed the huge coal furnace enthroned in the middle of the room, bounded through the dining-room that was dark because the yellow blind was down, and burst into the kitchen, exclaiming in his flute-like voice, "Duplessis! It's me! Here I am!" He stopped dead in his tracks beside the table, overjoyed at the sight of his love curled up in a silky ball by the oven door. He rested his head on the table-top, which came up to his ears, unable to speak and panting as if he'd been running for hours. Duplessis opened one yellow eye and stared at Marcel without moving. The cat was so violently happy he thought he might faint. "He's here! My love! All this time I knew he was prowling around the house, but I was too weak to go to him ... and now he's here!" Only the tip of his pink muzzle quivered, opened, closed, then opened again. "Ah! He still gives off that lovely smell of dried peepee! What's he waiting for? Why doesn't he take me in his arms? I've been waiting so long." The independence of cats is exaggerated, but it's true that they're very proud, and Duplessis would never have made the first move. He waited breathlessly for Marcel to come to him. But Marcel couldn't move. He had stuck one finger in his mouth, and two big tears were rolling down his cheeks. "Duplessis, you'll have to come, I can't even move!" But Duplessis yawned a great yawn that showed his teeth and his black palate. He got up, had a long, voluptuous stretch, first one hind leg, then the other, next stretching his two front legs as if making a bow, scratching himself a little; then he blatantly turned his back on Marcel and curled up in a ball again. Thus do cats behave. With his one eye he stared at the back of the oven, saying, "Let him come! Let him come. That's all I want!" Then Marcel gathered what strength he still had and walked across the kitchen. He knelt beside the stove and pressed his head against Duplessis's somewhat mangy fur. "Won't you talk to me? Don't you love me any more?" He lightly kissed Duplessis's ear and the cat felt his head swim. Slowly he turned on his back and delivered himself of the finest purr of his life. Marcel wrapped his arms around the big cat. The lovers wept, wordlessly. On the balcony, Rose, Violette, and Mauve became very still. Florence, their mother, stood near the door. When Violette spoke, her voice sounded strange, as if something was caught in her throat. "Will he be strong enough to keep the secret?" Florence ran a hand through her hair. "I don't know."

When Sister Saint-Georges pressed the bell button, it was eleven thirty-two. Two minutes late. Six hundred anxious pairs of eyes had been watching the classroom clocks for a good five minutes; the twenty classrooms in the École des Saints-Anges were even starting to fill with an inquiring hum and with protests that were less and less discreet. Leaning against a window in the recreation hall that would be crammed with fidgety, disgruntled students when the weather was bad, Sister Clump Foot hadn't noticed the time passing, and for more than an hour she'd forgotten all her responsibilities: she wasn't at her post in her office, and if anyone rang the bell at the main door, the Principal would be forced to answer it herself; she had not yet—as she was supposed to do every morning—run a lemon-oil-soaked rag over Mother Benoîte's window sill and office furniture, where a single speck of dust was considered to be a personal affront; and now classes were over and she hadn't even noticed the time! It was because Sister Clump Foot wasn't used to lies, and the one she'd just told her superior had plunged her into nameless torments. She sensed that justice was on the side of Sister Sainte-Catherine and Sister Sainte-Thérèse, who must be protected and kept together, but lying to her superior was so serious – unthinkable yesterday, yet so easily done today, and so happily – that guilt, which she was quick to feel, was bending her under its weight, bowing her down as if to break her in two. She had been told that lying is the ugliest sin because it can hide others, which are added to it and aggravate it because it makes them harder to own up to; to get to the heart of a sin concealed by lies, you must start by confessing all those lies, every one, without exception, and remembering a lot of lies is nothing to brag about. One lie leads to another, which is soon followed by yet another, and so on till you're caught or give yourself away, lost in your own muddle and unable to distinguish between true and false. Sister Saint-Georges was almost sorry she hadn't delivered the letter herself the day before. What complications she would have avoided! "If Mother Benoîte calls Mother Superior and asks who brought her the letter, she'll tell her it wasn't me and then there'll be trouble!" Sister Saint-Georges pressed her forehead against the sill of one of the windows, which was open part way because of the heat. She was watching the grade six pupils romping about in the school yard, surrounded by the props for the repository, and she wished she could go out, as she did every year, to help them find the flaws, spots and bumps she would note in Sister Sainte-Catherine's little black notebook, feeling so important, so useful; but going out would mean confronting Sister Sainte-Catherine, the cause of her disgrace, and how could she bear the gaze of the young nun, so beautiful and full of energy, who had asked her, out of the blue, to *lie* for her? For more than a quarter of an hour, Sister Saint-Georges had been loitering in the recreation hall, running her hand absent-mindedly over the games of Mississippi and croquinole, absorbed in the guilt that was stifling her, exaggerating her lapse, allowing it to take on ridiculous proportions, seeing herself on the brink of Hell's abyss, because of a lie. She limped across the hardwood floors, unaware of the passing minutes and, for the first time since she'd been assigned that important task, the time for class to end had come and the bell had not run out through the École des Saints-Anges. When she leaned against the window again she noticed that something was wrong in the school yard: the little girls seemed less wrapped up in their work and Sister Sainte-Catherine was looking at her watch, frowning. Eventually it was her former best friend, Sister Sainte-Philomène, who made her aware of her lapse. When all activity in the school yard ceased without the intervention of Sister Sainte-Catherine or Sister Sainte-Thérèse, Sister Sainte-Philomène turned toward the bell and shouted, "If it doesn't ring in one minute I'm going to yell so loud Saint-Georges'll think it's an ambulance coming to get her!" Sister Saint-Georges immediately looked at the clock and the panic that swept over her was so acute that, for a good minute, the poor nun could only stare, wide-eyed with horror. Then everything happened at a dizzying pace: Sister Saint-Georges rushed to the stairs that went up to the second floor, climbed them, holding her skirts with one hand and the bannister with the other, and rushed into the corridor, panting—she who always took her time going about her tasks, who had the reputation of always being ahead of schedule, whom the École des Saints-Anges could *trust* to keep things running at the proper pace, at a set rhythm, in peace, for so many years now. Sister Saint-Georges burst into her office, veils swirling, face sweating, coif awry, her wood and metal cross slapping her chest. Standing quite straight beside the bell button, watch in hand, was Mother Benoîte des Anges. "You're two minutes late, Sister Saint-Georges, and you're a sorry sight. Take the afternoon off and rest. I don't want to see you in the school. I'll ring the bell myself. And I'll answer the door as well. And dust my own office. But I don't want this to happen again, Sister Saint-Georges. Ever." Sister Clump Foot threw herself at the bell button as if it were her last chance, before they finished her off.

The school yard was empty in less than thirty seconds, the school in under two minutes. The three nuns and Gérard Bleau were alone, scattered about the hecatomb, motionless, as in a naïve tableau. Gérard was sitting on a truncated papier-mâché column, elbows on his knees, staring fixedly at the ground. Sister Sainte-Philomène was gazing at a statue of the Sacred Heart with a broken hand; she seemed hypnotized by the white plaster stump that clashed with the vivid red of Christ's mantle. A platform about two feet high separated Sister Sainte-Catherine and Sister Sainte-Thérèse, who didn't dare look at each other for fear of seeing in the other's expression the despair that each knew was in her own. Amid all the shouting, laughter, orders to be given and energy to expend, they had been able, for almost half a day, to forget their imminent separation, but now that calm had been restored and they would have to wait until after lunch to start working again, escape was no longer possible, and they could see the future in all its mediocrity; Sister Sainte-Thérèse saw herself alone at the school, under the yoke of Mother Benoîte, who would certainly take advantage of Sister Sainte-Catherine's departure to lavish on her once again the syrupy, greedy solicitude with which she had pursued her for so long; Sister Sainte-Catherine, for her part, found it hard to imagine life without her naïve and gentle friend who had become the focus of her thoughts, her reason for living, the vital core without whom her existence would lose all meaning, becoming useless and even sterile. The word "love" even appeared for the first time in Sister Sainte-Catherine's brain, and rather than fearing it or being tempted to run away from it, she allowed herself to be seduced by it, opening her soul and breathing it in, like the perfume of a flower you know won't last long, in which you want to steep yourself while it's still at its peak. All four remained motionless, lost in their own thoughts, unaware of the sun, though it was beating down. It was Sister Sainte-Philomène, finally, who pulled them out of their torpor. She brought her hand to her stomach and said with a sigh, "This is all very nice, but we mustn't forget to keep our strength up if we want to start work again after lunch. Let's eat, Sisters!" Sister Sainte-Catherine turned to Gérard with a smile. "If you'd like to share our meal, Monsieur Bleau, you're welcome. I can bring you something to eat out here." Gérard started like a cat that's just been awakened. He got up, mumbled some feeble excuse, turned his back on the nuns and almost ran from the school. "Will you be back this afternoon? We still need you!" As she received no reply, Sister Sainte-Catherine came back to Sister Sainte-Thérèse, whom she dared to look at this time, but whose own gaze was firmly lowered on the asphalt. "It's true, we have to eat if we want to keep up our strength." Sister Sainte-Philomène had already disappeared into the nuns' house, and the two friends found themselves alone in the very middle of the school yard. "How can you talk about eating at a time like this!" And then Sister Sainte-Catherine was bold enough to do something she would never have thought herself capable of: she put her right arm around her friend's shoulders and Sister Sainte-Thérèse began to tremble. "Do you really think I've given up so easily, Sainte-Thérèse? Believe me, I'll find a way."

Mauve was seated at the piano. With infinite care, as if she was getting ready to officiate at some important ceremony, she raised the cover. Then she gazed at the keyboard, wrinkling her brow, looking, perhaps, for some secret she alone could read on the even teeth of ivory and ebony, apparently simple in their monotonous regularity, but infinitely complex for those who knew how to sort them out, decode them, resolve them. Before her was an open notebook, dog-eared and yellow, at which Mauve cast a timid glance from time to time. Rose was standing on her left, ready to turn the pages when Mauve nodded. Violette, who didn't know a thing about music but loved it passionately, was sitting in a wing-back chair, where she waited, visibly excited. Florence was not in the living-room. She stood in the middle of the hallway, looking toward the kitchen as if trying to guess what was going on there. "Play, Mauve .... Play!" Violette's voice was high-pitched and trembling, and it made her sisters' heads turn. She looked down before responding to their silent question. "I can't wait. It's been so long ...." Mauve sighed. "Yes. A long time." Florence came in and stood very tall, in front of the lace curtain that hid the window. "Go ahead, Mauve. They're ready." Duplessis and Marcel were still at the stage of caressing and tickling and wrestling on the kitchen floor when the music rose through the house, astonishingly pure and transparent as a morning in spring when the mist has just risen and the sun, now that its thirst has been quenched, is round and smooth, yet still imperious, brazenly making its way into the darkest corners of every room, invading everything, captivating everything that lives

149

and pulverizing the rest, wiping out those objects that can't appreciate it, the better to seduce and intoxicate those beings who, with their hearts and ears and brains, can taste it and live it. The house no longer existed; only the music remained, overwhelming, devastating. The little boy and the cat were perfectly still on the clean kitchen linoleum. Duplessis's ears were pointed toward the living-room. Marcel looked into the hallway, head bent, ecstatically happy. Time was suspended, yet staved in, shaded, broken by the notes of music that breathed so powerfully they exploded in fragrant bouquets and made you numb with joy. When the first movement of the sonata ended, Marcel and Duplessis rose as if at a signal they alone had heard. Very slowly they walked the length of the house, wondering what creature it was that had made them so happy, what form did it take and just how much they could trust it (did it lure cats and little boys into its den and eat them?). Florence was waiting at the living-room door. She picked up the cat and pushed Marcel toward the middle of the room, where the little boy always sat, close to the coffee-table whose taste he was so fond of. Rose, Violette and Mauve were smiling, but it was Florence who spoke. "You always wanted to know what that big box was, Marcel. It's called a piano. Mauve was playing it just now. And she's going to do it again. You can shut your eyes if you want, or you can watch her play. It's beautiful either way." The second movement, a long lament that made you ache for some great misfortune that you would happily die of, blew its gentle breath over Duplessis and Marcel, who huddled close together, lost in happiness, on the verge of fainting. Diaphanous swirls, pink, amber, green, whirled through the room and it seemed there were odours that Marcel was discovering for the first time, but which Duplessis seemed to be rediscovering deep down in his memories, as he trembled contentedly. The little boy looked around as if to gather the music into his arms, but

150

the cat had shut his eyes and seemed to be concentrating on inner joys that were enchanting him: birds, perhaps, that he was pursuing as he savoured his own cruelty, or mice that he scoffed at or insulted as he tracked them. When it was over, when the last note was snuffed out in a sob so discreet you'd have sworn it hadn't really happened, Marcel put his thumb in his mouth, shuddering. Florence came and knelt beside him. "Marcel, music is one of life's great gifts. It's a consolation, a reward. It helps you get through the business of living. The hardships ahead of you, Marcel, can always be allayed, numbed, almost forgotten in Mauve's music. If you're so miserable you want to die, because someone's been mean to you, come and see Mauve. Later on, when you're grown up, when you can understand more, I'll tell you about the great rewards that Violette and Rose can lavish on you, but you're too young for that now. For the moment, the music will be enough." Marcel didn't understand everything Florence said, but he listened with avid curiosity. Mechanically he stroked his cat, who purred mechanically. "But you must keep all this to yourself. You can't say a word to anybody. Not about Duplessis, who will teach you things wherever you go, or about Mauve, who will console you whenever you need it. If you tell anybody, they won't understand, and that'll make things a lot harder for you." She got up again and went to her place at the window. The third movement of the sonata made Marcel laugh. Quick little notes of every colour skipped all over at once, and made you want to run and jump fences and try to catch the clouds; it went so fast it left you breathless and dizzy, even though you felt very happy. And it ended so abruptly that Marcel thought he was falling from the third floor, and he held his little arms out in front of him, with an exclamation of panic. Then he burst out laughing as he realized how absurd his gesture was. Florence smiled. "You can go home now." "With Duplessis?" "Yes, but remember to keep him just for you." Marcel picked up the cat, whose motor started up immediately, got up and walked toward the door. Then, for the first time, before leaving the house he turned around toward Rose, Violette, Mauve and Florence, their mother, and happily thanked them. When he had gone, Mauve slowly closed her music book. "It's been so long." Florence came and sat beside her on the big square bench. "Yes, a long, long time." "The last time was for Josaphat-le-Violon. Nobody's seen us since then." Rose pushed a lock of hair off her forehead. "But Victoire, if she'd wanted to ...." Florence sighed. "Victoire didn't want to. And neither did her children. But it's so good there's somebody in the young generation who needs us." "But are you sure he's the right one, momma?" "We'll try ... and we'll see."

"My mother asked you for lunch." Simone and Pierrette both turned their heads. Thérèse burst out laughing. "I guess I just put my foot in it. She meant you, Simone. I told her you looked gorgeous with your new mouth and she said she'd like to see it ...." Simone frowned. "I'm not a monkey." "And I'm not offering you peanuts!" Simone broke from her friends' embrace. Thérèse stood in the middle of rue Gilford, which they were crossing. "You aren't going to make another scene! Jeepers, we just made up! If you don't want anybody to see your damn mouth, stay home!" Pierrette pulled on Thérèse's sleeve. "You're blocking traffic ...." "I am not, there isn't one damn car in sight!" "If there was you'd be blocking it!" "You get on my nerves!" Thérèse crossed her arms and clicked her heel against the asphalt to show that she had no intention of moving. Pierrette shrugged. "Stubborn mule!" "I'll be as stubborn as I want, Pierrette Guérin!" "I know you, you'll get run over just to show us you can do whatever you want!" Pierrette turned her back on Thérèse and grabbed Simone by the waist. "Never mind her, she's plain crazy!" Thérèse watched them move away toward rue Fabre, and decided to turn her back on them and go home along the lane that joined Garnier and Fabre, parallel to Gilford. At that very moment Gérard Bleau entered the same street, after running past Saint-Stanislas church. He was already out of breath when he saw Thérèse in the middle of the street. He stopped, bringing his hands to his mouth like a little boy caught doing something wrong. When Thérèse saw him she recoiled a few paces. She stepped on to the sidewalk mechanically, not watching where she was going. She couldn't take her eyes off Gérard. "There he is! What does he want now?" She felt suddenly numb; she couldn't move, like the birds she'd seen Duplessis chase last summer, that helplessly let the cat hypnotize them, pounce on them, and let themselves be devoured almost without a struggle. But Gérard seemed as much a victim as Thérèse; he couldn't move either. Great fear could be seen in his staring eyes, and he, too, folded his arms across his chest. "Is it time now? So soon! Is it already here! What am I going to do? How am I going to do it?" Suddenly Thérèse saw him bend double and drop to his knees, his arms still folded. He uttered a small cry, like a wounded animal. He pressed his head against the cement, moaning. The street separating Thérèse from Gérard was still empty. No passer-by. No cars. Thérèse was leaning against a wrought-iron fence. "He's sick! I have to help him!" She ran across the street, not really aware of what she was doing, and stopped in front of Gérard, who was still moaning softly. "Are you sick?" The moaning stopped. Gérard raised his head without unfolding his arms. When she saw the young man's expression Thérèse shuddered in astonishment. The park attendant's face, which she'd thought was so handsome, which she'd been dreaming about for a month now, had changed. In his grimacing mouth, his creased forehead, his wild, dilated eyes with

153

madness bursting from them like a dark flower, she saw such suffering that she couldn't keep from holding out her arms to help him. Gérard shrank back, sat on his heels. "Don't come near me!" "Do you need anything?" "Don't talk to me! Go away!" "Get up, and I'll go. I can't leave you on the ground like this." "You really don't know what I want?" "No." Dragging himself along on his knees, Gérard approached Thérèse, who put her hands on his head. "I want something terrible, Thérèse!" She saw herself again kissing the park attendant's silky lips; she felt again the sweet turmoil that had warmed her body. A sob rose in her throat. "I hoped it was going to be nice! I just wanted a kiss!" Gérard wrapped his arms around Thérèse, rested his head against her stomach. "Hurry up and go away! Don't stay there! You feel so good! Hit me while you've still got the strength! Scratch me! Pull my hair! Put out my eyes! Shout! Yell! Call for help before it's too late!" He suddenly opened his arms, freeing Thérèse, who didn't move. "Go away!" He shouted so loud that Thérèse started running without realizing it. "Don't worry! You'll never see me again!" Thérèse's uniform disappeared in a bluish haze. Gérard leaned against the fence that surrounded the back of the church. He placed his hands on his swollen sex. The black dress had disappeared around the bend in the lane. Gérard rubbed his trousers furiously. "One last time! Just once before I go away for good!"

Thérèse found her brother sitting on the steps in front of their house. "Aren't you going to eat?" Marcel had one arm bent as if he was holding something and moved his free hand as if he was stroking some imaginary animal or a doll. "I'm not hungry." "My Lord, that's news!" She sat beside him. "I'm not very hungry either." Thérèse was certainly disturbed, but mainly she was disappointed by what had just happened on rue Garnier. She had never, at any time, been afraid of Gérard; on the contrary, she had lived long moments of expectation: during those few moments when Gérard had clasped her waist, her body had vibrated, and more than ever she had felt the urge to kiss him, but his wild look and the words she didn't understand had held her back. She knew now, she was sure of it, because he had told her, that he wanted something besides a kiss. But what? "I don't know any more than I did before. Maybe I ought to ask momma. No, she'd likely spank me 'cause I didn't tell her about it before!" So once more she pushed to the bottom of her heart the questions that had been weighing so heavily on her for a month. And surprisingly, she felt relieved; she even caught herself smiling at her brother. "Quit acting so silly, Marcel! If you want a dolly to play with you can have my old one, I don't need it any more, I'm too old. But don't pretend like that, you look really dumb." "I've got my own dolly, Thérèse, I don't need yours!" Marcel looked at her with his big round eyes as if he had something important to tell her, the way he looked when he went in his pants. "Did you pee your pants again? Good grief, Marcel, you're four years old, you aren't a baby any more!" She took him by the arm, picked him up without a fuss and they started slowly up the stairs. Marcel kept looking behind him, which got on his sister's nerves. "Quit looking back like that, you'll fall! When you go up the stairs you look up, and when you come down them you look down. That's not so hard to understand! If you look up next time you come downstairs you'll smash your head and we'll have to pick up your brains with a spoon!" She laughed at her witticism and Gérard disappeared from her mind altogether. When they got to the door Marcel turned around one last time. "Come on, Duplessis, we're going to eat." He had spoken very softly; Thérèse didn't catch his words. She wasn't listening in any case. As Thérèse was reaching for the handle, the door opened and Albertine burst out with such force that the balcony seemed to shake under the feet of the little girl, who couldn't repress a mischievous smile. "I've got two children, just two, and they have to gang up and make trouble for me! If you start being late at your age, what'll it be like when you're older? What are you trying to do to me? Richard and Philippe are already eating dessert! And where's your friend, Thérèse? You made me cook enough calves' liver for an army, then you show up all by yourself!" The two children went into the house, followed by their mother, who continued her harangue. "I've got other things to do besides hang around making lunch for the bunch of you! I've told you a thousand times, I want everybody to eat at the same time, because it makes life easier for me: can't you get that through your thick skulls? Are your hands clean? Marcel, wash your hands! Thérèse, help him!" Victoire hadn't returned to her room after "Francine Louvain." She even insisted on helping Albertine make lunch (although, to the old woman's great humiliation, her daughter only let her set the table and mash the potatoes). When Philippe and Richard came home from school – Philippe in stitches because he'd succeeded yet again in making his brother's ears turn red by telling him a dirty story neither of them understood, but which they sensed was very daring, Richard sad and miserable because his ears had betrayed him yet again – Victoire had decided to eat with them. She hadn't done so for a long time, but that day her leg didn't hurt as much as usual and she needed company. But the meal had been much less pleasant than she'd hoped, for when her children didn't come home Albertine started pacing the kitchen, cursing and knocking things over as she went: the teapot, a glass of milk, a chair. Philippe and Richard stuck their noses in their plates, where there were several pieces of liver, which they both hated but were forced to eat once a week "because it's good for your blood." Victoire chewed slowly, with a vacant expression, as she looked out the kitchen window which looked on to the gallery. All three were about to get up from the table when Thérèse and Marcel, followed by their mother screaming at them louder than ever, came into the kitchen. "Sit down before your hands are washed and I'll cut your throats, both of you!" Just before he went into the bathroom, Marcel, without thinking, turned to his mother and asked candidly, "Momma, can Duplessis have some calves' liver, too?" Albertine stopped dead in mid-curse. Philippe burst out laughing. Richard rolled his eyes to heaven. Albertine slowly put down the fork she was holding, from which a bloody piece of liver was hanging, went over to Marcel, bent down and, to everyone's great surprise, spoke softly. "Marcel, if you say one more word about that god-damn cat I won't be frying calves' liver, I'll fry your little behind!" Thérèse took her brother's hand and pulled him into the bathroom. She ran the water and started soaping Marcel's hands. "Don't talk to momma about things that don't exist, Marcel, she doesn't understand and it upsets her." Marcel stiffened. "Duplessis does so exist!" He spoke with such certainty that all heads turned toward the bathroom. Taking advantage of the fact that his sister was now soaping her own hands, Marcel ran out of the bathroom, through the kitchen and behind his grandmother's chair, where Duplessis was lying curled up in a ball. He picked up the cat and brought it into the kitchen. "See, here he is! So don't keep saying he doesn't exist!" At the sight of Marcel's empty arms, so slender but tense, as if they were carrying something heavy, Philippe and Richard burst out in cruel, childish laughter. As for Albertine, she had trouble containing her growing rage. She merely sighed, though, and threw the rest of the liver (it wasn't calves' liver at all, in fact, but pork; they just called it calves' liver because it didn't sound so poor) in the white-hot frying-pan. "I've got a crazy son! He's the only one I've got and he's crazy! What can I do? The asylum costs too much, and my nerves won't take much more of this! My life's no bed of roses, it's a pile of shit!" Only Victoire didn't react: she went suddenly pale when Marcel came back into the kitchen. In the little boy's arms she could *see* a huge tiger-striped cat that seemed to be scoffing at her with his one yellow eye. She leaned against the table, unable to take her eyes off the animal, which fascinated her. "It's my turn now! God help me, it's my turn!"

The pale green armature of the Jacques Cartier Bridge rose above the skittish, choppy St. Lawrence River, which was angrily caressing St. Helen's Island – so calm with its brand-new lawns, its trees bursting with health, a serene oasis seldom visited at that time except by a few connoisseurs who knew it as "Ass Island" – and was transformed right under the roadway into surging rapids with jagged rocks jutting out that gave you the shivers just looking at them. Gérard Bleau was standing just above these rapids. He was leaning against the guard-rail of the bridge, elbows on the round parapet that vibrated every time a car drove behind him. "It's too high! I'll never make it!" He had crossed part of east-end Montreal on foot before he realized that he was heading for the Jacques Cartier Bridge, high spot of his child-hood games, then of his adolescence, when he would go several times a week with his gang from rue Dorion to run or ride their bikes on one of the two cement sidewalks that went around the bridge; intentionally dangerous games ("If you stand on the edge you're a man, if you don't you're a fruit!") long on physical strength and totally lacking in intelligence: cowboys and Indians happily beat each other up, but the Indians had to lose because they were the bad guys; the *filles du Roy* were raped very realistically, complete with ejaculations and, O supreme joy, they actually tortured little English strays, calling them square-heads, goddamn dirty

158

dogs or blokes (whence the song: "The English live at the top of the hill/ And tell us to go to hell;/ But we'll throw rocks at the goddamn blokes/ And the Tremblays will ring all the bells!"). The rain washed away the blood that flowed during these little games and when it didn't rain, the blood would dry so that next time you could tell yourself, "That's mine! That's from when I smashed open Pom Pom Pomerleau's face 'cause he wouldn't climb the side of the bridge!" A large part of Gérard's life had been spent running, leaping and laughing on this bridge that started at the bottom of his street, and which his mother had given him as a present when he was little. (She'd just had her teeth replaced with what she called by the English name of "bridge," and she'd told Gérard, "I just bought myself a bridge. Looks good, but I had to pay through the teeth!" Gérard, in his great naïveté, thought his mother had just acquired the Jacques Cartier Bridge, and he'd run out into rue Dorion squealing with joy, trumpeting the news to everyone, and setting a toll – one cent for pedestrians, five cents for bikes. The whole neighbourhood had a good laugh at that one, and found out at the same time that Gérard's mother now wore false teeth.) "At least if I jumped from the Montreal Swimming Pool side there wouldn't be so many rocks! I'd still drown, but it wouldn't hurt so much." Gérard really did want to die. He saw no other solution to the desire that was tormenting him, which he'd been able to resist – he didn't know how – that very morning, but he knew it was insidious, demanding, and, in the end, really too much for him; but the laziness of this little bum with no ambition, for whom life had always been fairly easy, given his handsome mug and the shortage of men on rue Dorion, was more powerful than anything else, and even the truly dreadful despair he felt as he stared at the rapids and whirlpool wasn't able to overcome it; he wanted to die, but he wasn't going to kill himself. He thought of jumping off the bridge; he imagined himself falling, arms flapping as if in flight; he felt first dizzy, then the joy of knowing that for five or ten seconds he was absolutely free to do as he wished; he delighted in his fear between bridge and water, he waved at the city, his feet pointed toward the rocks, he sent kisses to the tower on St. Helen's Island, made the up yours sign to the east end of Montreal where he'd been born and, now that he was sacrificing himself, was turning its back on him; but deep down he knew he was still dreaming, as he had years ago, in this very place, when he'd masturbated thinking about Madame Veilleux, who made advances he didn't respond to because he didn't yet know how, about Madame Cinq-Mars, of whom it was said that she had five breasts, or of the little Simard girl who knew how to use her crossed eyes to check out men's pants. He had caressed his fantasies in this very spot and now he was doing it again. The eye of God had disappeared; so had his guilt. For the moment, even Thérèse was absent from his thoughts. All that remained was the beauty of the sacrificial gesture of which he was dreaming, blowing it up though he knew full well it was beyond his reach, because he wasn't worthy of it. He spent hours like this, drifting between sky and water, creating falls that were dizzying and exalting or calm and pacifying, but never thinking of the reasons for them. The sun had already started its slow descent toward Mount Royal when Gérard dragged himself back to the city, drained, exhausted, but still a bit ashamed of his cowardice. When he walked into one of the many taverns on rue Ontario, his friends gave him a long ovation.

That evening, a hairy creature staggered into the Canadian Army enlistment office at Place Viger on the Champ-de-Mars, obviously loaded and howling obscenities as he pounded his chest and demanded pen and ink from every man he encountered, soldier or civilian. "I wanna sign up, *tabarnac*! I wanna sign up! Take me with you. I'm young, I'm healthy, *ciboire*! Haven't got flat feet! But I'm a son of a bitch! I'm a son of a bitch that's sick of life and just wants to kill some poor buggers to atone for his sins. I wanna sign up! Let's get moving – while my slate's still clean! It'll be too late tomorrow! If you don't look after me right now, this time tomorrow it'll be all over. I want it so bad, and Thérèse is so beautiful! Let me die over there!" He slumped onto the chair that was held out for him and signed without reading a paper that sentenced him to go fight on the other side of the great waters for three long years. God had paid him another visit.

THIRD
MOVEMENT

---

*Allegro
giocoso*

"Never trust a man you find on the street!" "You're quite the expert on men, Sister Sainte-Philomène!" The nun blushed, just long enough to bring her hand to her heart. "God protect me from them, Sister Sainte-Catherine! But I know what they're like! Just because I stay away from them doesn't mean I can't see how they operate! Anyhow, we don't need a hired man, we've got lots of strong sisters." With that, she picked up the life-sized statue of the Sacred Heart of Jesus (a truly hideous thing that scared the children, with its staring eyes and poorly painted lips, but they were obliged to find it beautiful because it depicted the Saviour in the prime of life and at the peak of his brief career), lifted it with a loud "Whew!" that echoed off the brick wall, and with small quick steps hurried out of the school yard, her back stiff, her mouth pressed against the bleeding heart of Jesus, which seriously needed mending. Sister Sainte-Catherine laughed as she watched her move off. This Wednesday morning, on the eve of the Corpus Christi celebration, the grade-six students were in a state of rare feverishness: in a few hours the girls would be chosen who would have the honour of playing the Virgin, the angels, Sainte Bernadette Soubirous, and the little hanging angel in the tableau it was their custom to create for the repository. As far as the Blessed Virgin was concerned, the die was already cast: some years before it had been decided that the honour would go automatically to the grade-six student with the best marks in religion, who would be allowed to drape herself in the white robe, blue veil and narrow gilded belt of the Mother of Jesus; but her name was kept secret until the eve of the great day, so that, every year, speculation was rampant, with every class wanting to see its champion crowned. (Blessed Virgins in the past had been obese, rickety, cross-eyed, with rotten teeth, noses too long or too flat. Once there'd even been a hunchback who couldn't stand up very long, who they'd had to put on an improvised throne. The nuns deplored the fact that it was often the ugliest girls who came first in religion, but they couldn't change the rules that rewarded knowledge over beauty; the soul, after all, is more important than the body!) All three little girls in the running that year were very popular, but for different reasons: Six A was represented by Pierrette, whom the nuns were very fond of because she'd had some trouble hoisting herself into first place, but she had one serious flaw: her teeth were far from straight and, though her face was pretty enough, her mouth didn't quite shut, which would give the Blessed Virgin – in the event that she won – a goofy look that already had them worried; in Six B, Thérèse had easily won first place, and Sister Sainte-Philomène swelled with pride at the prospect of seeing her Thérèse, so bright and pretty, too, climb up on the Virgin's pedestal, as the whole parish looked on ecstatically; as for Six C, one of the most hopeless classes, where laziness was the norm and the most boneheaded sort of ignorance reigned, to the great despair of its teacher, the gentle Sister Sainte-Thérèse de l'Enfant-Jésus, it had crowned Ginette Chartier, a homely child in glasses, two-faced, sneaky and scheming, who had cheated all year so she'd come first in religion, because her mother had promised her a balloon-tired bike if she got the part of the Blessed Virgin, and whom her classmates respected because they were afraid of her. But despite blackmail and the liberal use of threats, the poor child didn't have a chance: everybody knew the real contest was between Thérèse and Pierrette, who weren't getting too worked up because they knew that the one who didn't climb onto the Blessed Virgin's pedestal would get the consolation prize – playing Bernadette Soubirous; thus they were both sure of being singled out. (And as Pierrette put it so well that very morning when the trio

166

"Thérèse-'n'-Pierrette" was turning the corner of Gilford and Garnier, talking about their chances and how they couldn't care less about the whole business, "I'd rather be Sainte Bernadette, 'cause then I'd have my back to everybody and they couldn't see my crooked teeth." To which Thérèse had replied, "You're right, I'm prettier." Simone looked angrily at Thérèse. "Just because you're pretty you don't have to hurt other people's feelings!") Sister Sainte-Catherine came out of the school yard on to rue de Lanaudière, walked around the school and up to the huge cement staircase that would be the base for the repository. It was very steep and Sister Saint-Georges hated it because she had to sweep it twice a week, and it was rather hard to stand up on, as her club-foot stuck out from the step she was standing on, making her balance very precarious. It must be said as well that it was a very ugly staircase, functional to the point of plainness, like an appendix stuck on the school that no one had taken the trouble to decorate; a cement mass devoid of interest, but which must be magnified so as to make it worthy of the Blessed Sacrament that would be placed there on Thursday night, as if the fate of the world depended on it. That morning, though, the staircase, which was generally deserted because Mother Benoîte forbade the students to use it, was filled with excited little girls taking useless measurements, offering opinions and shouting orders that nobody was listening to, climbing the stairs ten times in a row for no reason, then hurtling down them to go help a classmate who didn't need it, noisy, chattering, and red from excitement because of the great feat they were preparing. When Sister Sainte-Catherine arrived at the foot of the stairs, Lucienne Boileau, sucking a pigtail, as was her habit whenever she was nervous or concentrating, was trying, for reasons known only to herself, to move the statue of the Sacred Heart that Sister Sainte-Philomène had just placed on the sidewalk. The nun, sitting on the steps, was wiping her brow, puffing like an engine. Sister Sainte-Catherine smiled at her. "You see, Sister Saint-Philomène, men aren't altogether useless." The Six B teacher replaced her handkerchief in the sleeve of her habit. "If they only moved statues I might not be a nun!" Thérèse and Pierrette arrived with the huge wicker trunk in which the costumes were stored. They put it down beside Lucienne, who was still holding her statue. Thérèse spoke without even looking her way. "Did he ask you to dance or did you make the first move?" Pierrette added, without even a glance at the poor little fat girl, who had just set the statue down on the sidewalk again, "We just saw the Principal and she wants you to put the statue in her office so she can make a lamp out of it. But don't go up the main stairs; she wants you to go around." As they watched Lucienne's face crumple, they could sense the rising indignation of Sister Sainte-Philomène, who had leaped to her feet. "She's taken leave of her senses! Lost her marbles altogether! Give me that statue, Lucienne, I'll take it up to the Principal myself. And let me tell you, she'll get a piece of my mind!" Thérèse and Pierrette hid their giggles in the trunk they'd just opened. Sister Sainte-Catherine wiped Lucienne's forehead. "I think Thérèse and Pierrette are just trying to give us a taste of their sense of humour, Sister Sainte-Philomène, but I'm afraid all they've done is show us how silly they can be." Sister Sainte-Philomène leaned against the statue of the Sacred Heart and sighed with relief. "Oh, it was just a joke!" Then she looked at Thérèse and Pierrette, who had started to take out the costumes. "It sure fell on its face." Lucienne Boileau made a face at the two friends, who didn't see her, as it happened, because they were slapping their thighs, and walked away, chewing her pigtail. Sister Sainte-Philomène followed after her, snapping, "How many times do I have to tell you not to fiddle with that pigtail! You'll pull it off and your mother'll say we're trying to make a martyr out of you!" Lucienne started running toward rue Garnier, in tears. Sister Sainte-Philomène turned to Sister Sainte-Catherine, flinging up her arms in a gesture of helplessness. "She's crying again. She'll be dried up before the year's over!" Sister Sainte-Catherine let Thérèse and Pierrette take all the costumes from the trunk (twelve satin angels' robes, so faded that the colours – sea green, pale pink, butter yellow – had virtually disappeared, especially at the creases, where they had indisputably turned brown; the celebrated Virgin's costume that they made it a point of honour, every year, to declare "miraculously preserved" whereas it, too, in fact, was beginning to deteriorate badly; Sainte Bernadette's outfit, a checked skirt found by Sister Sainte-Philomène in her boxes for the poor, which didn't bear the faintest resemblance to any garment that might have been worn by a nineteenth-century Portuguese girl, but rather by a good twentieth-century French-Canadian farm girl obsessed with her country's folklore, and a very pretty beige peau-de-soie blouse trimmed with lace, inherited from Sister Sainte-Catherine's grandmother, which clashed wondrously with the big yellow and blue checks in the skirt; a few rags with which the shepherds were decked out whenever they wanted to toss a few into the repository, and full-dress sheepskin regalia with real fur that Sister Sainte-Catherine had never worked up the courage to use, because she thought it cruel to stick some poor child in fur in June, and thought it ridiculous anyway that French Canadians had chosen to represent themselves by an animal as stupid as a sheep), then she said to them, smiling mischievously, "Would you mind telling me what's the idea of emptying the costume trunk in the middle of the sidewalk?" Thérèse and Pierrette, expecting a compliment for their brilliant initiative, looked at each other in surprise. "Do you think we're going to try on the costumes in front of the whole parish? Honestly, sometimes I think the only reason you two come first is because everybody else is even dumber than you are!" She burst out laughing, ruffling their hair. "Pierrette, tell your mother that if she doesn't wash your hair for tomorrow night, I'll dress you up as a bird's nest! Meanwhile, will you kindly put all that stuff in the trunk and take it back to the school yard! That'll teach you!" All this time the other girls had been fidgeting, running, shouting into the wind. The tension was rising dangerously and Sister Sainte-Catherine thought she must put a stop to it immediately if she didn't want the day to end in tears. She climbed up a few cement steps, took her clapper from her pocket and struck it three times. The faces of all the girls, red with emotion and covered in sweat, turned toward her. "Now that you've shown me what you can't do, let's tidy all this up."

The day before, Thérèse hadn't had time to give any serious thought to the incident with Gérard before she went to bed. Too much had happened: dinner, with her mother ranting and raving at Marcel because of his phantoms and at her for being late, had taken place amid sobs and shouts, with Marcel screaming whenever his mother came near him, Thérèse as usual repaying insult with insult, blow with blow. Thérèse felt as if she was regressing several weeks, to the time before her mother had mellowed, after their conversation about Marcel and the fat woman's departure for the hospital. And yet the brief period of near happiness that was ending in tears had been the most beautiful time of their life. Albertine was slowly transformed into an almost normal mother, cajoling her children and speaking to them like someone sharing a secret, even trusting them, though her instinct was to spy on them; Thérèse, filled with questions about Gérard, had finally, thanks to her mother's delightful mood, been able to leave her little brother to himself, his games, his laughter – to his childhood, in fact – without worrying about his fate as she had always done before. Marcel was developing in a rather surprising way and required less care: he was more discreet now and, above all, less nervous than before. Sometimes he would disappear for hours, but no one worried because they knew he'd come home smiling, calm, with a bouquet of dandelions that stained his hands and some tall tale that would delight everybody. One day, Richard had said of his little cousin, "If he keeps this up he'll turn into a poet like *mon oncle* Josaphat!" Albertine merely hissed between her teeth, "I just hope he'll do a better job of earning a living." At noon, however, with his stories about an imaginary cat, everything had fallen apart in a matter of minutes and there was a layer of dust over the fine month of May that had just ended, as if to transfix it in utter stillness: Marcel was once more a nervous little boy terrified of his mother; Albertine had lost the gleam in her eye that Thérèse liked so much and Thérèse found herself once more filled with rage and contempt, whenever Albertine struck out indiscriminately at a child of hers or of the fat woman's, rarely actually selecting a victim because she wasn't annoyed just at them, but at the whole world, at life, at her very existence. As usual, around ten to one Pierrette and Simone were waiting for Thérèse at the foot of the stairs and the afternoon at school had passed very quickly. Gérard's absence hardly registered because he wasn't really needed for the remaining tasks – dusting the statues, washing platforms and pedestals in plenty of water, using Brasso on the candlesticks, liturgical objects, the columns supporting the canopy that had become tarnished over the winter – nothing, in fact, that needed a man's strength. Still, a few of the girls asked timid questions such as, "Where's the blond dream boat that was here this morning?" They heard Sister Sainte-Catherine reply, "He wasn't blond; he was dark. See how underdeveloped your powers of observation are?" "But we still don't know where he is! "What difference would it make if you did?" They soon forgot Gérard, though, in the midst of cloths soaked in Brasso, steel wool that scraped their hands and soapy water that reeked of Javex. At recess, Thérèse approached Pierrette and Simone, who were still scraping off the base of the statute of the Virgin, and told them, "I don't want to hear another word about the guy from the park. He won't be back." Pierrette looked up, pushed back the lock of hair that clung to her forehead. "Did he tell you?" "No. But I know." Pierrette got to her feet. "You're keeping something from me." Thérèse looked her straight in the eye. "Right. And when I'm ready to tell you, I'll tell you." That night, Thérèse clung to the plump, warm body of her cousin Philippe with whom she shared the living-room sofa, wrapped her arm around his soft little belly, placed her mouth against his shoulder. "You're sticking like glue – how come you're so lovey-dovey?" Be quiet, I'm not thinking about you!" Philippe pushed away his cousin's arm. "If you aren't thinking about me, hands off!" Then he turned his back and Thérèse started to laugh. "You're stuck on yourself, aren't you!" "What would you say if I kissed you and said I was thinking about Gramma Victoire?" "I'd say you were weird! Anyway, the guy I'm thinking about's a lot cuter than you are." Thérèse, who knew every one of Philippe's weaknesses, started to tickle him, exclaiming, "Kitchy-koo on Philippe's ears, and a little tickle on his arms, and his big fat belly, and his neck ...." Philippe, doubled over with laughter, begged for mercy, then surrendered, weeping, on the verge of fainting, groaning with pleasure. Thérèse had got to "a little tickle on your little thing" when Albertine burst in carrying a wooden ruler. At the same moment, Victoire's door opened, and the old lady stuck her head out and murmured very softly, almost inaudibly, "If you don't stop that ruckus right now, I'll die tonight and it'll be your fault!" Then she shut the door without another word. Albertine stayed in the living-room doorway, rooted to the spot, still holding the ruler over her head, eyes bulging, but silent. The children, by some miracle, had stopped moving, for their grandmother's face seemed so frightening, old and so pale it looked like wax, and with such big circles under her eyes it was scary. Albertine silently threatened the children with her ruler and then turned her back. Philippe took refuge in Thérèse's arms. "Think about whoever you want, but don't let go of me!" Thérèse laughed nastily. "Are you going to think about her now when I kiss you?" "Yuck! Don't make me sick!" When Philippe's breathing became regular, Thérèse pushed him away, tucked him in and gave him a peck on the fore-head. At last she could think about Gérard in peace. She knew she wouldn't see him again for a long time. Or maybe never. She had sensed it right after the scene on rue Garnier. She wasn't sure if that upset her or not. Yes, maybe a little. She had felt that something very serious had nearly hap-pened between them, but as she had no idea just what it was, she couldn't feel sorry and she couldn't feel relieved. "I want to know what it is! I want to know!" Exciting little shudders, a pain in her lower belly and palpitations dis-turbed her even more, leaving her panting, breathless, filled with expectation, yet convinced that nothing was going to happen. "I only wanted to kiss him! Like I kiss Philippe before he goes to sleep ... but with something else!" Suddenly a very precise image made her start: she saw Gérard again, putting his head on her belly. She covered her belly-button with both hands. She had felt so good, almost delivered, when he did that! She remembered a game of her cousins' that she thought was very stupid, one of those boring games you save for Sunday afternoons when you're all dressed up and aren't allowed to do anything: she pictured her cousin Philippe going up to Marcel and threatening him with his index finger, "I'm going to unscrew your belly-button and your behind'll drop off!" She saw her brother undo his shirt as he told his cousin, "Go ahead, let's see!" And every time, after Philippe had twisted his finger in Marcel's belly-button a few times, the little boy would turn around to see if his behind had fallen onto the sidewalk. Disappointed, he would say to his cousin, "You haven't got the right key!" Thérèse stuck her own index finger into her belly-button and moved it around, increasing the pressure. A tickling sensation she'd never felt before spread from her navel to her anus and she bent double. Then, without realizing what she was doing, she put her other hand on her sex. "That's where it is. Somewhere around there." Immediately, though, a vision of the confessional, the word "lust," Sister Sainte-Philomène's long fart and the memory of her mother telling her with a frown, "When you wash yourself there, do it fast, it isn't nice!" made her raise both hands and place them on her budding breasts. "I'll never figure it out by myself! And I don't know anybody that can tell me. Shoot!" She finally fell into an agitated sleep, in which there drifted the head of a man, so handsome and gentle, that came to rest on her belly, saying, "I could have shown you. I could have told you. But it's too late now and you'll never find out."

Posted in the vestibule of the presbytery, his nose pressed against the door pane that still smelled of vinegar, Monsignor Bernier waited until all the overactive little girls were off the stairs of the École des Saints-Anges before poking his nose outside. He didn't like children. For a long time they had represented Evil for him, the unfinished work of the Lord, hypocrisy, the fall of man after Original Sin, the fruit of that sin and the fruit of woman; but he'd had to get used to them when, thirty years earlier, he was named curé of the Saint Stanislas de Kostka parish, one of the most "fruitful"

174

on the Island of Montreal, and in the end he came to see them as a necessary evil, the disagreeable part of his priesthood, which still didn't keep him, whenever he could, from crossing the street to avoid them, or refusing to enter a house where he knew there were a lot of them. Actually, children embarrassed him. These small dependent beings, still unformed, who had to be force-fed, educated and straightened out, so ignorant as to drive one to despair, and with so little interest in shedding their ignorance, unsure of themselves when very young, then cocksure by the time they were six or seven, either too timid or not timid enough and, above all, liars, such liars that they made him uncomfortable, because he'd never taken the trouble to try and understand them: a child's expression, no matter how pure, concealed dirty, dangerous thoughts by definition, because that's what he had decided, to make his life easier. Every now and then he was expected to play the good priest who loves children, but it took a superhuman effort that he found harder and harder, now that he was past sixty-five. He could still sometimes be seen patting a head or pinching a cheek, but it had become so rare that children thus favoured were considered by their mothers to be "chosen," almost "holy." ("The priest stopped and touched my Raymond on the chin! I couldn't get over it and I couldn't say a word! I always said there was something special about Raymond! He's different from the other kids and the Monsignor saw it, too! Well anyway, I've decided he's going into the priesthood and nothing'll stop me.") His embarrassment around children and his contempt for their naïveté —which he took for hypocrisy — were what he had in common with Mother Benoîte, who shared his feelings as a silent and efficient accomplice. Both spent their lives surrounded by children (not so much Monsignor Bernier, who had actually banned them from the presbytery, pleading the frequent acute migraines brought on by their noisy games) and should have focused their lives on them – it was part of the day-to-day business of their positions – but their aversion was so strong that it led them to ignore the most elementary rules of professional ethics, joining together to erect an impassable barrier about themselves that cut them off almost completely from the world of children. Actually, the subject of children hardly ever arose between them. They spoke freely about the "business" of the school, about its needs (monetary) and its efficiency, but rarely about its products, from which they strangely dissociated themselves. Monsignor Bernier waited, then, until Sister Sainte-Catherine had led her flock into the school yard before risking a step outside his presbytery. He crossed the first part of boulevard Saint-Joseph, and came to a stop on the grassy median. He took a long look at the school, shaking his head. "It's all very well and good that the repository get us attention, but meanwhile the school looks like a garage!" It must be said that the sidewalk and lawn were strewn with rags of all sorts (not all of them thought of as rags) and statues, lying or standing, that seemed lost amid the platforms leaning against the fence and the decorations (plaster cherubs' heads, friezes and plinths) tossed any which way, as far as the steps. "All this has to be tidied up before tonight. Tomorrow's Corpus Christi and I have to be relaxed when I prepare for it." He sped across the other half of the street and the sidewalk in front of the school, then started up the cement staircase, walking around the objects with which it was littered. When he rang the doorbell, his heart was pounding and he was out of breath. "Those damn steps will be the death of me! And there's still another set to go!" The door opened at the top of the wooden staircase inside the school, and Sister Saint-Georges threw up her arms at the sight of the old priest. Every time Monsignor Bernier came to the school, she tried to rush down the stairs so he wouldn't have to wait too long; this accentuated her slight limp and she swayed left and right like a

176

disarticulated toy. And every time, Monsignor Bernier would close his eyes so as not to see her. "Poor Sister Saint-Georges, one of these days she'll roll right down the stairs and into the front door!" Sister Clump Foot pulled on the door with unaccustomed vigour. She seemed very worked up. "Father! I'm so glad you're here! I wanted to see you!" The priest frowned. "If you want me to intercede with the Principal again to readjust your budget for paste wax, Sister Saint-Georges, you might as well save your breath!" But the old nun was so overwrought she interrupted the priest for the first time in her life. "That's not it, Father, it's more serious .... I want you to hear my confession." Monsignor Bernier pictured the long list of boring little sins that Sister Saint-Georges had been confessing as long as he'd known her and he felt suddenly drained. She'd probably eaten too much dessert again, or been impertinent to the Principal or scolded a student or who knows what else. "I haven't got time for your confession this morning, Sister Saint-Georges; I'll forgive you without hearing it." He raised his arm to bless her, but she threw herself to her knees on the stairs, exclaiming, "You can't, Monsignor, it's too serious!" The priest put his hand on the nun's shoulder. "You've never done anything serious, Sister, and you certainly won't start today." He gave her a rapid blessing and went up the stairs as fast as he could, for fear she might persist. Sister Saint-Georges remained prostrate on the stairs, as if thunderstruck. When the priest walked into the Principal's office, she lumbered to her feet, hiding her face in her hands. "But what's my punishment? I deserve a severe punishment, otherwise I can't be forgiven. Nobody can help me!"

"Don't trust her, Sister. I wouldn't put it past her to paint the face green!" Thérèse and Pierrette burst out laughing and grimacing as Simone threatened them with her paintbrush. "I would not, Pierrette Guérin, I know my colours a lot better than you do!" Simone was sitting on the edge of an improvised table that Sister Sainte-Philomène had quickly thrown together using an old wooden door she'd found at the back of the shed and two metal uprights that later would support part of the repository, and she was peering intently at the face of the statue of the Virgin that had to be freshened up. Pierrette's remark had offended her deeply because, as it happened, her notions of colour were really quite unsound (for a time she was even thought to be colour-blind), though she stubbornly refused to admit it. "If they'd just let me paint in peace, I'll show them what a good job I can do." Sister Sainte-Thérèse had gathered around her the smallest (and the weakest) grade-six girls, telling them, "We'll let the bigger girls do the heavy work, and meanwhile we'll try to brighten up the statues." She picked Simone up, sat her on the edge of the table, put paintbrushes in her hands and some jars of paint around her. "Simone, I'm giving you the Blessed Virgin and I want you to give her a lovely red mouth and a pretty flesh-coloured face; the poor thing needs some work." Simone knew the red mouth wouldn't be a problem: among the jars of paint she had already spotted a marvellous bright red that she'd apply delicately, without going outside the well-moulded plaster lips; it was the colour of the face that concerned her. She looked for flesh-coloured paint, but in vain. "I'm not very good at mixing, maybe I ought to ask Sister." But her pride, wounded to the quick by Pierrette's dart, kept her from asking for help. Slowly she opened a jar of yellow paint. "Is this ever yellow! The Blessed Virgin's face can't be this colour." Then she spotted a tube of white. "White would just make the yellow paler." Then she picked up a jar of red. "Red would make her look like an Indian." She grabbed a jar of blue. "And blue would just look crappy!" At that point Lucienne Boileau blew

178

in, after watching Simone for several minutes. She leaned against the table. "Need any help?" Simone replied without even looking at her. "Go suck your braids somewhere else, drip!" Thérèse and Pierrette were now at the other end of the school yard; Thérèse was vigorously rubbing a censer that certainly needed it, while Pierrette was taking costumes, one at a time, from the wicker trunk. Simone turned her head in their direction. Pierrette could help. Her drawings were always among the best in school. Lucienne followed Simone's gaze. "Sister didn't ask Pierrette to paint the Blessed Virgin's face, she asked you!" Simone looked at her for the first time that day. Since that morning, she'd sensed that Lucienne was watching her and she'd done all she could to avoid her gaze. "Then how come you're hanging around bugging me? I guess I didn't tell you off enough yesterday, so you came back for more. Why don't you make yourself useful instead of getting in everybody's way!" Simone pushed Lucienne, who stumbled into the statue and nearly knocked it down. "Okay, pighead, do it yourself, we'll see tomorrow night what colour you paint the Virgin's face!" She turned and walked away toward Sister Sainte-Philomène, who was nailing a platform together. Simone picked up the jar of red paint again. "I'll just mix some red and some white. After all, skin's pink." Pierrette had placed her wicker basket between the two sets of cement steps that led to the recreation hall. She unfolded each costume and spread it out on large sheets of canvas she'd placed on the ground, following Sister Sainte-Catherine's instructions. "Look how pretty it is, Thérèse! Did you ever see a green like that? And with the gold it's gorgeous! I wonder what kind of costume it is, though. Doesn't look like an angel's to me." Thérèse stopped rubbing her censer, pushed the lock of hair off her forehead. "Don't you remember, two years ago when we were in grade four, they put the Three Wise Men in the repository." "No, I don't." "Sure you do, remember, Jeannine Trépanier nearly dropped her gift right in the middle of the ceremony and the priest gave her heck in front of everybody." "Oh, now I remember .... Was that the Three Wise Men? I didn't know. I thought they were just ordinary saints." "Anyway, it was the nigger that wore that costume." Pierrette laid the apple-green taffeta costume next to a pair of crumpled wings she'd had a terrible time unfolding. "It's a swell costume for a nigger." Around them, the activity went on without let-up; little girls came at regular intervals, looking for the costumes Pierrette put out to air, announcing, "Sister wants the archangel Saint Gabriel's robe. She said it's pink with red wings" or "Did you see a big white wig with square bangs?" or "Let me know if you find a round box with jewels in it, I have to count them!" Others ran past carrying hammers or rulers, red and breathless from the effort Sister Sainte-Philomène demanded of them; while still others were examining all the statues, looking for blemishes to be repaired as soon as possible. "Saint Joseph's got a broken nose!" "The big ugly angel hasn't got any paint on his face!" "Gee, Saint Christopher lost his head!" When the recess bell rang the children kept on working, exchanging grimaces or winks. No recess today! The whole day would be one long recess, which they'd talk about with pride as long as they lived. When the bell rang, hundreds of heads appeared at the windows of classrooms and the recreation hall. Students in the other grades called out to their friends in grade six, waving and teasing them a little for form's sake, but envying them their day off and their great responsibility in front of the whole parish. The grade eight and nine girls were in the recreation hall, but the other grades were condemned to stay in their classrooms. They could draw or read, but none of them followed the rules, because they knew that toward the end of recess Sister Sainte-Catherine would announce the names of the girls who would appear in the repository, and they were so agitated that some of the teachers had been obliged to act ruthlessly. Pierrette finally emptied the trunk, then slammed it shut and sat on it with a contented sigh. "Whew! Let me tell you, those costumes don't smell like roses!" Thérèse finished polishing her censer. She was getting sick of rubbing. "The sisters'll clean them for tomorrow." "They'd better! I don't want to spend three hours in a dress and veil that stink!" Thérèse looked up, smiling. "Who do you think's going to play the Blessed Virgin, you or me?" Pierrette brushed imaginary crumbs from her skirt. "I told you – it's got to be you 'cause you're prettier. Unless that weasel Ginette Chartier got on to Sister Sainte-Cathcrine." Their attention was attracted by applause coming from the recreation hall, and they turned toward the school. Sister Sainte-Catherine was just coming out, raising her arms for silence. "Here comes the big moment .... C'mon." Thérèse took Pierrette by the hand and both girls went and leaned against the cement steps where Sister Sainte-Catherine was standing. The nun smiled as she waited for total silence. "The names of the pupils who will have the honour of appearing in the repository have just been chosen by Sister Sainte-Philomène, Sister Sainte Thérèse de l'Enfant-Jésus and myself. Here they are!" Thérèse and Pierrette hugged each other, embarrassed, blushing, close to fainting. "Sainte Bernadette will be played by pretty Thérèse from Six B!" Applause rang out as Pierrette kissed her friend. Thérèse whispered in her ear, "By gosh, if you get to play the Blessed Virgin I'll make you laugh so everybody can see your crooked teeth!" When silence was restored, Sister Sainte-Catherine began speaking again. "This year the Blessed Virgin will have the lovely face of Pierrette, from Six A!" Pierrette brought her hand to her heart. "I won! I won the Blessed Virgin!" It was Thérèse's turn to kiss her friend. "And I'm going to make you laugh till you wet your pants in your blue robe!" Sister Sainte-Catherine went on. "The trumpeting angels will be Claire Morrier, Lucie Pineault and Ginette Chartier.

The Archangel Gabriel will be played by Lucienne Boileau, and the little hanging angel by Simone Côté!" More applause, in the school yard and inside the school. Pierrette was devastated. "What'll I do with my teeth?" "Stick 'em in your pocket!" "Promise you won't make me laugh!" Thérèse walked away from her friend, maliciously humming a little tune. Pierrette followed her. "Promise, Thérèse!" "Okay, you choose: either I make you laugh or I put itching powder inside your costume!" Thérèse laughed and hugged Pierrette. "Do you think I'd really do a thing like that? I'm really glad for you!" The girls crowded around Thérèse and Pierrette and even Simone who, hard at work, concentrating on the face of the Virgin, with the tip of her tongue sticking out and the brush shaking a bit in her hands, hadn't heard the announcement. Lucienne Boileau rushed over to her, clapping. "Aren't you glad, Simone, aren't you glad?" Simone sprang from her torpor as if she'd been awakened from a sound sleep. "Glad about what?" "Didn't you hear? The names are out! I'm Saint Gabriel and you're the hanging angel!" Simone's heart leaped. The hanging angel! The most beautiful angel of all! The one with the fanciest costume and the biggest wings! The one everybody talked about the most because it was the most visible! She put down her jar of paint, trembling. Sister Sainte-Catherine, Thérèse and Pierrette all arrived at the same time. Simone's friends slapped her thighs, while the nun squeezed her tight and whispered in her ear. "You'll be so lovely up there, Simone!" Simone wound her arms around the nun's neck without a word. Behind the three girls and the nun, the statue of the Blessed Virgin's face was tomato red, as if she'd been flayed alive.

Mother Benoîte's fat body overflowed the straight-backed

182

chair on which she was sitting, the uncomfortable one generally kept for visitors but which she'd never dare impose on the old priest, more for political reasons than out of deference. Monsignor Bernier, as it happens, had known the score for a long time now and enjoyed the position of inferiority in which the Principal placed herself whenever he came to visit her: he always ensconced himself in her easy chair without hesitation, making himself at home, gripping the arm rests as if he owned them, his thumb and index finger enjoying the coolness of the little nails that held down the leather under the arabesques of fretsawed wood trim, even going so far as to rest his head voluptuously against the small cushion that crowned the chair, making it look vaguely like a rather comical barber's chair. Like most parish priests, Monsignor Bernier was susceptible to flattery, but he was a wily soul who didn't shun this precious commodity but always sniffed it out in the end, figuring out how it worked and using it himself to the detriment of his flatterer, who didn't even know what was going on. Which was what happened with Mother Benoîte, who thought she was manipulating him but strongly suspected, from the look on his face whenever she brought up the subject of money, for instance, or the occasional ironic glint in his otherwise glum or totally vacant eyes, from the little smiles floating above his double chin that he had trouble repressing, that something about him – the perfidious intelligence of a sycophant, perhaps, or more simply cold cynicism – was escaping her and she wanted to track it down, uncover it, control it and master it in such a way that she would be the sole mistress of the situation, with no fear of seeing the old priest pull any sudden tricks that would be both unexpected and effective. She hadn't often known defeat, and this week, which had got off to such a bad start, had her so worried she could hardly sleep. She even surprised herself in the middle of the night, muttering insults to one or other of the nuns

as she lay in bed, trying out threatening gestures and pointing to a hypothetical Hell somewhere in the cellar, in the
vicinity of the furnace, and she would blush with shame.
This controlled, logical woman, almost maniacally organ-
ized, had for two days been letting herself be undermined by
a tough-minded little nun and a pupil who, two days before,
had been frighteningly ugly, but whom everyone suddenly
seemed to want to protect, simply because she'd undergone
a slight operation that made her mouth almost normal! It
was even more depressing because she hadn't managed – as
she'd always done before – to carry on despite these really
insignificant problems, but was letting herself be ruined
almost without reacting, and, above all, without understanding why she didn't react more vigorously. "I'm getting
older, it's true. That must be it. That's what it means to get
old ...." To satisfy the great thirst for victory that had always
ravaged her and made her do so many delectably imprudent
things that she savoured all the more because they were
dangerous and sometimes even highly compromising, the
tension between her and Sister Sainte-Catherine would have
had to blow up more dramatically so that she – Principal of
the school, after all, *and* the directress of the nuns – could
crush the younger nun under all her weight, make her cry
for mercy and surrender her arms, humiliating her publicly
(that was always the most delightful moment of all) and
toss her out like an old rag, an object henceforth useless
and even harmful; instead she was obliged to spare her
loathed adversary because the parish, which was more
powerful than she, with a reputation to uphold and all the
publicity the damn repository brought to it, still needed
Sister Sainte-Catherine for another few days. Mother Benoîte
was annoyed at the priest, at the churchwardens, at the
Ladies of Sainte-Anne, the Girl Guides, the Boy Scouts, and
even at the Daughters of Isabelle who, the next evening,
would parade, stiff and ridiculous and all dolled up in their

184

fancy clothes, while she champed at the bit and looked daggers at the mistress of the event, the focus of the evening, her sworn enemy who would be the object of public praise that Mother Benoîte would be helpless to do anything about. A childish rage was making her seethe with impatience on her small chair, and beads of sweat were running underneath her starch-stiffened wimple when the priest began to talk. He had no notion that what he was about to say would finish off Mother Benoîte, drive her to the wall of despair and make her commit irreparably stupid deeds that would precipitate her fall. "I had a phone call from your superior, Mother Benoîte. Yesterday afternoon." The Principal, growing tense, hiked up her black tunic on either side, as though pulling back her overflowing flesh. She managed the merest hint of a cold little smile. "Oh yes? And I suppose she told you about Sister Saint-Georges's visit ...." "No, she didn't mention it. She did say, however, that Sister Sainte-Catherine had brought her a certain letter written by you ...." Mother Benoîte rose abruptly, resting one hand on her desk while with the other she clutched her ebony cross, as if she wanted to pull it off. Misinterpreting the reason for her anger, the priest stood up as well. "Mother Notre-Dame didn't commit any indiscretion, Sister. All she knew was that Sister Sainte-Catherine is very useful to the parish and she wanted to let me know that she was leaving." Mother Benoîte was so humiliated she couldn't speak. She saw Sister Saint-Georges again recounting her visit to the Mother House, particularly her great cow's eyes in which Mother Benoîte thought she saw the usual beatific fidelity and inexhaustible loyalty as the limping old nun described the superior's tea-service. So even Sister Saint-Georges, the faithful dog, the night watchman, was deceiving her! "Sit down, sister, you seem quite shaken. Your superior warned me that your letter indicated a state of mind that was, to say the least, disturbing, but I'd never have thought you were in such a bad way." Gathering all her strength, Mother Benoîte managed to answer the priest in an almost normal voice as she resumed her place on the straight-backed chair. "I'm not in a bad way at all, Monsignor ... I ... I'm just rather surprised to learn that my superior didn't phone me right away to let me know ...." "She was going to call you this morning .... If she hasn't, it's because she hasn't made her decision yet." "Her decision? About what?" The priest slowly sat down in the Principal's chair, rested his head against the cushion, examined the ceiling for a moment, as if searching for his words. "Don't interrupt me, Mother Benoîte. What I'm about to say will probably shock you more than what I've said already, but the decision's almost made and there's no going back." This time Mother Benoîte put both hands on her cross. "I think I can guess what you're going to say, Father. So our superior has chosen Sister Sainte-Catherine after all." "Your superior hasn't chosen, Sister; I have. Or rather, I've strongly suggested a solution which your superior is considering at this very moment ...." He leaned across the Principal's desk as she herself had done so many times, to impress her interlocutors, to intimidate them, to nail them to the straight-backed chair on which it was her turn now to tremble with indignation. "As far as I'm concerned, losing Sister Sainte-Catherine is out of the question. And you know why, Sister. I don't have to praise her merits to you, you know what they are, and in your present state you certainly aren't in the mood to hear me list them. Nonetheless, the repository that Sister Sainte-Catherine is preparing at this moment represents a singular opportunity for the parish ...." Mother Benoîte broke in, her voice filled with veiled despair, filtered through pride but still so obvious the old priest was amazed. "So you've chosen Sister Sainte-Catherine! And you've come to ask for my resignation!" "Not at all! Where did you get that idea? There's no question of your leaving the school, and no question of Sister Sainte-Catherine leav-

186

ing either. We need you both, Sister, you as much as her! I know your pride will have some trouble accepting this state of affairs, but I think I've persuaded your superior to keep you both." Malicious pleasure could be seen in the priest's eyes, which Mother Benoîte discovered as she was about to make a very cavalier reply, deliberately ignoring the respect she owed the old man, spitting out her hatred for Sister Sainte-Catherine, whose insolence went beyond the bounds of decency. But the sight of that ironic spark and of the smug little smile she thought she could glimpse on Monsignor Bernier's lips kept her from blowing up. In a flash she understood exactly what the priest was looking for, thinking that by humiliating her like this he'd pay her back for all the hours he'd spent in this very office, talking about money and petty contracts, he who was always trying to interfere in the affairs of the École des Saints-Anges, whom she had always managed to brush aside, inventing pretexts that were often lame but always carried, and always relegating him – the leader of the parish – to the background, where his role would be limited to signing the papers she had decided on, planned and written herself. Caution. Never take revenge in the heat of the moment. She drew a long breath, closing her eyes. "I'm going to think about all this, Monsignor." And the old priest released his last dart, the most poisonous, the one he knew would be fatal, which he'd kept for the end. "You have no choice, Sister. We're the ones who decide." He slowly got to his feet in front of the closed mask that Mother Benoîte's face had become, walked around the huge desk that dominated the middle of the room and left her office without another word. Mother Benoîte sat motionless on the straight-backed chair for a very long time. She didn't hear the bell ring to announce the end of morning classes, the sound of footsteps on the stairs, six hundred little girls racing through the corridors and shouting, free now after a morning filled with surprises. Nor did she hear everyone talking about the little hanging angel, whose role they had given ("They" being, of course, Sister Sainte-Catherine, who else?) to another of her *bêtes noires*, in fact the source of all her present problems: Simone Côté, the ugly duckling who to her great misfortune had been transformed into a swan.

"What do you call that? I always forget." "A piano." "Piano. That's a nice word." "Yes." "I wonder if she plays it very often. I never heard her before." "Me neither." "If I ask her to play me the same thing as yesterday, do you think she can do it?" "Of course, dummy, she reads it out of a big book!" "Don't call me dummy, Duplessis, I don't like it." "If you don't want me to call you dummy, don't act dumb!" They were sitting in the fat woman's chair, on the balcony. Marcel began to rock energetically, holding Duplessis against his heart, but after a moment the cat asked him to stop. Looking at Marcel with his round eye he said, "I'm better now, Marcel, but not that much better! When you rock hard like that I feel sick." In a great burst of compassion, Marcel asked, "Are you going to throw up?" Do cats laugh? In any case, Duplessis produced something that resembled a laugh, but not exactly, and Marcel slapped his thighs. "You're sick to your stomach but you're still having fun, right?" They had come quite naturally to talk about Rose, Violette and Mauve, and of their mother, Florence; Duplessis even caught himself telling about his convalescence. "They were really nice, you know. Specially the mother. They waited on me hand and foot. Milk twice a day, liver every morning, and calves' liver, too, not pork like that other loony used to give me because it was cheaper." "Don't say that, Duplessis, Marie-Sylvia isn't a loony; she's nice, too!" "You're right, she is. Anyway, I'm really grateful." "What's that, grateful?" And just as naturally, Duplessis had started to educate Marcel, in his fashion.

And that was how the word "grateful" entered the little boy's vocabulary. They'd come to the piano, then, to the beautiful sounds it made and the ticklings of joy it had stirred in Marcel's heart when a noise to their right, behind them, made them turn around. Victoire was opening her bedroom window, which looked out on the stairs. "Gramma's opening her window, Duplessis. We'd better stop talking." (Victoire had shut herself up in her room after lunch the day before. She had carefully shut her bedroom door and window and got under the covers, despite the nearly suffocating heat, and for most of the afternoon she could be heard muttering and whimpering. That evening, when her grandson Richard went into the double room to go to bed, he found her sitting on the edge of her bed, holding a prayer book. "I thought you were asleep, gramma. I was trying not to make any noise so I wouldn't bother you." "I slept this afternoon ... but at night I'm scared of dying." Richard approached her timidly. "Why do you say that?" She put her prayer-book on the bed beside her. "You can tell when the end's coming, Richard. I can feel death prowling around my bed. I can feel it smelling me, like a dog sniffing at a fence .... I can hear it walking, I can hear it breathing ... and I'm so scared!" Richard finally sat down beside her. He put his arm around the old woman's neck. "You're talking yourself into it, gramma. You aren't going to die so soon, you're still good and strong." He didn't believe a word he was saying; he saw again all the nights when he thought he'd seen his grandmother die, so fragile in her sleep, so ugly, too, her open mouth revealing her white gums; he could hear her grunt, then cough lightly, then spit; worst of all, he heard her breathe, making that awful noise, like a clogged pipe, and he thought, "Maybe it's true this time. Maybe her time's really up." And suddenly he didn't want her to go. Though he had wished for her death at least a hundred times: when he woke up in the middle of the night because she was

189

moaning so loud, or often at dawn when she started talking in her sleep, screaming insanities or insulting God; and also when he contemplated the greyish grotto of her mouth by the light of the bedside lamp she so often forgot to switch off. But now that the old lady had named death, Richard didn't want to lose her. He rested his head, with his long red ears, on Victoire's shoulder. "I've got an idea, gramma! Let's play a trick on death! You sleep in my folding bed tonight. Take my place, and then if death comes sniffing around the bed you won't be there and he'll go away! He won't do anything to me, I'm too young, I'm too little. That way you'll be able to get a good night's sleep." Then he opened out his bed, struggling with the springs as usual, and settled his grandmother in it. She let him do as he wished, saying nothing. Then he climbed into Victoire's bed, which smelled strongly of camphorated oil and other odours of old age, convinced he'd spend a sleepless night wrestling with his grandmother's phantoms; instead, he was filled with a great peace when he lay on his back in the middle of the soft little mattress. Was it because Victoire had fallen asleep almost immediately, free of her fears, or was it because he was pleased with himself? He didn't know, but there was a smile on his lips. When his Uncle Edouard came staggering in, around midnight, he merely said, softly, "I'm in gramma's bed, *mon oncle* .... We switched places for tonight... Go to bed now, and don't make any noise!" Edouard started giggling, not even trying to hold it back. "Playing musical beds are you? Count me out! I wouldn't want to see my old mother turn up in my bed! You, though ...." He didn't complete his thought, but lay down silently. Ten minutes later he was snoring loudly, as usual. Richard didn't sleep much that night, but he felt very happy. Duplessis jumped off Marcel's lap and headed for Victoire's window. "Don't scare her, Duplessis. She can see you, too, but I don't think it makes her very happy." "I'm not going to scare her, I just want to say hello!" He hesitated for a moment, then jumped up on the window sill. Immediately, a cry rang out from the back of the room and Duplessis shot on to the stairs, head over heels. Victoire appeared in the window, haggard, her arms in the air. "Scat, you damn cat! Get out of here! Scram! Damn ghost! Damn death! Goddamned death!" Marcel ran to the window. "How come you're yelling at Duplessis like that, gramma? He didn't do anything!" His grandmother gave him a nasty look and Marcel stepped back, at the risk of tumbling down the stairs. She spoke more gently to him than to Duplessis, but the same fright could be heard in her voice. "You go away, too! I don't want to see you. You're crazy and you're driving me crazy, too! You're carrying my death in your arms!" Marcel turned around, went slowly down the stairs, clutching the wrought-iron railing, and sat on the bottom step, where Duplessis joined him, purring in spite of everything. When the cat was comfortably curled on his lap, Marcel asked the question that kept preying on his mind. "Duplessis, what's death?" And that was how the word death became part of his vocabulary.

Bernadette Soubirous, the Virgin Mary and the little hanging angel came back to school arm in arm, bellowing "J'irai la voir un jour" at the tops of their lungs and slightly off-key, so happy that even their classmates who were most jealous of them thought they looked lovely. The other students gathered around, giving them compliments and slaps on the back, and pulling their hair – just a little; all three, suddenly taking an ounce or two of magnanimity from the heart of their joy, went so far as to give Lucienne Boileau a hug, as if they actually liked her. But right afterwards, Thérèse started calling Lucienne "trumpet," a nickname that would stay with her all her life, so well did it describe her, with her greasy braids and her voice that rang in your ears like a battle-cry, and the poor child, who for a few minutes thought she'd been accepted into the Holy of Holies, once again went home alone, following a few steps behind the trio "Thérèse-'n'-Pierrette," savouring her defeat along with her left braid. "I'm so excited! I can't wait till they hang me up above the Blessed Sacrament!" Simone's excited laugh slightly darkened the fine line of red flesh that still ran through her upper lip. "Everybody'll be looking at you, Simone, I'm telling you, you don't want to be caught napping!" Pierrette was dancing from one foot to the other. "Aren't people going to be looking at me? Gee, I can't wait to tell my mother. I'm the first one in my family that was ever in the repository .... I don't think my sisters were very good in religion." Pierrette was picturing her three sisters, Germaine, Gabrielle and Rose, pregnant to the eyeballs, standing before their youngest sister dressed as the Blessed Virgin. "They'll be so proud of me! It'll be fun to have the three of them leaning up against the school fence with their big bellies." Thérèse kicked a little stone that disappeared under a car. "And meanwhile I'll have my back turned so I can't see a thing! Bernadette Soubirous doesn't see anything." Her friends looked at each other. "Before, you said you were glad they picked you for Bernadette." "Oh, sure I'm glad .... But I was just thinking, I won't get to see the parade." "It's not a parade, Thérèse, it's a procession!" "Come off it, Pierrette Guérin, just because you're going to play the Blessed Virgin doesn't give you the right to correct my grammar! I'm better than you are anyway!" "It's still a procession." Thérèse sighed. "So what. Okay, it's a procession. Geez! You want me to say I'm sorry? Anyway, I won't be seeing it because I'll be down on my knees in front of the Blessed Virgin with crooked teeth who'll be scared to smile!" They were in front of Simone's house. "Hey, I don't know how my mother's going to take this." "If she isn't glad she's crazy! Wow, the hanging angel! You might even get your picture in *La Presse* like Lise Bellemare last year!" Simone, who hadn't thought of this possibility, blushed deep red. "My picture in the paper!" Thérèse smiled sadly. "I've always dreamed about being the hanging angel, but I'm too big ...." Simone started up the stairs to her house. She stopped suddenly and turned around, frowning. "I don't care about it that much, you know .... I can ask Sister if we can trade places .... Even if people just see the back of me, I'll still be happy." "Come on, Simone Côté, you've got a chance to show yourself off for once, take advantage of it!" Thérèse had awakened from her torpor and was pulling up one stocking, which was slipping down her leg. "Let me tell you, if I got a chance like that I wouldn't be so generous to my friends!" Relieved, Simone ran up the stairs and disappeared. The other two girls silently walked the fifteen or twenty feet that separated Simone's staircase from Thérèse's. On the bottom step, Marcel was chatting with his imaginary cat. Thérèse raised her eyes to Heaven. "You see what I'm like, Pierrette? Five minutes ago I was singing *'J'irai la voir un jour'* to beat the band and now I'm as sad as soapsuds." She leaned against the fence. Pierrette hesitated for a moment before she spoke. "Thérèse ... you know I don't care that much about the Blessed Virgin." Thérèse interrupted her with a slap on the shoulder. "Geez, will you cut it out and quit offering me your parts, you're really a pain in the neck, both of you! You're the ones the Sisters picked, not me!" She rushed up the stairs, jostling her little brother. "And you, birdbrain, stop talking to yourself and come eat!" Marcel put Duplessis on the ground while Pierrette walked away, head drooping. "I don't think you'd better come up for supper, Duplessis. Go see *ma tante* Florence, maybe she'll feed you." Duplessis sat in the patch of dirt and watched Marcel labour up the wooden steps. "*Ma tante* Florence? He'd better not start calling me *mon oncle* Duplessis!" Once Marcel was inside the house Duplessis stretched out on his back in the sun. "Oh joy! A little nap!" Thirty seconds later he was asleep.

Mother Benoîte found the list of the elect on her plate, on top of the napkin that had been folded into a triangle. This was the first time the list had been drawn up without her and she sensed, even before she read it, that it would contain some unpleasant surprises. All faces in the refectory were turned toward her; the nuns were waiting for her blessing before they started to eat. She decided to say a prayer before reading the list; that way they wouldn't be able to guess that she was displeased or see her face turn red. All the coifs were bent down during the brief invocation, except Sister Saint-Georges's, which remained obstinately turned in Mother Benoîte's direction. Sister Clump Foot hadn't seen the Principal again since the previous day, since the dreadful moment when Mother Benoîte had sent her away for the rest of the day because she'd been two minutes late with the bell to signal the end of classes. At first, she went to hide in her small room, the only one on the ground floor of the nuns' house, a grey cell with one tiny window that had once been a cloakroom but had been converted into an almost livable bedroom when Mother Benoîte decided that Sister Saint-Georges could be portress in the nuns' house, even if they didn't really need one. She hadn't gone to bed, but sat on the straight-backed chair by the window, her nose pressed against the glass as if she were looking for something on rue Garnier, and she thought of dying. Not violently (suicide would never have occurred to her, it was far too great a sin), but very gently, very discreetly; it would happen without anyone's knowledge; they'd know she was sick in bed, but they'd say it wasn't serious, that she'd pull out of it, bravely, and be back at her post in a few days; meanwhile, she would

194

let herself fade away, refusing all nourishment and happily feeling herself grow weaker; then when the time came for her to depart, she would call for Mother Benoîte des Anges, confess her sin, ask for mercy and die in a great moment of exaltation. The Principal would throw herself on the body, crying aloud, beseeching her forgiveness ... and finally she, too, would die of chagrin. This waking dream, childish as it was, did her enormous good. She imagined the Principal's hysterical cries after her death, and bursts of joy rose in her throat. "She won't realize how much she needs me till I'm not around!" Then gradually her pleasure lost its edge and sad reality gained the upper hand: she'd been punished because she had sinned, which was only fair, but no one had yet offered her absolution. She jumped up, as if powered by a spring, and walked out of her room, leaving the door open behind her. She wandered through the corridors of the house, sticking close to the walls, head down, limping more than usual. Ten times she almost threw herself at Mother Benoîte's feet, but the picture of Sister Sainte-Catherine and Sister Sainte-Thérèse came back to her, laughing as they ate fruit filched from the kitchen, and she stopped smack in the middle of the stairs or corridor. "I haven't the right to snitch on them either!" This dilemma was really too much for her; the more she thought about it, the greater her guilt – and her suffering. Not only did she not turn up for the midday meal, she refused the glass of water that would have quenched her terrible thirst; she wanted to suffer as much as possible, imagining this would expiate part of her sin. Then she had the ludicrous idea of washing every floor in the house, which definitely didn't need it. Armed with a bucket and a brush, she threw herself to her knees on the first floor she saw and started to scrub like a maniac. She'd been working for a good four hours without let-up, first washing the three main corridors and waxing them until they shone like mirrors, then attacking the floor in the kitchen, where she wasn't very popular with the cook because she was always getting underfoot, and finally she went to the refectory, where she worked with particular care, forehead sweating, head empty – at last! – her arms knotted with cramps. When she finished she was exhausted, purple, aching all over and unhappier than ever. Her physical effort had brought only passing oblivion and guilt was gnawing at her as much as ever. She dragged herself off to her room then, lay on her bed without washing, thinking she could get a few minutes' rest before the evening meal, which was around half-past five, and immediately fell asleep, without a struggle, like a tired child. She had slept for a solid twelve hours without waking, and if she dreamed she didn't remember, so deeply did she sleep. Mother Benoîte didn't turn a hair when she read the list that Sister Sainte-Catherine had drawn up for her. After the blessing, she had slowly unfolded her napkin, pushing aside the piece of white paper as if it didn't matter, and started to eat the barley soup that had just been ladled into her dish. It was too hot; she grimaced slightly and then, to disguise her lack of composure, picked up the salt-shaker. Next she conscientiously blew on each spoonful of soup without once looking up at the other nuns. When her almost empty bowl was taken away, a drop of liquid fell onto the list and, mechanically, Mother Benoîte wiped it with her fingertip. The paper wasn't folded; Simone Côté's name leaped out at her. She didn't move a muscle, but picked up the list and read to the end. So Sister Sainte-Catherine had had the gall to choose the entire "Thérèse-'n'-Pierrette" trio, just for spite! The hanging angel, the pride of the repository, would be that ridiculous child on whose account everything at the École des Saints-Anges had been going so badly for the past three days! She wished she could let her anger explode, let the river of her spleen overflow, scream, publicly condemn and punish those heretical nuns: the scheming Sister Sainte-Catherine, lying Sister Saint-Georges, Sister Sainte-Thérèse, who in the past had refused her protection and followed the plots and the bad example of Sister Sainte-Catherine; she wished she could strike them, wound them, whip them until the blood flowed; but nothing showed in her face, which remained as impassive as ever. She looked for Sister Sainte-Catherine, but didn't find her. Sister Sainte-Thérèse wasn't there either. Cowards! The only grade-six teacher who was present was Sister Sainte-Philomène, who was happily slurping her second bowl of soup, Sister Saint-Georges's needless to say, since she couldn't eat a thing. But Mother Benoîte immediately caught the eye of Sister Saint-Georges, who was watching her like a beaten dog. And all her rage crystallized on that ignorant, unintelligent nun whom she'd always despised in spite of her great devotion, who had dared to disobey her and lie to her. She spoke in the icy voice that made hearts stop and those it addressed tremble. "Sister Saint-Georges, get up if you please." Amazingly, Sister Sainte-Philomène was the one who started. With her mouth full of barley, which she was chewing with obvious pleasure, she looked at the Principal, then at Sister Saint-Georges, who had just got to her feet beside her. "Come here, Sister Saint-Georges. Kindly present yourself before me." Sister Sainte-Philomène put her spoon on her plate as she watched Sister Saint-Georges limp off. She frowned. Everybody knew that the noon meal was Mother Benoîte's favourite time for inflicting punishment and reproaches before the assembled nuns; a deathly silence fell over the refectory. No one dared to move, not even the cook on the other side of the hatch through which the plates were passed. When Sister Saint-Georges was before her, Mother Benoîte got to her feet. The poor portress grimaced pitifully, her lower lip trembling like a baby about to be scolded. "So, Sister Clump Foot, you dare

197

to lie to me!" Sister Saint-Georges brought her hands to her heart. She tried to speak, but nothing came out of her throat. Her head twisted first to one side, then the other, as if she was desperately trying to catch her breath. Then the Principal really let loose. Taking advantage of her adversary's weakness, she poured out – in a very ugly scene in which Sister Saint-Georges was spared nothing – all her frustrations of the week and some that were even older, reproaching the entire school through the poor limping nun, for the disrespect she imagined herself to be victim of, the plots she claimed to see being woven around her, the base deeds that were hidden from her and those they dared to show her; the disobedience, lies, hypocrisy she claimed that most of the nuns exhibited. Her paranoia burst like a rotten fruit: she screamed, she threatened, her arms stretched out on either side of her, her immense body shaken by rage; she stamped her foot and pounded the table with her fist; she sputtered and in her fury seemed about to faint. Sister Saint-Georges fell to her knees beneath the burden of accusations, and buried her face in her hands. Then suddenly, in the midst of a particularly unfair insult, Sister Sainte-Philomène sprang to her feet and started banging her spoon against her soupbowl. "All right, all right, that's enough!" Mother Benoîte stopped short, as if she'd been unplugged. Eyes wide, she stared at Sister Sainte-Philomène, who walked over to Sister Saint-Georges and took her in her arms. "C'mon, Saint-Georges, don't just stand there ...." Sister Saint-Georges clung to her former friend as to a buoy. Sister Sainte-Philomène helped her up and looked the Principal in the eye. She was still staring incredulous. "If you say one more word I'm going! And you won't just be losing the organizer of the repository, you'll be losing the best mathematics teacher in the city!" She headed for the door, holding up Sister Saint-Georges, whose head was on her shoulder. Before she went out, Sister Sainte-Philomène turned toward her Principal. "You nearly killed her, you know. You practically killed her! That's going to be held against you, too!"

"The Blessed Virgin! You?" Rita Guérin took from the stove the pan of frying bologna – one of Pierrette's favourite foods, bologna shaped like little hats – and wiped her face on her apron. "How come?" Pierrette was leaning against the doorpost, pink with emotion. "Well – I guess I came first in religion or something, but anyway, they picked me for the Blessed Virgin this year!" "For the parade?" "It isn't a parade, momma, it's a procession! And you know very well the Blessed Virgin stays on the lawn." Rita Guérin approached her daughter, so impressed she didn't dare to touch her. "My little girl's going to be the Blessed Virgin! Never in my wildest dreams – I've got to call the others!" "Call them later, momma, I'm hungry." Rita Guérin went back to her frying-pan. "Good Lord, I can't give the Blessed Virgin bologna! Do you want some ham? I've got some left – or how about ground beef? Heck, I haven't got any!" Pierrette was ferreting about the stove, sticking her nose in the saucepans, her hair nearly touching the grease in the cast-iron frying-pan. "Little hats are fine, momma, you know I love them." Rita put the pan back on the stove. "It's true, with mashed potatoes they're okay." Pierrette picked up a piece of carrot she'd found in the colander. "And Sister said I should tell you to wash my hair. She said it's as stiff as a bird's nest." Rita Guérin gestured impatiently. "She sounds like a jerk, your Sister." "No she isn't momma, she picked me to be the Blessed Virgin!" "Blessed Virgin or no Blessed Virgin, she's got no business telling me when to wash my children's hair! I'm no slob, I know when my children's hair needs washing!" "Don't get all worked up, momma ...." "Here's something she doesn't know, and you can do me a favour and tell her:

you've got naturally oily hair! Does she really think I'd let my daughter be the Blessed Virgin without washing her hair? That's nuns for you: give you a present with one hand and slap your face with the other!" While she spoke, she set two places at the table. Gesturing furiously, she served their lunch. Pierrette ate heartily, while her mother picked at her food. When she was finished, Pierrette got up from the table, wiping her mouth and fingers. Rita seemed a little calmer. "Will they give you the white gown and the blue veil and the gold belt and the works?" "Momma, you know very well the Blessed Virgin always wears the same things!" "I just can't believe it! Germaine's going to be so jealous! She always wanted that!" Pierrette came back and sat down across from her mother, holding an apple. "She'd've been a fat Blessed Virgin!" "She wasn't that fat when she was your age.... She wasn't a dry stick, but she wasn't a tub of lard like she is today." Pierrette poured herself a glass of milk. "There's something else I'm worried about, momma." "My Lord, what now?" Pierrette hesitated for a moment. "Well, my teeth ...." "Not your damn teeth again! Did the nuns tell you your mouth looks like a rabbit's?" "Gee whiz, momma, every time I mention my teeth you laugh at me!" "That's because it's silly the way you carry on. First of all, they aren't all that crooked, and second of all, we can't do anything about them by tomorrow night! Anyway, you don't see the Blessed Virgin's teeth, she smiles with her mouth shut. Have you ever seen the Blessed Virgin with a big grin on her face? No? Well, you just smile the same way she does!" Pierrette slapped the table. "Momma, even with my mouth shut, my teeth still stick out when I smile!" "Do you think anybody's going to notice from fifty feet away?" Rita's voice had suddenly risen. She couldn't hide her impatience. "Anyway, last year the Blessed Virgin had pimples the size of your thumb all over her face, so two little white teeth aren't going to ruin anybody's day. They aren't spotlights, Pierrette, they're teeth! Maybe they're a bit big, but they aren't ugly." Pierrette sprang up from the table and ran out of the room. Rita Guérin heard her door slam. She shrugged. "If she goes on like that I'll punch out those damn teeth with my own two fists!" She smiled at the thought. "Honestly! I must be really upset to be thinking things like that! I wouldn't hurt a fly ...." To clear the air a little she broke into a deafening "Marinella" as she cleared the table. When she finished she went to her daughter's room, knocking softly on the door. "I haven't got time to wash your grubby little head at noon hour; it won't have time to dry, but tonight I'll give you a nice shampoo, the kind you like." No answer. She sighed. "Are you dead, Pierrette, or just pretending?" She heard Pierrette laugh. "I'm dead and you killed me!" It was Rita's turn to laugh. "Right! And the wake won't cost me a cent, the nuns'll show you off tomorrow night." She rushed to the telephone, still singing, to call her daughter Germaine.

"Why should I be excited? They'll only see your back." Thérèse had beat around the bush for a long time before announcing the big news. The presence of her brother and her two cousins embarrassed her; she was afraid they'd laugh at her. The family wasn't fanatically religious and tended to jeer at any overly pronounced outward gestures. (Oh sure, they went to mass, the bare minimum, but never to Vespers, and they didn't recite family prayers. As the fat woman once put it so well, "Let other people be Pharisees; it doesn't mean we have to be. When I get down on my knees in church, it's to pray; at home, it's to wash the floor!" In fact, that was one of the reasons – along with lack of money – why Richard and Philippe had never gone into the Crusaders: their mother had a good laugh describing the white satin costume, the ridiculous little cape and the beret with a red pom-

pom. Now that Richard was eleven, with ears that turned red at the slightest provocation, he was glad he'd missed all that, but Philippe occasionally still looked longingly at the rows of little boys all dressed in white who were so admired because they carried on the great tradition of the crusaders. (Philippe didn't have the slightest idea what the crusaders were, but he kept hearing how brave and even heroic they were, and that was all he needed.) So it was very hard for Thérèse to come right out and announce point-blank that she'd be donning a saint's costume and standing motionless at the feet of the Virgin, played by Pierrette Guérin, for hours and hours... She waited until they were having dessert, when her mother sat down and ate with the rest of them. Instead of laughing, as she'd expected, Albertine shrugged and went on with her soup, which she ate very hot. The three boys, on the other hand, had a ball. Richard climbed up on a chair and Philippe threw himself to his knees, crying, "Hey, Blessed Virgin, let's see your teeth!" Albertine, who normally would have reacted very badly to such clowning, didn't move a muscle. Marcel laughed delightedly, banging his dessert spoon on the table, even though he had only a very vague idea of who the Virgin was and hadn't even heard of Bernadette Soubirous. "It's an honour, momma!" Albertine held her spoon midway between plate and mouth and stared intently at her daughter. A bit of soup was dripping onto her chin and she wiped it off with the back of her hand. "Listen, Thérèse, if you want to give me the thrill of a lifetime tell me the war's over, or your father's been reported missing or we've become millionaires, but really – I'm not going to wet my pants over Bernadette Soupirous!" Thérèse's reaction was quite unexpected: while the three boys went into gales of laughter at the thought of Albertine with wet pants, Thérèse placed her hand gently on her mother's arm. "What's wrong momma? For a while there you were so nice! You'd laugh with us kids and play with us and the other day

202

I even heard you singing when you were doing the dishes. But – ever since yesterday you're just like you used to be. You're as grouchy as a bear." Richard, Philippe and Marcel, foreseeing an imminent storm, stopped in mid-giggle and quietly made off before lightning struck the kitchen. But Albertine remained very calm. She even ate three or four spoonfuls of soup before replying. And when she spoke it was in a gentle voice, without looking at Thérèse, as if she were speaking to herself. "What difference does it make if I change; my life's still the same. I no sooner turn my back than everything falls on my head! How do you expect me to be in a good mood when my own child thinks he's talking to an imaginary cat and sees three women knitting baby bootees in an empty house! And when my mother shuts herself up in her room and says she wants to die! How do you think that makes me feel? Like I've driven my own kids crazy and pushed my own mother into her grave; that's how I feel! I'd like nothing better than to be an ordinary woman, nice and happy, but my bitch of a life always manages to come and shit on the doorstep! If I was another mother maybe I'd be glad you were playing Bernadette Soupirous in the Corpus Christi parade, but with all the crap I've been handed since yesterday I can't help thinking something's going to happen to you, and it sort of spoils my fun." "What can happen, momma?" Thérèse was thinking about Gérard, telling herself she'd spared her mother a much bigger worry by not saying anything about him. Albertine finally looked up at her daughter. Tears veiled her eyes but didn't fall. "I don't know. And I hope nothing will, Thérèse. But let me tell you one thing, I'm not coming to see you and neither is Marcel." "Because you'll only see my back?" "No. Because that stuff's just a pile of foolishness." "But you'll let me go?" "The only way to keep you from going would be to lock you up in your room, you know that. And I haven't got the strength. Go ahead, be Bernadette Soupirous if you want, but if you come home with cramps or bloody knees don't come crying to me!" Thérèse kissed her mother's temple. Albertine suddenly embraced her daughter, who was standing now, and put her head in the very place where, only yesterday, Gérard Bleau had put his. Thérèse felt dizzy and leaned against the table. Her mother was sobbing. "I wish I was like other mothers, Thérèse. I would have liked that so much!" It was then that Thérèse decided that Bernadette Soubirous would not pass unnoticed, and that the entire parish would see her from the front.

"Hanging! You're going to be hanging! Where? What from?" "Oh momma, you know; we went last year and you thought it was lovely." "It's lovely when other people's children are hanging in mid-air, but not mine!" Charlotte Côté put down her cup of green tea, shaking her head. "And what if you have to pee, eh? Did you think about that? What'll you do then? Are they going to take you down and tell everybody, 'Sorry, our angel has to go to the toilet!' I don't want to look up and see you staring into space like when you were a little girl and still went in your pants!" Simone was playing with the edge of the table-cloth, a sullen look on her face. "For once, something's happening to me!" "That's just it, I'm worried something might happen to you, Simone, that's why I'm not glad something's happening to you." Maurice laughed with his mouth full, and some noodles fell out. His heart leaped when Simone announced that Pierrette was going to be the Blessed Virgin; at last he'd be able to look at her for hours at a time and she couldn't brush him off; all he had to do the next morning was volunteer to play a Roman soldier, and he could swoon before her all evening. (Six sturdy grade-nine boys were chosen every year to hold back the crowd of the faithful that lined boulevard Saint-Joseph, across from the École des Saints-Anges, and sometimes turned rowdy. They were dressed as Roman soldiers and served to trim the repository with red and to police the crowd.) When Simone added that Thérèse would be Bernadette Soubirous, he exclaimed, "She ought to play the devil!" The antagonism between Maurice and Thérèse had become legendary on rue Fabre: they'd been fighting as long as they'd known each other, Thérèse punching Maurice whenever he gave her a rough time. Actually, they were too much alike for their friendship not to be stormy. And it was a friendship: beneath the slaps, the insults and the cries hid a great affection that would take them years to come to terms with, but from the moment it saw the light of day, shooting a fountain in the sun, it would last until death. Meanwhile, they called each other all sorts of names, maligning one another with a lively, malicious pleasure, making up the most shocking stories, putting so much energy and imagination into them that in the end they believed them. His mother turned to him impatiently. "At fourteen you haven't improved with age, have you? Whenever you open your mouth, rubbish comes out!" Charlotte Côté was often exasperated by her son's mediocre performance in school and by his lack of intelligence and, above all, by his immense laziness which easily turned him into a profiteer who would never miss a chance to fool somebody in order to obtain some little favour or big present. Sometimes she even hated the big good-for-nothing who already, at fourteen, would rather sneak a beer than prepare for the future by conscientiously doing his homework. When he came home, staggering and reeking of beer, she felt like wringing his neck, but she knew he was stronger than she was and already mean when drunk; so she'd settle for insulting him, as her husband looked on, smiling sardonically, for he rather liked this oafish young man – his son – who was going off on his first escapades at the same age at which he'd gone off on his own. Maurice blushed violently at his mother's insult. His only real sore spot was his intelligence, which he knew was shaky, and it gave him a complex around people he thought were smart. He spun his fork furiously in his noodles, muttering unintelligible but surely unflattering remarks at his mother. And when Simone broke the news, as if it was nothing out of the ordinary, that she was going to be floating above the repository for two or three hours, suspended from the pediment of the École des Saints-Anges, in a long white robe and pink wings, Maurice and Charlotte stared incredulously at each other, suddenly reconciled, united in the absurdity that had just descended on them, Maurice because he was dizzy, Charlotte because she thought that Simone was. "But how will they hang you up? Will they put a corset on you or what? How will they get you up in the air? And get you back down when it's over?" Simone let go of the tablecloth. "I'll be finding out this afternoon, momma, we're having a practice ...." "Oh no, little girl, you won't be practising this afternoon and that's that!" Charlotte got up and drained her teapot into the sink. Then she rinsed it with cold water, splashing it all over. Maurice and Simone hadn't moved. Maurice's stomach turned at the thought of his sister swaying at the end of a rope, like a hanged woman, over the repository. "Come and see the practice this afternoon, momma, there's nothing to worry about!" Charlotte wiped her hands on her apron. "I said no, Simone! I had one fit at your school day before yesterday, that's enough; if I turn up there again this afternoon they'll think I'm the police! Or that I want to join the nuns!" She pointed to Maurice. "And you stop laughing, nitwit!" Maurice, who was about to let out a loud snigger, stopped in mid-breath and nearly choked. Simone got up from the table, took her plate and empty glass to the sink, and started to rinse them, copying her mother's gestures. "Please come, momma, I'd like it so much!" Then she was silent for several seconds, as if searching for the words. "I'm pretty, momma, and now everybody's going to know."

He had fallen asleep in the shade; he woke in the sun, the fur on his belly burning, his tongue thick and dry. He had slept on his back, wanton and trusting, front paws folded on either side of his head, the tip of his pink tongue protruding, his muzzle damp and mobile. He woke up cursing a little because he hadn't expected to sleep so long; he tore up some dandelions to work off his rage, and ran after their seeds that were brazenly dancing around him. Next he went under the stairs of Florence's house and conscientiously deposited his excrement, opening his eyes wide as if someone had just told him some tremendous, incredible secret, then buried it, comically serious, sniffing the earth twenty times, stirring it up and burying it with determination until all trace of odour had disappeared. "A good job well done!" He hadn't been out for a month and he'd often dreamed, while he was recovering his strength on the apron of the stove, of the lawns on rue Fabre, the ones that were cut too often and the ones that never were; the patches of dirt where so many fragrant weeds grew that were so pleasant to rub against, purring; the fences and trees too, that always smelled of rutting dogs or unclean cats that had to be tracked down and chased off his territory, without mercy. The day before, he had resisted all these bewitching odours to stay with Marcel, curled up against his plump belly, chatting on and on, laughing at the *bons mots* and even at the bad ones, nestling in the warmth of their reunion; but today he was going to resume his strolls through the neighbourhood in search of dissolute adventures or heinous, but delicious, crimes; he would visit dark backyards where occasionally a mouse or even a rat (yes, he'd once seen a rat!)

would try to make its nest out of the garbage and dust; he could climb the Jodoins' tree, which rose proudly in the middle of their yard, immense and full of stupid, excitable squirrels it would be such fun to chase, watching them shiver as he meowed at them. Perhaps he'd even push on as far as rue Mont-Royal to see if Godbout still reigned there, in bloody terror. He had a good long wash, rubbing his muzzle and head with a moistened paw, then running his rough tongue all over his fur, licking it, even rummaging in it with his teeth in search of fleas, which he hadn't had since Violette (or Rose? or Mauve?) had coated him with some ointment that smelled terrible but rid him of the loathsome creatures; then he cleaned his anus, one paw sticking straight up in the air, assuming comical poses to avoid losing his balance (when he did it in front of Florence, she would always say to her daughters, "Look, Duplessis's playing the cello!"). When he had completed his serious cleaning for the day he lay in the grass for a moment, out of breath, worn out by this exhausting exercise; he felt like taking another little nap, but told himself that would be really lapsing into laziness. Instead, he shot off after a fly, swallowing it whole before it was even dead. He crossed rue Fabre and headed automatically, without thinking, for the restaurant owned by Marie-Sylvia, his former mistress whom he despised because she'd fussed over him so much. He crossed the lane in four leaps, feeling a sort of prickling on the side where his heart was. And when he came to the cement steps that went up to the restaurant, a real burst of emotion rose to his head. "Duplessis, my friend, you're getting soft! If the prospect of seeing that old bag is giving you palpitations, how will you feel when you run into the lady cats who gave you so much pleasure in the past!" He stood on his hind paws, stuck his muzzle against the glass in the door. Nothing had changed. Marie-Sylvia was still in the same place, in her "mysterious armchair," between the two candy counters; her head was turned toward the window and she was sadly sucking at a Coke, probably a warm one. In a flash he saw again all the years he'd spent in this shop, with its strong smells that seeped right into his fur; the summer nights when he wanted to go out because the lane was full of cats in heat, announcing their distress, the winter nights, so mild despite the raging wind, that he spent under the stove, curled in the foetal position, purring contentedly; he thought of his box of sand that Marie-Sylvia changed too often for his liking and laughed to himself. "That's all over now. Fini. But I might as well say hello." He wiggled the door latch as his mistress had taught him when he was still a kitten, and Marie-Sylvia started. He stuck his muzzle against the glass again and saw Marie-Sylvia's huge body (she was, of course, wearing her Wednesday dress, the most ordinary of the seven, because as she'd often said, "On Wednesday there's not even a cat in sight, and if there is, it's asleep!") walk through the restaurant, taking quick little steps. "Lord, how she's aged!" Marie-Sylvia opened the door and loudly called, "Duplessis!", which the cat interpreted as an exclamation of joyous surprise but which was, in fact, the anguished cry that she'd been uttering at any given moment for a month now, since the cursed day when she told him never to come back because his escapades were becoming more and more numerous and lasting longer and longer. When Marie-Sylvia looked from side to side, grieving, Duplessis remembered that she couldn't see him, and for the first time he felt real pain. He craned his neck toward her and meowed as loud as he could – but to no effect. After a few more "Duplessis!", increasingly feeble, Marie-Sylvia lowered her head (she was looking at the precise spot where the cat was standing) and wept. Shattered, Duplessis rubbed against her legs; he'd have given anything just then for her to feel his cool fur against her ankles. But she went back inside the restaurant and slowly shut the door. He heard the little bell and told himself that it was the last time.

Pierrette shrank back when she saw the pedestal on which she'd have to climb. "It's so high, Sister!" Sister Sainte-Catherine put a wooden table beside the pedestal for Pierrette to climb on. "Just four feet, Pierrette, it's not the end of the world .... And you'll see, the platform's bigger than it looks." Pierrette got up on the table with no trouble and approached the plaster column on which she'd have to spend a good part of the evening tomorrow. "If you ask me, it's tiny!" "Do you feel dizzy?" "Dizzy? No ...." "All right, let's try it then. Put one foot on the platform, very slowly, then when you feel ready, give yourself a good push ..." Rather than follow the nun's advice, Pierrette turned completely around and sat down on the pedestal. Sister Sainte-Catherine came and sat on the table, at her feet. "If you don't think you can do it, Pierrette, you'd better tell me now .... I'm sure Thérèse would be glad to replace you ...." "No, no ... I want to do it, Sister. It's just ... it's just that this is the first time .... I'll be okay after I've done it once." Trying not to think about it too much, Pierrette stood up and climbed onto the pedestal in one motion. The sight of the room she knew so well because she'd gone there so often at recess, in the winter or in bad weather, from a brand new viewpoint, amazed her: the croquinole or Mississippi tables looked different and the square tiles on the floor had never looked so even. Familiar objects that she didn't even notice when she walked into the vast hall – folding chairs piled up in the corner, the flags on the walls, the upright piano on the stage – had a new, almost threatening appearance that oppressed her. She felt a little as if she was dreaming, that she was floating somewhere between the floor and the ceiling and that her presence there was disturbing. "Do you feel dizzy now, Pierrette?" Pierrette swallowed before replying, "Nope! I love it up here! And when I'm outside it'll be so much fun to be high above everybody, in front of the school!" Her voice was unsteady and her hands were shaking. Thérèse had just tip-toed into the hall. Pierrette noticed her and waved timidly. "You look so tiny up there on your column, Pierrette!" Thérèse came and sat beside Sister Sainte-Catherine. "Is my pedestal lower than that?" Sister Sainte-Catherine smiled discreetly and showed her a sort of rectangular box a few feet from the plaster column on which Pierrette was now bravely standing, hands clasped, gaze fixed. "Is that all? No body'll be able to see me!" The nun put her arm around the little girl's shoulder. "Go and try it out, Thérèse." She ran over and knelt on the box. "That's it, eh? I have to stay on my knees all the time and look ecstatic!" "Never mind the ecstatic look, Thérèse, no one will see it, as you've pointed out yourself! And we'll put little cushions under your robe so it won't be too hard on your knees." Thérèse and Pierrette looked at each other and burst out laughing. Pierrette blew kisses to her friend, who put both hands on her heart and fluttered her eyelashes. "Hail Mary!" "Hail you, too!" Sister Sainte-Catherine took advantage of this exchange to remove the table that was leaning against Pierrette's pedestal. The child immediately stopped laughing and crouched down on the platform, crying, "Momma! I want down!" The nun came and took her hand. "Come now, Pierrette, be brave .... It's always like that the first time we take the table away.... But nothing's changed. If you could stand up a minute ago you can still do it." "Okay, but at least hold on to me while I stand up!" Clutching the nun's shoulder, then her head, Pier-rette just barely managed to stand up. "Don't look down, Pierrette .... Look straight ahead .... Look toward Thérèse, but don't look *at* her, she ... not now, anyway ...." Pierrette looked up and her vertigo disappeared at once. "You're right, it isn't so bad like this!" Sister Sainte-Catherine stepped back a few paces and looked at the two girls, smiling. "It's going to look lovely. You'll be beautiful in your costumes, both of you." Pierrette looked in the nun's direction. "Do I have to smile?" As if at a signal, Thérèse got up and pulled up her stocking, which was sliding down her leg again. "I got an idea, Sister ... about Pierrette's teeth .... I think it's a good one!" Thérèse was speaking in that wheedling tone Pierrette had learned to be wary of, because it inevitably announced some trick or an insult disguised as a compliment. She wriggled on her plaster column. "I want to get down now, that's long enough for the first time!" But Thérèse was drawing Sister Sainte-Catherine over to the Mississippi tables. "Thérèse, come and help me down!" Thérèse merely waved. "Quiet! I'm saving your life!" Sister Sainte-Catherine returned to Pierrette's pedestal, smiling. "Thérèse, if you have anything to say about Pierrette, say it so she can hear you." Thérèse followed her, dragging her feet. Pierrette was becoming really impatient now. "Can't I get down?" The nun tapped her foot lightly. Thérèse turned her back to her friend as she explained her plan. "I had an idea. If we switched the pedestals around and put mine further back and Pierrette's closer to the fence, then we could change them around and the Blessed Virgin could look at the school and Bernadette could look at the street." Sister Sainte-Catherine covered her mouth with her hand and pretended to clear her throat to hide her giggling. Thérèse continued. "See, that way Pierrette could smile as much as she wants and it wouldn't bother anybody 'cause nobody could see her teeth!" She had assumed a triumphant expression that didn't escape the nun. "And then I, well, *I* could look ecstatic and I promise, I'll do a good job!" Pierrette, on her pedestal, was jubilant. "Hey, that's a good idea, Sister. What I was most worried about was my teeth. And Thérèse is so much prettier than I am!" Sister Sainte-Catherine was dazed by Thérèse's skill and Pierrette's naïveté. She didn't dare acquiesce, but told

212

herself she'd have time to think it over before the next evening. Thérèse sensed that she'd won, though, and winked at Pierrette, who was jumping up and down with excitement.

The pediment at the front of the École des Saints-Anges, which overhung the stairs where Sister Sainte-Philomène and the more robust grade-six girls were bustling about amid total chaos, was surmounted by a square, squat cement cross that rain, snow and wind had patiently worn down, smoothing its edges and giving it that greyish patina, far from its original white, proper to monuments roughly treated by the elements. Above the cross, between the second- and third-storey windows, you could read an inscription carved in absolutely ordinary letters: ACADÉMIE DES SS. ANGES. And it was on this sloping pediment, beneath this inscription, that Sister Sainte-Catherine, Sister Sainte-Thérèse de l'Enfant-Jésus and Simone Côté were now crouching on their heels, wildly excited. Simone had been strapped into a sort of harness of cured leather that ended, at the neck, in a metal ring to which a long rope was attached. She was taking deep breaths to hide her nervousness, but her trembling hands gave her away and she felt that she had to keep saying, "No, no, I'm not scared .... I'm not scared .... Everything's fine." They had just explained that she was going to be pushed over the edge and slowly lowered, an inch at a time, until she was level with the semi-circular rose-window above the main entrance. Ten times, Sister Sainte-Catherine asked if she'd changed her mind, if she still felt brave enough to cope with the vertigo that would be sure to overcome her once she was suspended in space, and ten times Simone replied that she trusted them, that she knew they wouldn't drop her and that she even expected to enjoy her little journey in the void. Charlotte Côté, stunned, was standing

213

at the bottom of the steps, arms outstretched, in spite of herself, toward her child whom she hadn't recognized for several days now, who she felt was drawing away from her. "Think it over, Simone, you can still change your mind, sweetheart!" Simone stuck her head over the triangular ornament and smiled at her mother. "Don't worry, momma, it's safe!" Charlotte realized how ridiculous the situation was and laughed bitterly. "That's right; make me feel better! You're the one being dropped out of the school, and I'm the one that's scared!" When she saw Simone sit on the edge of the pediment, in a very precarious position, and then let herself sway forward, she felt her legs turn to jelly. The two nuns, wearing thick leather gloves, were letting the rope slip slowly through their fingers. "She really doesn't weigh much ...." Sister Sainte-Thérèse was trying to sound cheerful, but there was a strange hint of concern in her voice. Sister Sainte-Catherine leaned over the pediment a little. "She's not saying anything. She's better than last year's; remember she started screaming before we even put the harness on ...." As soon as she felt herself floating, Simone shut her eyes. "I mustn't yell! If I do, momma won't let me come back tomorrow. I have to like it! I have to!" She pinched her lips together and didn't dare move; she wished she could wave her arms or legs, give her mother some sign to reassure her, but she couldn't loosen her muscles, which had knotted up in spite of her. She suddenly felt that she'd never come down again. She must have been just in front of the red and blue stained-glass window she'd always dreamed of seeing from up close. "Now's the time, dumb-bell, it's right beside you!" But her eyes remained obstinately shut and her brow was creased, giving her a stubborn look. Sister Sainte-Catherine's voice rose above her, soft and caressing. "How are you, Simone? Not too scared?" "I don't know yet, Sister, I haven't opened my eyes!" Charlotte Côté had climbed up a few steps and was sitting on a platform just under her daughter, thinking that if Simone were to fall she could catch her, at the risk of being felled by the impact. "I'm dreaming! This is silly, it can't be really happening! That's it, I'm dreaming! I'll wake up and have a good laugh at all this!" Without showing her concern, Sister Sainte-Catherine continued talking to Simone. "You can't spend two or three hours with your eyes shut, Simone .... Now really, there's no danger .... Open one eye if you want... Just for two or three seconds." Simone was starting to feel the onset of panic: the void all around her, with nothing to lean on and nothing to cling to, seemed to be sucking her down; her feet felt heavy, her head very light; there was an unpleasant prickling sensation along her back and when she lifted her head she could feel the metal ring against her nape and the end of the rope in her hair. "I mustn't yell! That would spoil all my fun!" She was about to scream when a mocking voice that seemed to come from far away suddenly extinguished her fear and made her open her eyes. "Close your legs, Simone, your pants are showing!" She saw Thérèse and Pierrette, on the opposite side of boulevard Saint-Joseph, waving at her and doubled up with laughter. She happily waved her arms and started to laugh along with them. "It's pretty up here! And so much fun! I feel like I'm flying! Hi, momma! Don't sit there on the steps like that, you'll get dirty!" Suddenly happy as a fish in water, Simone assumed poses and pretended to be swimming, under the amused gaze of several passers-by who had stopped to look at her. "Don't move around too much, Simone!" Simone looked up and saw the nuns' coifs sticking up comically over the cement pediment. "Don't lean over too far, you'll lose your coifs!"

When Sister Sainte-Philomène came into the linen room, Sister Saint-Georges had just finished ironing the Blessed

Virgin's blue veil. She was gaily humming a hymn to which she'd forgotten the words. "Have you decided to go back to work, Saint-Georges?" "It's quite a job, ironing around all that gold lace!" She wiped her forehead with the back of her sleeve. Sister Sainte-Philomène had approached, awkward and blushing, as Sister Saint-Georges was talking. "I just came to see if you were feeling better." Sister Saint-Georges put the iron on its metal stand and didn't dare look up at the friend with whom she'd been newly reunited. "Sure, Sainte-Philomène, everything's just fine." After the terrible scene with Mother Benoîte, Sister Sainte-Philomène had taken her friend back to her cell, helped her get undressed (a serious infringement of their community's rules) and put her to bed with gentle, reassuring words. The two nuns, holding hands, had mingled reproaches, apologies, memories, grievances; moved to tears, they finally asked the questions they'd been burning to ask for years. "Why did you give me that nickname, Sainte-Philomène?" "Why did you take it so hard? It was just a joke!" "A joke that lasts your whole life isn't a joke; it's a curse! Did you never think of that?" Then they lingered over all those years of friendship wasted because of a crude joke, and finally swore never to let anything come between them again. Caught up in their reunion, they didn't talk at first about Mother Benoîte and the danger she now represented for them: Sister Sainte-Philomène preferred to keep this problem for later, after the Corpus Christi celebrations, which would take up every minute of their time until the following evening. Sister Saint-Georges hadn't gone to sleep, but she shut her eyes as she talked. And she kept her hand on her friend's. Then at one point in a rather banal conversation about the splendid plants at the entrance to the nuns' house, which Sister Saint-Georges was particularly proud of because they'd given her a lot of trouble, she suddenly confessed to her friend what she considered to be her great sin, the pangs of conscience she felt at her grievous lie, the unbearable situation in which she'd been struggling for two days now, and finally she dissolved in tears at the thought of the punishment that was surely awaiting her. As for Sister Sainte-Philomène, she burst out laughing, a straightforward guffaw that rounded her already plump cheeks and brought the blood to her face; then she wiped her forehead with a handkerchief already stained by a half-day of toil, and even got up from her chair to try a few dance steps. "Your conscience is giving you trouble over *that*? Come on, Saint-Georges; you may not realize it but you've made one of the greatest dreams of every single nun in this school come true: you put one over on Mother Benoîte and she doesn't suspect a thing." "But she'll find out, that's what's so terrible!" "You still deserve a reward for it, not a punishment!" Sister Saint-Georges finally tried a timid, uncertain smile, telling herself it was all very well to have a laugh at the Principal's discomfiture, but Mother Benoîte would certainly find some way to take revenge. Sister Saint-Georges snatched up the iron again. "I'll be done in a jiffy, then I'll take them the veil ...." Sister Sainte-Philomène took the last costumes from the cupboard. "I hope the fittings go all right; the girls are pretty keyed up ... and so are we ...." "Don't start without me, I don't want to miss anything." Sister Sainte-Philomène walked around the ironing-board, puffing a little. "I'm telling you, we have a sweet hanging angel this year!" Sister Saint-Georges picked up the veil gently, shook it, and folded it with broad, delicate gestures. "Is the Blessed Virgin really going to have her back to the crowd this year?" Sister Sainte-Philomène, who had just opened the door of the linen cupboard, turned around. "How come you know that already?" "News travels fast in a girls' school, Sainte-Philomène. You should know that!"

217

The door was wide open, but there wasn't a breath of air. The three parallel beds were occupied: the first one, closest to the door, by a skinny little thing who was always eating and talked with her mouth full, sputtering things that at times were somewhat disgusting; the middle one, by a jovial, red-faced woman who made everybody laugh with her dirty stories, of which she had an impressive repertoire that she would belt out in a powerful, raucous voice, to the benefit of the whole floor, which had nicknamed her, of course, "the comic"; and the third (the one near the window on which a particularly brazen pigeon had just landed, a bird known as 'Romeo' because he came to serenade them punctually every afternoon), by a mass of flesh oozing from under the cotton sheet that barely covered it: the fat woman, hardly recognizable for she'd put on so much weight in the past few weeks, the end, she thought, of the pregnancy that had left her pale and undone, and short of breath. She'd had to sleep sitting up for the past ten days, and she snored so much that her room-mates took turns shaking her so she would change position. She apologized profusely then, but the other women, who were very fond of her because she was so calm and so sensible, told her not to worry, they understood and sympathized. But the fat woman didn't want anyone feeling sorry for her and she tried to explain that she was happy despite her difficult pregnancy, but they didn't seem to believe her. Some nights, so as not to disturb them, the fat woman wouldn't go to sleep and she'd watch the day break over Parc Lafontaine. As she was always sitting and her bed was high, she had a fine view over the first trees and even over the path that ran parallel to Sherbrooke, with its green-painted benches occupied all day by squirming children or overly calm old men who spent hours motionless, eating peanuts in the shell. She had never before seen the day break, and when she felt the night air becoming gradually transparent, turning first grey, then white, until a ray of yellow light touched the tree-tops as though to bring them back to life, she felt her soul rise, and it almost seemed as if she was leaving her bed, flying out the window and soaring above the park where, with uplifted arms, she would conduct the concert of light that was bathing her in comforting warmth. It was at these moments that she most missed rue Fabre; and her children, who weren't allowed to come and visit her (children could come inside the Hôpital Notre-Dame only at Christmas and Easter), whom she hadn't really had a chance to talk to before she left: Philippe, who hadn't seemed to understand that he wouldn't see her again for a long time, and had kissed her absent-mindedly, and Richard, who understood only too well and had clung to her, howling; and her husband, whom she adored, from whom she'd never been separated since their marriage, whose absence weighed so heavily on her. In fact she missed everybody. Though she'd been saying for months that she wanted to move at any price, she suddenly missed Albertine and her children and even old Victoire, who was such a nuisance but so lovable too. When the sun had risen completely she fell into a noisy sleep. They left her then, because it was breakfast time and her snoring didn't bother anyone, with all the conversations, the din of metal carts carelessly pushed by the Grey Nuns, and the morning ablutions that were performed amid singing and laughter. When Gabriel came into the room that afternoon the fat woman was reading *The Charterhouse of Parma*. She was so absorbed in her reading that she didn't hear her neighbour say, with a laugh, "Look, here's your other Romeo!" She started a little when he touched her arm. "How are you feeling today?" She barely smiled when he kissed her forehead. "This is terrible, a poor youngster locked up in a dungeon, trying to send messages to his beloved ...." She put the book on her bedside table. "I hope he can get in touch with her!" Gabriel pulled a chair close to his wife's bed. "Is it good, at least?"

"Oh yes, it's really well written, but it's so complicated and, my Lord, it's so sad! Didn't they ever write anything funny in those days?" Gabriel ran his hand delicately over his wife's enormous belly, hoping to feel a bit of life, a kick or a few heartbeats, as he often had these past few days. "Is he still being such a nuisance?" The fat woman took Gabriel's hand and put it on a precise spot on her belly. "I don't call that a nuisance! Know what he did last night? He turned over, my dear! If you ask me he's getting sick of being in there!" When she talked about her child the fat woman was transformed: her colour came back, she grew animated and seemed on the verge of laughter. "Sometimes I even play with him, it's so easy! Honest! I tap myself there and I touch one of his little arms or one of his feet, and then I push on it .... And does he ever react! Sometimes I do it for hours, talking to him; it's so much fun!" Gabriel had buried his head in his wife's belly. She was gently stroking the nape of his neck. Her two room-mates, who were astonished and even embarrassed by these shows of affection, because their husbands would never dare do such a thing in front of strangers, looked at each other, making discreet little signs, got out of bed and slipped out of the room. "What about you, how are you getting along?" "I really miss you a lot." The fat woman gently ruffled Gabriel's hair, then gave him a little tap on the head. "Quit telling me that, one of these days I'll believe you!" "Believe me, it's true! I'm sick of listening to Albertine shouting and the children hollering and my mother complaining .... When you aren't there I realize how poor we are and it's so depressing! Come home quick, with the baby, we all need you." Suddenly, as if replying to his father, the baby kicked the fat woman's stomach and she moaned, as much from joy as from pain. "Touch, right there. The little beggar's saying hello!"

Allegro energico
e passionato

Gold and white streamers hung from the roof of the school, partially masking the third-floor windows. Each one bore a golden letter sewn onto the bottom of the cloth; when you stood far enough away (from the front steps of the church, for instance, the view was impressive), you could read: PRIEZ POUR NOUS in big block letters that swayed in the wind up above the repository. As night fell, the letters would disappear one by one, for want of adequate lighting, until, by the time the ceremony was over, they would form only a faint veil over the façade of the school, like a cloth hanging from a table. The repository itself transformed the old cement staircase in an amazing way: the steps had disappeared altogether beneath a profusion of cloths spread over small platforms, or masked plinths or pedestals holding vases of paper lilies or freshly repainted statues with ecstatic expressions and brand-new smiles or clumsily spruced-up bleeding hearts; an improvised altar (two Mississippi tables tied together side by side) where dozens of electric candles blazed and on which a makeshift tabernacle, put together a few years before from a white satin-covered wooden crate, partially concealed the door to the school, which was itself hidden behind heavy black velvet so that the predominant gold and white stood out even more; cushions – small ones for the children who would occupy them, big ones for the priests who would have to kneel on them – had been meticulously set out in strategic places (Monsignor Bernier's was gold brocade and bore the papal emblem), first on the bottom step, where a row of pink-clad angels would remain prostrate during the whole ceremony, then at the foot of the altar where the upper crust of the Saint-Stanislas-de-Kostka parish (the churchwardens and vicars, actually) would position themselves so everyone could see them. All the second-floor

223

windows that were anywhere near the repository (Mother Benoîte's office window as well as the others) were caving in under papal banners of every size – from small ones no bigger than a handkerchief to the huge parade flag decorated with gold tassels and cords – arranged in a fan that the wind had trouble disentangling, they were so numerous and close together. Everything glowed softly and trembled under the tender gaze of Sister Sainte-Thérèse, who went across boulevard Saint-Joseph to get an overview (one last quick look is always a good idea, it uncovers those little flaws you might have missed) while Sister Sainte-Catherine arranged the flowers on the altar. "Goodness, it's lovely! Absolutely perfect! And to think that this is the last time!" Sister Saint-Thérèse didn't go so far as to wonder where she might be this time next year, but something told her she wouldn't be at the École des Saints-Anges and she was grieved at the prospect of never again seeing the repository all aglow in the setting sun. The six o'clock sunlight was gilding the façade of the church when Sister Sainte-Catherine turned to leave the repository. She replaced a cushion that she had probably moved as she was making her way to the altar, then very cautiously went back down to the sidewalk. She smiled at Sister Sainte-Thérèse, who was watching her and even waving at her from the other side of the street. "We should eat, Sainte-Thérèse. We'll need all our strength to-night." Sister Sainte-Thérèse gestured to her friend to join her, and Sister Sainte-Catherine ran across boulevard Saint-Joseph, holding her skirt with one hand and her head-dress with the other. A bus drove past, blowing its horn, and the driver gestured appreciatively toward the repository. Sister Sainte-Catherine came and leaned against the fence that surrounded the church lawn, beside her friend who had hidden her hands in her broad sleeves when she crossed her arms. She looked at her handiwork for a good two minutes without speaking, peering at everything – the banners,

224

statues, vases of flowers, embroidered altar cloth, flags, electric candles – squinting like a connoisseur. Then she dropped her judgement like the blade of a guillotine, at one stroke cutting the repository from her life, forever. "It's very ugly. And very vain." Sister Saint-Thérèse de l'Enfant-Jésus looked at her, offended. "You don't think it's beautiful, Sainte-Catherine?" "I've always thought it was hideous, Sainte-Thérèse, today more than ever!" She too had hidden her hands in her sleeves. "But that's all finished now. For good."

"It didn't seem this long yesterday!" "That's because you were standing on a bench when you tried it on, dumb-bell!" "Don't call me dumb-bell, Pierrette Guérin! I'm no dumber than you are!" Simone had already put on the white angel's robe, which she had to hold with both hands to keep from trailing on the ground. Pierrette was sitting on a little bench beside her, eating an orange. First she'd carefully peeled it, cautiously putting each strip of rind in her uniform pocket, then she shouted, "Stand back, it's going to squirt!" She tore the orange apart as the little girls around her looked on covetously, then started to eat it, gravely, chewing each mouthful for a long time, eyes shut, concentrating on the joy that burst first in her mouth, piquant and sweet, then poured deliciously into her throat, where it disappeared leaving a prickling sensation in her nose. Between two sections of her orange she noticed Simone, who was standing in front of the long mirror Sister Sainte-Catherine had put up on the stage in the recreation hall. Simone was simpering and bowing, blowing kisses and craning her neck, as she tried to see herself from the back. Pierrette sat beside her, licking her fingers. "We aren't supposed to get dressed till seven o'clock, Simone. It's just twenty to, how come you've got your robe on already?" "Getting an early start! There'll be too many people later, and too much fuss." Simone turned, lifted her robe above her bottom and sat on the edge of the stage. Pierrette spoke with her mouth full. "You're going to get all dirty. Move over." "Where'd you get that orange?" "From Thérèse. Want some?" "I don't want to get my robe dirty. Where'd Thérèse get it? You don't just find oranges, and besides they cost a fortune!" "Her Uncle Josaphat brought them." "He must be rich!" Pierrette swallowed the last section of her orange, took out a piece of rind and rubbed it carefully over her teeth. "What are you doing, you nut?" "Cleaning my teeth! Didn't you ever clean your teeth with an orange peel?" Simone dropped her head and ran her hand over her robe as if to smooth it. "I never ate an orange ...." Pierrette put the piece of rind back in her pocket. "Never ate an orange! Why didn't you take the piece I offered you?" "When I eat an orange I want the whole thing, not just one piece!" At that moment Thérèse arrived, followed by Lucienne Boileau, who had taken advantage of the fact that Thérèse was by herself to trail along after her. Thérèse hadn't said a word, but Lucienne walked proudly at her side, certain she'd just won one of the greatest victories of her life, though Thérèse hardly noticed she was there. Thérèse had carefully combed her hair and her magnificent tresses fell gracefully to her shoulders, glossy and just slightly wavy. At the corner of Garnier and Saint-Joseph, Lucienne had asked in a falsely naïve little voice, "Is your hair naturally curly? It's so pretty!" Thérèse merely answered, "If I give you the slap you've been asking for, you'll have a naturally curly mouth for the rest of your life!" Lucienne, who had no pride whatsoever, laughed. "Hi everybody! Sorry I'm late, but my Uncle Josaphat was visiting and he's such a gabber and everything he says is so interesting, I didn't notice how late it was ...." Thérèse ran up the six steps to the stage. "You managed to find the school all by yourselves?" First she gave Pierrette a kiss, and

226

said, holding her nose, "You stink of orange! Did somebody give you a present?" Pierrette took the same piece of chewed-up rind from her pocket. "Gee, it was so good! My fingers are all sticky, but I don't care, I'll wash my hands afterwards." Thérèse then went over to Simone, who was pouting in a corner, her robe bunched up between her legs. "How come you put on your robe before your harness? Are they going to hang you up by the scruff of the neck? Sister Sainte-Catherine told us not to get dressed yet, Simone, are you deaf?" "Leave me alone and stop picking on me! I can take care of myself!" Thérèse turned away without replying and went and sat on the edge of the stage with Pierrette. "Stay away from Simone, she's so touchy she nearly bit my head off just now!" She took a huge orange from her uniform pocket and held it over her head, as if looking at the light through it. "Too bad she's in such a rotten mood, I had a little present for her!" She heard something like a stampede behind her, and the orange disappeared. "You brought me one! At last! I'm going to eat an orange! What does it taste like? Orange candy?" "No dummy, it tastes like cherry candy! Now take off your robe or you'll reek of oranges all the way to boulevard Saint-Joseph tonight!" Simone nimbly took off her robe, hung it up and withdrew into a corner, gripping the orange in both hands. "Gosh, I hope it'll taste as good as I expect!" She sat on a stool, placed the fruit on her lap. Lucienne Boileau came over and cordially sat at her feet, on the floor of the stage. "You're going to eat that nice orange, Simone?" Simone smiled broadly and Lucienne's hopes went up a notch. "Yup! And if you stay there, you can watch me!" The recreation hall was gradually filling with nervous, noisy little girls, chattering like monkeys as they glanced enviously at the stage, a place of privilege reserved for the grade-six girls who had had the good luck, and the honour, to be chosen to appear in the repository. The grade nines, braver than the others, quicker to jeer as well, came right up and leaned on the edge of the stage, laughingly tossing off rude remarks about the chosen, who were impatiently nosing about in the costume cupboard. "Don't forget your wings, girls, or you'll look like you're in your night-gowns!" "This year's going to be the ugliest one we've ever seen!" "Just imagine, the Blessed Virgin played by a rabbit!" "Hey, Mary, don't bite baby Jesus when you kiss him goodnight; he might get rabies!" But Sister Sainte-Catherine put a damper on their fun when she burst into the recreation hall, followed by Sister Sainte-Thérèse, Sister Sainte-Philomène and Sister Saint-Georges, who was smiling broadly and limping almost jauntily. Silence fell immediately, and the grade nines disappeared from the edge of the stage as if by magic, mingling innocently with the other pupils who were starting to mill around the four nuns. Sister Sainte-Catherine didn't stop to talk; she issued her orders in a strong, clear voice as she headed for the stage. "Everybody out, please! I don't want anybody here except those who have permission. Everyone else, into the school yard! And I wish the grade nines would stop acting like babies and look after the grade ones, who must not under any circumstances get their first communion dresses dirty .... Make yourselves useful for once, instead of just acting silly!" There was a dreadful uproar in the hall as the nuns got up on the stage, where they were literally assailed by little girls whose nervousness and stage fright you could see in their eyes and hear in their voices. Sister Sainte-Catherine gave a few additional orders and the other three nuns headed for the tasks that had been assigned to them: Sister Sainte-Thérèse glided into the dressing-room (a huge screen in front of the mirror), Sister Sainte-Philomène and Sister Saint-Georges went out of the hall pushing the wheeled coat rack that held the Roman soldiers' costumes for the grade-nine boys from Saint-Stanislas school, who were waiting in the basement. Sister Sainte-Catherine found Simone in the midst of her feast, with orange juice on her chin and a look of ecstasy lighting up her face. Thérèse pulled on the nun's sleeve, murmuring, "Don't give her heck, Sister, it's her first orange." Sister Sainte-Catherine, who had other things on her mind, walked away from the two friends with a shrug and pointed at Lucienne Boileau, who was once again sucking one of her braids. "Lucienne, one of these days you'll poison yourself!" She clapped her hands to get the attention of the girls, who had started chattering again. "Everyone listen to me please! I want everything to go smoothly, so we're going to follow a very precise plan: first I want the pink angels for the base of the repository to go to Sister Sainte-Thérèse for their costumes; after that, the trumpeting angels, and finally, the Virgin, Bernadette and the hanging angel .... Understand?" There was no problem putting the angels' robes on the girls: they had tried them on the day before, the hems had been adjusted, the sleeves shortened or lengthened; but the wings were another matter: they were too heavy for some of the girls, too long for others; they caught everywhere, on the doors, in curtains, on the screen, their class-mates, the nuns; someone burst into tears, slaps were exchanged by two sworn enemies, each of whom thought the other looked prettier, and Sister Sainte-Catherine had to scold and even deal harshly. The little girls eventually calmed down a bit and they were put on two long wooden benches, with instructions to stay perfectly still until they were called to go out. Then they were hot. And the windows had to be opened. The trumpeting angels were considerably calmer and only Ginette Chartier caused any trouble, more out of bad faith, actually, than for any other reason. Their costumes were elaborate (these were chic angels), more varied, too, but just as ugly: one was sea green with pink wings and a silver trumpet; there was a pale blue one with white wings and a gold trumpet; a canary yellow one with silver wings and a white trumpet; and, finally, a pink one with red wings and trumpet (they'd decided this was the Angel Gabriel, who was always placed to the right of the altar). Lucienne Boileau had inherited this costume and she was more than a little proud of it: she paraded about for some time, assuming poses and even trying to play *"J'irai la voir un jour"* on her papier-mâché trumpet, which had the inevitable effect of getting on everybody's nerves and drawing a few more gibes from Thérèse and Pierrette. The dressing of Thérèse was quickly settled: her costume was quite simple and presented no problems. Thérèse muttered as she sat down between the two most flamboyant angels, "I look like an orphan! They'll think I came to the wrong party!" When Pierrette, pink and trembling and so lovely in her white robe and blue veil – so vulnerable, too, with her mouth carefully shut and her anxious eyes – came out from behind the screen, the rows of angels became silent. Sensing that they were all looking at her, she turned away, wanting to hide in the dressing-room; but Sister Sainte-Catherine held her back, kissed her cheek and signalled the other girls to applaud. Thérèse got up from her bench and gestured to Pierrette to take the place she'd just vacated. "Sit down, Pierrette ... you'll be on your feet all night!" Sister Sainte-Catherine found Simone in the same place, on a corner of the stage. The floor around her was strewn with orange peels. The little girl looked up at Sister Sainte-Catherine with a look of utter despair. "I'm not going. I feel sick to my stomach."

Maurice Côté thought he looked so ridiculous as a Roman soldier that he stayed in the corner as if rooted there, distraught. The tunic in particular was cruelly mortifying: he had never shown his legs to anyone because he knew they were soft and chubby, and now the whole parish was free to make fun of them – and to make matters worse, it was his own doing! All that just to get a good look at a girl who wanted nothing to do with him! He'd tried to sneak away discreetly, but at the last minute Sister Sainte-Philomène had caught him and put him back in line. She didn't want to lose a single Roman soldier this year, because only five had turned up, though the grade-nine boys usually fought for a place .... The fat nun manoeuvred among the fifteen-year-old boys, half-naked and smelling suspect, with surprising ease: she handed out helmets and Roman sandals with brusque gestures, barking an occasional searing insult or a brisk compliment that made everyone start. Sister Saint-Georges was helping the boys to put on their costumes and was mortified by it; as were the boys, who flatly refused to get undressed in front of this witch whom they laughed at for ten months of the year, and behaved like little girls, prudish and very comical, as they hid behind the furnace to drape themselves in their rags. (The Roman soldiers hadn't been touched up for years and they were becoming seriously shabby.) When everything was finished and the young men were decked out as well as possible and blushing as much from embarrassment as pleasure, Sister Sainte-Philomène decided to inspect them and was profoundly depressed by what she saw. "I think this guard looks pathetic, don't you Saint-Georges?" Sister Saint-Georges, who considered it quite a feat to have dressed five boys in a single day, muttered a reply that was hard to interpret. Sister Sainte-Philomène leaned against a door, wiping her face. "Haven't you got any brothers or cousins or friends who'd like to come and help you make fools of yourselves? We could use another three." As no one replied, Sister Sainte-Philomène estimated their I.Q.s and turned her back on them with a sigh. "I think we've got a bunch of dim-wits this year, Saint-Georges! They're either too tall or too short, they stink and they're stupid!" The five boys (of whom three, at least, were the terrors of their school, who made all the other pupils tremble) looked down, twitching and squirming with embarrassment before this fat abrupt woman, whom they were irritating and who was making fools of them. The grade threes and fours, who, some mornings, had to pay a cent or even two to get into school, would have been very surprised at the sight of their torturers falling to pieces and dissolving with embarrassment before a simple nun. Sister Sainte-Philomène opened the door that gave on to the staircase on rue de Lanaudière. "Go and report to Sister Sainte-Catherine in the recreation hall. You can remember her name, all five of you, I hope? Sainte-Catherine! Like the street! And meanwhile, Sister Saint-Georges and I are going to have a last look at the repository." The poor Roman soldiers disappeared down the stairs, not daring to look at one another. Sister Sainte-Philomène followed them with a look of contempt. "When you're old enough to fight, if the war's still on, for goodness sake don't sign up! They'd laugh you out of the army!" Sister Saint-Georges had started up the steps, one at a time, gripping the handrail. "How come you're so mean to them, Saint-Philomène? They didn't do anything to deserve that!" "I'm mean because I know what they *could* do!"

They walked Simone around the recreation hall; they told her to breathe deeply, to hold the air in her lungs, then let it out slowly in irregular little bursts. All the windows had been opened but there wasn't a breath of air in the large room. Simone had managed to release one or two little belches, to the great relief of Sister Sainte-Catherine and her two friends, who were surrounding her like a queen bee. "Feel better now, Simone?" Simone didn't answer yet: she was concentrating on her nausea, which from time to time seemed about to go away, but then suddenly came back, making her stomach heave dreadfully. Suddenly, at the very moment the five Roman soldiers came bursting in, Simone retched horribly and shot off toward the bathroom behind the stage. On the way, she jostled her brother, whom she didn't recognize, and he followed her, asking what was wrong. When she she saw the Roman soldiers, so awkward and pitiful in their ridiculous get-ups, Sister Sainte-Catherine raised her eyes to heaven and got back up on the stage, trying to compose her features as serenely as she could. "Boys, go and take your places on the curb immediately .... I think your teacher, Brother Martial-Rosaire, has already explained what you have to do." The bravest boy plucked up his courage and took two steps toward her. "The fat sister told us to come and see you .... We don't really know what we're supposed to be doing." "Sister Sainte-Philomène sent you here? Very well ... but she should have realized that boys your age, in a roomful of girls, could only cause problems .... Well, it isn't your fault .... Now, go back and tell her I said she was to look after you till the procession starts." The four soldiers, more pitiful than ever, slouched out of the room. "And straighten up! You're soldiers, don't forget!" Meanwhile, Thérèse and Pierrette had followed Simone and Maurice into the toilet. At the sight of Pierrette dressed up as the Blessed Virgin, Maurice started slightly and they both blushed to the roots of their hair. Then Thérèse was obliged to carry the conversation; she knew the others would remain silent, each in his corner, trying to avoid the other's gaze. "Simone, where are you?" Two little legs could be seen under the door of one of the cubicles. "Simone, are you in there?" She heard only a faint gurgling that made her feel queasy. "Unlock the door, Simone! Didn't your mother ever tell you not to lock the bathroom door when you're going to throw up?" The door opened a crack and Thérèse rushed inside the cubicle. Pierrette and Maurice realized then that they were alone in the girls' bathroom, and their embarrassment increased tenfold. They managed to avoid each other's eyes, staring instead at their shoes or turning their heads every now and then toward the cubicle, from which some very unpleasant sounds were emanating. When Sister Sainte-Catherine came into the cold, damp room that was perpetually filled with the uproar of all the toilets being flushed at once and the persistent odour of green soap, they still hadn't said a word to each other. "Pierrette! Who is this boy? The idea! The Blessed Virgin in the washroom with a Roman soldier!" Thérèse's voice came to them from the cubicle, where things seemed to have calmed down. "He's Simone's brother Maurice, Sister! And Simone's feeling better, so you can tell him he can go now ...." Sister Sainte-Catherine didn't need to repeat Thérèse's remark; Maurice left the room, reeling with embarrassment and rushed into the recreation hall where he thought he'd find his four friends. The door to the cubicle opened wide and the two girls came out. Thérèse was supporting her pale, dishevelled friend. Sister Sainte-Catherine approached them and took Simone by the chin. "Feeling better, Simone?" The little girl swallowed several times, then replied, "Please don't tell my mother I was sick. She might not let me go. I was so excited and I ate my orange too fast." Then she looked reproachfully at Thérèse. "You and your bright ideas, Thérèse!" Just then the bathroom door opened and several little girls inched their way inside, their wings already clipped somewhat and their haloes askew. Among them was Lucienne Boileau, holding her trumpet like an ice-cream cone. "We'd like to go to the bathroom, Sister!" "We, um, we have to ... is it all right?" It was the same thing every year and Sister Sainte-Catherine was resigned to it; she had no choice. But before Simone left the room, she took her aside. "Are you sure you want to go, Simone? It's not too late, we can decide not to have a hanging angel this year." "No, no, Sister, it's all right ... I'll be okay.

Anyway, nothing worse can happen to me now!"

The Ladies of Sainte-Anne, the Daughters of Isabelle and the churchwardens of Saint-Stanislas-de-Kostka parish were all assembled on the church lawn, with their standards and banners depicting the saints in spangled and sequinned gowns, lambs of God of real wool on gold backgrounds, flaming Sacred Hearts that showed Jesus with the face of a naïve young girl, or bearing quotations from just about anywhere: the Bible, the Gospels, hymns, even *La Bonne Chanson*; all this high society, the Ladies of Sainte-Anne draped in purple, the Daughters of Isabelle in blue and white and the churchwardens simply dressed to kill, with creaking shoes and hair slicked down with brilliantine, squawked along the central path from boulevard Saint-Joseph to the church steps; the women were already swooning over the beauty of the unfinished repository, while the men coughed into their fists to conceal the fact that they had nothing to say. Madame Duquette, the president of the Ladies of Sainte-Anne, talked more and said it louder than anyone else; she gave orders that nobody listened to in a tone that everyone hated; two great rings of sweat on her black taffeta dress indicated just how nervous she already was. The president of the Daughters of Isabelle, Mademoiselle Thivierge, a spinster known to everyone in the parish as Mademoiselle Grosse Vierge because she was so hugely fat, muttered so that everyone could hear, "Look at Duquette getting all worked up! She's going to reek to high Heaven! I feel sorry for the poor Ladies of Sainte-Anne who'll have to put up with *that* all night!" Above the two huge buildings could be heard the boys from Saint-Stanislas and the girls from Saints-Anges getting excited in their respective school yards; it was time for something to happen. At ten past seven, ten minutes behind schedule, Sister Sainte-Philomène walked briskly across boulevard Saint-Joseph and presented herself to Monsieur Charbonneau, the dean of the churchwardens for a scant two months (his predecessor, Monsieur Saint-Onge, died of indigestion brought on by eating canned corn in March) who was still very embarrassed by the honour. "Monsieur Saint-Onge, you can go and get the canopy; it's all ready in the school yard." "Charbonneau, Sister, not Saint-Onge." "I'm sorry, Monsieur Charbonneau, it's because you're new ...." The old man gave a sign to the four churchwardens he had chosen to carry the canopy through the streets of the parish, and followed Sister Sainte-Philomène, who had set off again, at a run. In the school yard were deposited the grade-one girls (squeezed into first-communion dresses and veils that their mothers had already consigned to moth-balls, forgetting they'd have to take them out at the beginning of June, excited because they were going to watch the Corpus Christi procession, singing *"J'irai la voir un jour"* and *"Oh! Jésus, doux et humble de coeur,"* but impatient because they were supposed to stand stock-still) in the space between the two sets of cement steps. The grade-nine girls told them they looked like the monkeys in the Parc Lafontaine zoo and pretended to throw them peanuts. The canopy, dazzling and breath-takingly ugly with its red and gold lace border and its uprights draped in cords, pom-poms, crêpe paper, tassels and fringes of every colour, was in a corner waiting for its four bearers (four pushers, rather, because two years earlier it had been decked out with huge wheels that creaked horribly and jammed every fifteen feet), and the dean of the churchwardens who would walk ahead of it, with his gold-headed cane. The pushers took their positions, the dean took his place ahead of them, and the signal was given to the grade one girls to move forward by classes, as they'd been rehearsing for three days, and go and stand in the middle of rue de Lanaudière. The double gates to the school yard had to be opened so the canopy could be taken out unscathed. Only then was the door to the school that opened onto rue de Lanaudière opened, and the repository's extras came out one by one and stood under the canopy. Some of the curious were already congregating on boulevard Saint-Joseph and when they saw the angels coming out of the school, then Mary and Bernadette, there was a scramble toward rue de Lanaudière. Simone led the way, in her white robe and pink wings, followed by Thérèse and Pierrette, who were standing so straight they seemed taller and, then the other angels, who weren't used to their trumpets yet and didn't know what to do with them. There were applause and whistles and "Hoorays," and Simone was happy. Her mother was in the front row of spectators, hands pressed to her heart. The mini-procession set off slowly, turned on to boulevard Saint-Joseph and advanced toward the repository. The grade-one girls stopped at the corner of Garnier and, at a signal from Sister Jeanne au Bûcher, turned toward the repository to see the angels take their places. The trumpet-ing angels climbed up first, walking around statues and candlesticks, and kneeling at the base of the altar, where they made as if they were playing their instruments. Luci-enne Boileau, drunk with pride and pink with pleasure, blew a timid kiss to "Thérèse-'n'-Pierrette," who didn't even notice her. The Roman soldiers were in position, standing straight as fence posts. When Pierrette, pale with stage fright in her blue veil, her mouth hermetically sealed, walked past Maurice, he raised his eyes to keep from blushing. Thérèse and Pierrette walked through the little gate in the fence and headed for the two pedestals covered with crêpe paper that, in a manner of speaking, imitated the stones of a grotto. Thérèse was furious because Sister Sainte-Catherine hadn't taken her advice and had left the two pedestals where they'd always been; she knelt so that her profile squarely faced the crowd, telling herself that showing half of her face was better than nothing. As for Pierrette, she was quite nervous as she got up on the table that Sister Sainte-Catherine had placed next to her damn column. When she was up on the little platform and Sister Sainte-Catherine had taken the table away, there was a veritable ovation on boulevard Saint-Joseph, and Pierrette thought she was going to faint. In the front row her mother and three sisters were waving papal flags and howling with delight. Then it was Simone's turn. At the last moment, while she was dressing Simone with all the delicacy of which she was capable, Sister Sainte-Catherine got an idea that was picked up immediately by Sister Sainte-Thérèse, Sister Sainte-Philomène and Sister Saint-Georges: instead of dropping the little hanging angel from the pediment of the school, she'd be hoisted up from the repository. That way Simone wouldn't have to dangle in space. Sister Sainte-Philomène and Sister Sainte-Thérèse were kneeling on the pediment, waiting for Sister Sainte-Catherine's signal to pull Simone up over the altar. Simone, so small and fragile it seemed as if she might actually take flight, very cautiously climbed the steps to the repository, holding her gown, which was slightly too long. She saw nothing, heard nothing; she wanted to die then and there. Sister Sainte-Catherine slipped the heavy rope into the ring that protruded from her costume; she tied two sturdy knots and gestured to Sister Sainte-Philomène to pull. There was absolute silence as Simone rose in the air. Even Madame Duquette shut up, wiping her face with her handkerchief soaked in "Tulipe Noire" by Chenard. Just as Simone came to a standstill right in the centre of the rose-window, Sister Saint-Georges, who was in charge of the lighting for the repository and was waiting for this very moment to spring into action, turned on the cloakroom lights, and the hanging angel was awash in red and blue. She stood out against the stained glass like a little living saint, a delicate silhouette floating above the altar as if to protect it. All the boys from

238

Saint-Stanislas school were lined up along rue Garnier now, and the girls from the École des Saints-Anges were waiting impatiently on rue de Lanaudière. Everything was ready; the procession could begin. Monsieur Charbonneau walked ceremoniously through the presbytery garden and rang the bell, hat in hand. Monsignor Bernier, preceded by Mother Benoîte des Anges and Mother Notre-Dame du Rosaire, came out on the steps and made a broad sign of the cross, but nobody noticed.

The previous day, Mother Benoîte had left the school very early in the afternoon. She took it on herself to call a taxi (an almost unthinkable expense for a member of her community, but Mother Benoîte des Anges couldn't see herself taking the bus as Sister Sainte-Catherine had done a few days earlier, going along the same route, perhaps in the same vehicles), in which she had forced herself to say her rosary, eyes shut, arms folded over her vast bosom. She had come to throw herself at the feet of her superior. Mother Notre-Dame du Rosaire talked about humility, Mother Benoîte about humiliation; Mother Notre-Dame talked of obedience, Mother Benoîte of anarchy, revolt, rebellion. The Principal of the École des Saints-Anges begged her superior to remove her from the school if she didn't want to get rid of Sister Sainte-Catherine, predicting that the problems with the Six A teacher would multiply tenfold in time; she had stated coldly that a reconciliation was absolutely impossible, that war was inevitable and that everyone would suffer as a result. There was nothing to be done. Urged on by the demands of Monsignor Bernier, who headed one of the most important parishes in Montreal and wanted to keep the two nuns where they were, but also by a political need to impose her will on these two rebels, who were suddenly starting,

239

despite their vow of obedience, to ask, to demand, to criticize and threaten, Mother Notre-Dame was intractable. Mother Benoîte recounted her week in the greatest detail, not omitting a single insult and humiliation to which she had been subjected, although everyone in the school owed her respect and obedience, but now they were suddenly taking malicious pleasure in contradicting, insulting and even ignoring her (the choice of the trio Thérèse-'n'-Pierrette for the repository was a glaring example). But the decision had been made and it was irrevocable. Both the Principal and the Six A teacher would keep their positions and they'd just have to learn to put up with each other. Mother Notre-Dame du Rosaire suggested to Mother Benoîte des Anges that she spend the night at the Mother House in humble reflection and prayer, accepting this lesson with resignation. Once again, Mother Benoîte blew up. "A lesson! Mother, all I did was punish a nun who had it coming to her! Everything that followed was her fault! Everything! She's the one who deserves a lesson! She and her three acolytes will turn our school upside-down if something isn't done immediately! Even the Sister portress, I assure you, is telling outright lies, looking me straight in the eye and not even blushing!" Mother Notre-Dame du Rosaire dismissed her without further ado, and she left the Superior's office harrowed and distraught. Lying on the hard bed in the cell that her superior had offered, Mother Benoîte des Anges wept with rage, fulminated and blasphemed for a good part of the night. When she walked out of the presbytery, with Monsignor Bernier and Mother Notre-Dame on either side of her, and caught sight of the crowd, already large and noisy, gathered in front of Sister Sainte-Catherine's repository, Mother Benoîte des Anges became aware of the exaggerated importance and, above all, of the futility of this grotesque play-acting that was used to numb naïve souls; for the first time she realized how ugly was this display of gussied-up children and paint-daubed statues, insipid, laughable leftovers from medieval mysteries, and she was horrified. As the three of them headed toward the canopy that was waiting for them, the monstrance that would be proudly borne by the *curé* and the banners that would follow, pitching and tossing at the ends of their poles, she caught herself smiling maliciously. "I'll go to the depths. The very depths. Of humiliation and despair. And of ridicule. But I'll come out of this the winner! I still have a year to get to the bottom of all this! A year from now the repository will no longer exist, Sister Sainte-Catherine will no longer exist, and I'll spend the evening of Corpus Christi day at my window, savouring my victory!" All grew silent as they approached boulevard Saint-Joseph. The *curé* took his place under the canopy, picked up the monstrance and raised it to eye-level. The crowd knelt and Monsieur Charbonneau struck up a hymn that everyone sang in chorus, while the *curé* gave the starting signal.

The big hands of Josaphat-le-Violon enclosed the frail wrists of Victoire, who didn't get up to greet her brother as she usually did when he arrived during her nap. She didn't even smile when he kissed her forehead; half-heartedly she pushed away the orange he held out to her. "You're usually a lot more excited than that at the sight of an orange, Victoire! Remember how wrought-up we'd be when we found one in our Christmas stockings? We'd eat just one orange a year, and we ate it so fast that five minutes afterwards we'd already forgotten it!" Victoire turned to the wall. "I'm going, Josaphat...." "You're going? Going where?" "You know! Don't be hypocritical! I've started seeing things and death's just waiting for me!" Josaphat brought a chair to his sister's bedside, and took her wrist in both his hands. They had never held hands; some old sense of propriety, an old fear of sinning through overly intimate contact, had always kept them from truly kissing or openly embracing. For Josaphat, taking his sister's hand would have meant inciting her to something forbidden between brother and sister; and so all his life he had held her by the wrist, delicately, never pressing his fingers too hard on the veins he could feel throbbing. Yet they had often said they loved each other, passionately and unequivocally; but words fly away and they could always pretend they hadn't heard them, whereas deeds are so compromising! "What did you see exactly, Victoire?" Then she told him about the cat no one could see, which followed Marcel everywhere and which she thought she'd heard *talking* and *laughing*; the four women in the house next door whom she'd seen going out to the yard, in the back, in May, to sow seeds in the sunny part of their garden, how they had waved at her before going back in the house and the mother's look of complicity when she smiled at her. "Marcel sees them, too, the cat and the women! But Marcel's crazy, Josaphat, not me! He's no ordinary child, Marcel, I've always said so! It means that I'm going crazy too!" She turned abruptly toward her brother and gazed intently into his eyes. "You, too, Josaphat, you used to say you saw things when you were little! I remember, once *ma tante* Zonzon told you to stop talking about it, or she'd send you to the insane asylum, and you never brought it up again .... Do you still see things, Josaphat? Have you been crazy all your life, too, and never told anybody? Does it run in the family?" After a long silence, Josaphat-le-Violon started to tell his sister everything: about Rose, Violette, Mauve and Florence, their mother; their age-old vigils and their eternal knitting; Mauve's music, Violette's songs, Rose's poetry; the years he'd spent with them as a child in Duhamel, learning the oral legends of their country, filled with marvels barely hinted at, that could be developed and infinitely multiplied and never brought to an end because you don't want them to

242

end; the spell, the nest of sensations woven by the violin, in the pit of your stomach, that you can burst when you want to because music exists inside as well as outside; the bawdy songs and the other, more proper ones, that are printed in books, all those songs brought from the old country but touched up, straightened out, transformed and transfigured here by foot tappers, spoon players and accordionists and fiddlers, whose nasal voices help you get through the winter without becoming gloomy. He praised the beauty of the things you can't understand and tried to make her acknowledge how lucky they were – she, Marcel, and he himself – because they could taste all that, while others were condemned to a bland, ordinary existence. But Victoire was struggling in her bed, tossing her head in all directions and pushing her brother away when he bent too close to her. "That's craziness! It's all just craziness, Josaphat! I'd rather go! I'd rather die! You don't start learning things like that at my age, don't you see? I'm too old, I just want to be left alone! That's all I want, to be left alone in my corner! Before ... before, maybe, when I was little ... maybe with you . . the two of us together, maybe we could have .. but now .... Just let me die with an honest soul, Josaphat!" Josaphat tried to calm her, but Victoire kept repeating "No!", plugging her ears and kicking under the sheet. Having run out of arguments, Josaphat seized Victoire's hands and she suddenly grew still. They looked at each other for a long time without moving; fear could be seen in Victoire's eyes, and in Josaphat's an immense love that asked only to break free. The old man moved first; he slowly brought his sister's hands up to his mouth, then planted two long kisses on them. "You really don't want to, Victoire?" She withdrew her hands abruptly, as if they'd accidentally been dipped in dirty water. "No!" Marcel, who had slipped discreetly into the bedroom a few minutes before, approached his grandmother's bed. "It's so beautiful, gramma!" The old woman didn't answer; she didn't even look at him. Marcel walked around the iron bed and pulled on Josaphat's sleeve. "It's time to make the moon rise, *mon oncle* ...." They left the room without a sound, Josaphat with his violin, Marcel with his cat. They silently descended the stairs and went and stood on Florence's front steps to watch the Corpus Christi procession pass. Rose, Violette and Mauve were drinking tea. Florence, their mother, was cutting a cake. Marcel smiled as he looked at Mauve. "*Mon oncle*, the other day Mauve played the piano.... And it was so beautiful!" Josaphat rubbed a bit of rosin on his bow. "In my day she played the violin."

That night, then, Albertine was alone on the balcony watching her God go past: her mother refused to get up, her daughter was making a fool of herself on the school lawn, her two nephews were in the procession, her brother had gone to visit his wife in the hospital, her son was on the balcony next door, listening to her uncle play the violin to seduce the moon. Albertine held her little papal flag, thinking, "If that's what life's all about, the good Lord ought to be ashamed of himself when he goes past my door."

"It's a lot worse than I expected .... Don't you think it's stupid, Pierrette?" Pierrette obviously couldn't reply to Thérèse without showing her teeth to the people watching her, and so she just frowned. Thérèse went on: "It was fun at first because there were lots of people, but now practically everybody's following the procession and it's starting to drag." Some time ago she had dropped the exalted but exhausting pose she'd adopted at first (arms stretched out before her, hands clasping her rosary, head thrown back) to

244

sit lethargically on her heels, arms folded, head turning constantly from side to side. "Know what, Pierrette? My damn stocking's undone again!" Fastening it was out of the question and it was driving her crazy. She could feel the garter digging into her thigh and kept wanting to scratch it. Luckily the cushions Sister Sainte-Thérèse had put down for her knees were very effective and she wasn't feeling any pain, only a slight stiffness in her left knee, which she was able to control by rubbing it as discreetly as possible with her fingertips. "Haven't you got cramps, standing up there as stiff as a board?" Pierrette slowly shook her head and Thérèse guffawed into her rosary. "Don't look like that, Pierrette, people will think you've got itching powder on your back!" Pierrette didn't have the slightest urge to laugh. At first she'd been very excited by everyone looking at her, and she'd felt her heart swell with pride when anyone smiled at her or if a child waved; but paranoia soon got the upper hand and now if she saw two heads leaning together or two chins pointing in her direction, she'd wonder, "Are they saying I look nice or laughing at me? Are they talking about my teeth? Can they see them? Are they saying I look embarrassed? Are they laughing at my hands because I'm holding them like a church steeple, just like a real statue? My hands aren't nearly as pretty as the real Blessed Virgin's! They're laughing at me, I know they are!" Her mother and her three pregnant sisters wept for a long time as they recited prayers and sang hymns, but when the procession finally got underway, Rita Guérin had shouted to her daughter, "We're going now, sweetheart .... The parade goes right past our house and I don't want my balcony to be empty! I took the flags out of the shed a while ago and put them all up on the balcony and in the windows .... It really looks swell! We'll be back for mass." Pierrette thought she'd die of shame. For a few minutes now the air had felt heavier and stickier, and from time to time a bead of sweat dropped from her forehead and made its way down her neck. It tickled terribly but she didn't move. She stood so still that she heard one old woman ask another, "Is she a statue or a real one?" Glancing discreetly at the repository, Pierrette noticed Maurice Côté gaping admiringly at her as he leaned on his Roman soldier's lance, hands at the level of his heart. She felt like shouting insults at him as she did so freely when she came upon him at a bend in the lane, spying on her with a look of ecstasy; she wished she could throw stones at him, smack him across the ear, send him home with kicks in the calves and the rear end. Meanwhile, he was well aware that she was looking at him and was blowing foolish little kisses at her, completely forgetting his role. The crowd had dispersed somewhat since the procession headed off toward rue Fabre, which it would take down to Mont-Royal, then go back up Chambord to boulevard Saint-Joseph. The Roman soldiers found themselves with time on their hands, and they were starting to push each other around and generally play the fool. Sister Sainte-Catherine, who wasn't following the procession so she could keep an eye on the repository, along with Sister Sainte-Thérèse de l'Enfant-Jésus, had had to intervene twice already, but the boys kept elbowing each other and making inane comments about the Blessed Virgin and the angels. Simone, meanwhile, was struggling against a powerful urge to sleep. It had come over her out of the blue, just after the procession turned onto rue Fabre. Until then she had been concentrating on her role, seeing everything as beautiful – the banners and flags that looked very different from up high, the canopy that completely concealed the *curé* and looked like a counter in a fancy store, the people shouting hymns as they admired her, her class-mates, who waved at her and her mother, who had finally relaxed and was accepting, with a blush, the compliments of other people in the parish; but now, suddenly, as she gestured to Sister Sainte-Catherine to let her know everything was all right, she was overcome by a crazy urge to go to sleep. Her eyes shut in spite of her, her head was nodding and she could feel her legs going numb. "Jeepers, it's hot!" The air was heavier and heavier, hotter and hotter, and at times a blazing little wind would make her sway at the end of her rope. "I hope I won't get sick to my stomach again!" Sister Sainte-Catherine had carefully explained that she should give her a warning sign if anything was wrong; twice she almost summoned the nun to her aid, but then she thought how humiliating it would be and decided to be patient a while longer. A gust of wind, stronger than the others, made her spin around, and she found herself facing the stained-glass window. "How do I get turned around again?" She swung her legs a little, but didn't move an inch. She stretched out her arms, pressed her fingertips against the stained-glass window and gave herself a slight push. She turned slowly back toward boulevard Saint-Joseph. She smiled at Sister Sainte-Catherine, who had approached the repository. She murmured, "Don't worry, Sister, I'll tough it out! But jeepers, it's long!" She thought of her cool little bed, of her soft pillow, and her heart turned over. Sleep! She sighed deeply, shutting her eyes, but a drop of water landed on the tip of her nose and she woke with a start.

Firt came the grade-one girls in their white first-communion dresses and starched veils, rhinestone rosaries in their hands and a tiny leatherette bag draped over their wrists. They were singing, generally very softly, embarrassed to be out in the street in a costume they thought had been relegated to the back of the closet forever, or at least until their younger sisters were old enough to wear them. Right behind them came the first communicants from the École Bruchési, squeezed into stiff shirts, embarrassed by armbands – each one more spectacular than the next, ablaze with gold, embroidered or dripping lace – that were draped around their left arms. Some were even wearing huge white bows, chiffon or peau-de-soie; they had red ears, too, because they were constantly assailed by stinging insults like, "Hey, nancy, are your panties silk, too?" or "Give us a kiss, sweetie, or I'll undo your pretty bow!"; "Put it on your head, you'll look like your sister!" They all sang very loud to put on a bold front, and their teachers, Mademoiselle Saint-Jean, Mademoiselle Karli and Sister Rose de la Croix, interpreted it as piety. Next came the entire École des Saints-Anges, marching in compact, well-behaved rows, the grade-nine girls at the head, calm and disciplined for once, the smallest ones at the very back; they were supposed to be singing the same hymn or reciting the same prayer, but often there was a big gap, two or three seconds, because of the length of the line, which produced an unpleasant cacophony that rose over rue Fabre in irregular, confused waves. All the girls, future housewives, obedient and discreet, perfect products of the Catholic religion, were constantly scanning both sides of the street where their parents stood waving at them, and most of all the good-looking boys from other parishes, who were eyeing them. The girls who were old enough to flirt did so shamelessly, interrupting a hymn or a prayer to laugh or wave or even blow a kiss quite openly. Just behind them, the boys from Saint-Stanislas-de-Kostka school were bored to tears, singing sluggishly, standing and gawking or even jamming their hands in their pockets and scratching their penises. It didn't matter that their teachers bellowed out hymns as they kneaded their rosaries, the boys' replies were scant and sometimes non-existent. Thumbless Buddha, the vice-principal, a huge Brother with a stentorian voice, fulminated, red-faced, from the back of the line, promising the younger boys (according to the older boys he always took on the youngest because they were defenceless) punishments, each

248

one worse than the last. As he was quite capable of carrying them out, the little boys trembled as they tried to respond to the prayers. Immediately behind the fat Brother, who kept going up and down the rows of boys like a German shepherd, came the various women's clubs and groups of the parish, the Ladies of Sainte-Anne, Daughters of Isabelle and other hordes of old maids or frustrated widows who met every week to tell each other their fears, be deeply shocked at nothing and out-gossip each other. They bore banners, flags, armbands, badges and standards proclaiming their great faith and their love of God; they sang louder than anybody, in stricter time and better; they marched, heads high, shoulders straight, their dry faces concealed behind thick veils that allowed only their voices to seep through. They were, in a way, the majorettes for the canopy that came behind them, tawdry and almost pagan with all its red and gold. The bystanders gathered on either side of the street bowed as they passed, crossed themselves and straightened up, certain they'd just experienced a great moment. Monsignor Bernier lavished great benedictions on his flock, holding the Blessed Sacrament in both hands as he did so: he had terrible cramps in his shoulders, but he held out valiantly. He had consecrated the Host just before setting out and sincerely felt that he was guiding Our Lord Himself through his parish, to show Him the piety of these poor naïve folk you could always count on – and with whom you could do whatever you wanted. Behind the canopy, Mother Notre-Dame du Rosaire and Mother Benoîte des Anges were calmly reciting their rosaries, looking down at their shoes. They were followed by the churchwardens, who marched in step, bellowing hymns that, in their mouths, sounded more like slogans. At the end of the procession came the men and women of the parish, in shaky and untidy rows. Strangely, neither piety nor joy rose from this procession, altough they had come together to celebrate the Body

249

of Christ. It was all deathly sad, and as Josaphat-le-Violon put it so well as he watched the almost funereal procession go past, "They should have an accordion, a piano, a fiddle! They should be singing and tapping their feet! We couldn't've dreamt up a parade like that, it's too boring! Let a few fellows do a jig; that'll perk things up!" He nodded his head as he caressed his instrument. Marcel was sitting on Mauve's lap, trying with devastating winks and cajoling smiles to seduce her into playing the piano. "Longer than last time, and prettier!" Duplessis was sleeping in the corner. Florence had squarely turned her back on the procession and now she was sipping her tea as she looked lovingly at Marcel.

When she heard the grade-one girls' voices mingled with those of the nuns, which dominated them without covering them altogether, Victoire thought she was dying. "It's the angels!" But when she opened her eyes and saw her small, almost miserable bedroom with the worn lace curtains yellow from too many washings, she heaved a sigh of relief. "The Corpus Christi procession .... It's just the Corpus Christi procession." She got up without difficulty – to her surprise – and impatiently pushed aside the curtains, which she had carefully shut before getting into bed. She pressed her nose against the window. "The little things are so pretty!" A faint smile drifted for a moment across her face, still ravaged by the nightmares she'd just had. The first communicants walked past, beribboned and pink with embarrassment, and Victoire saw herself some sixty years before, sauntering down the little dirt road in Duhamel, all in white and almost apologetic in her long dress with its many flounces. She smelled the scent of lily-of-the-valley from the wreath her mother had woven that very morning, and she saw her father, big Gaspard-la-Pipe, wiping his eyes with his checkered handkerchief, already dirty though it was early in the day. Her dress was too heavily starched and it cut into her neck, but she was so happy! Victoire gestured as if pushing her long, child's hair off her shoulders; she smiled more broadly and spoke in a high-pitched voice that contrasted strangely with her old face and wrinkled lips. "Don't cry, poppa, it's the most beautiful day of my life!" She heard her father's cavernous voice and her heart melted. "The most beautiful day of your life! You're only nine years old, for Christ's sake!" And suddenly she was filled with a fierce urge to live, so urgent and powerful that she had to support herself against the window frame. "Why should I die? Why should I let myself go without putting up a fight? Because I'm going crazy? So what! It's better than a hole in the ground!" The little girls were already far away; the boys were passing now, lamely reciting, "I believe in God." Victoire sat on her bed and bent down to look for her slippers. "Like Teddy Bear Brown used to say if he had to talk French on Saturday night when the drink was starting to get to him: 'If you can't beat 'em, join 'em!'" Victoire had a good laugh at the memory of Teddy Bear Brown's incredible mug; he had chased her for a long time, calling her "The Impossible Victory," which she'd taken as a compliment but which he considered a serious flaw. Oh, the scent of sun-warmed hay and clover; the well next to the house, built on top of a creek whose water was always icy, even on the worst days of summer, and infested with green garter-snakes that traced slow arabesques as they hunted for easy prey; her father's house was perched on the top of a hill that would later be sold to Singer and was already, back then, circled by a little railroad that carried more wood than passengers .... "I'm stifling in here!" She tottered out of her room and onto the balcony where Albertine was cautiously waving her little white-and-yellow flag. At the sight of her mother, Albertine started slightly and hid her flag between her legs. "Where're

251

you going?" Victoire was already on the stairs. "Never mind, Bartine, you wouldn't understand ...." "But momma, you're wearing your night-gown!" "What's wrong with that? It's a pretty night-gown, isn't it?" "But momma, the Good Lord's coming this way!" "To hell with the Good Lord! He just about got me today and I've heard enough about Him!" At the bottom of the stairs she hesitated for a moment, then slowly turned her head toward the balcony of the house next door. They were all there. The crazy ones. And the ghosts. The three knitting women. Their mother, who was drinking tea. Marcel. Josaphat, her brother, who was looking at her with eyes as big as saucers. And the cat, too. The goddamn cat, bearer of death. All four women turned their heads in her direction at once. She approached the fence, slowly pushed open the gate. Above her, Albertine was leaning over the railing. "Don't, momma, there's nothing in there!" Victoire looked up at her daughter. Smiled. "There's nothing at our place, Bartine!" She walked across the lawn, taking cautious little steps, climbed up the wooden steps to the balcony. "I decided not to let myself die!" Florence immediately got up and offered Victoire her chair, but the old woman waved it away. She sat down next to her brother, who put his arm around her shoulders. "I think you were right, Josaphat ...." Just as she rested her head in the hollow of his shoulder, the Blessed Sacrament passed the house. On the balcony, everyone looked the other way.

Sister Sainte-Catherine and Sister Sainte-Thérèse de l'Enfant-Jésus were leaning against the church fence. The procession was slowly making its way back to the repository; already you could see the first communicants turning the corner of rue Chambord and boulevard Saint-Joseph. The crowd was fairly dense again; mothers arrived, pulling their children by the hand, fathers in groups of five or six cut paths across the church lawn, chatting. Monsignor Bernier was going to celebrate a short mass, give communion and then it would all be over. Until next year. Sister Sainte-Catherine laid her hand on Sister Sainte-Thérèse's arm. They had just had a long conversation, in the course of which they had analysed their situation and realized there was only one way out. But Sister Sainte-Thérèse hadn't accepted this solution yet: she was very disturbed and didn't dare raise her head, so her face was completely hidden by her white coif. "You can't be serious, Sainte-Catherine – to go over the wall!" Sister Sainte-Catherine briskly withdrew her hand. "What a terrible way to put it! That's not the image I'd use to describe our happiness, Sainte-Thérèse!" Sister Sainte-Thérèse raised her head. "Our happiness! In ... in sin!" Sister Sainte-Catherine took a long look at the façade of the École des Saints-Anges before she replied. "The sins we might commit in the world are certainly no worse than the ones that are lying in wait for us in that school, Sainte-Thérèse! I told you once that I thought I'd made a mistake, that I wasn't really sure I had a vocation .... Well, I am sure now .... And it's up to you to examine your soul ...." "It would be beyond me to go back out in the world .... It's been too long .... I've been so protected from everything!" "But we could still teach, Sainte-Thérèse! People will point their fingers at us for a while, but they'll forget that we used to be nuns .... It'll take time and it won't be easy, I know that, but we'll make a life for ourselves." "And what about God? You seem to be forgetting about God, Sainte-Catherine!" Sister Sainte-Catherine put both hands on Sainte-Thérèse's shoulders and brought her face close to her friend's. "God is within us, Sainte-Thérèse. Not there." She pointed to the school. "Do as your conscience tells you. Everything will work out, in time ...." Sister

Sainte-Thérèse freed herself from her friend's embrace. "You're taking on the role of my conscience a bit too much, Sainte-Catherine! Let me think it over ... by myself." The procession arrived, somewhat dishevelled now; the children were becoming really tired: the little girls were yawning, the boys were dragging their feet. The banners weren't so high or so straight, and even the Ladies of Sainte-Anne weren't singing quite so loud. They cleared a space for the canopy, which had arrived in front of the repository. Then the storm broke, so quickly that no one saw it coming. For several minutes, big clouds had been gathering over Montreal, quickly turning yellow in the west, where you could see the crest of Mount Royal at the end of boulevard Saint-Joseph. Just as Monsignor Bernier was about to gesture to the four bearers to push the canopy toward the sidewalk, there was a cloudburst and cold rain came streaming down, soaking everything in seconds. Cries rose in the crowd, children started running in every direction, the canopy was picked up by a gust of wind and came crashing down on the side-walk with a splash and Monsignor Bernier rushed off toward the church, hugging the monstrance to his chest, followed by Mother Benoîte des Anges and Mother Notre-Dame du Rosaire, whose habits were already soaked. In the repository, Pierrette was the first to be knocked over. As soon as she saw the rain start to fall, she crouched on her pedestal, calling Thérèse to come and help her. But the wind that carried the canopy away had wrenched her from her plinth and now she was down on all fours on the dirty lawn. "You hurt yourself, Pierrette?" "Damn it all anyway, I knew something rotten was going to happen, I just knew it!" And up above the improvised altar, Simone was screaming as the trumpeting angels and the Roman soldiers left the repository and followed the crowd, which was surging into the church. Somewhere in the west, lightning rent the sky and, almost immediately, thunder roared. Sister Sainte-Catherine and Sister Sainte-Thérèse ran across boulevard Saint-Joseph, and Sister Sainte-Catherine ordered Sister Sainte-Philomène, who was standing at the bottom of the school stairs, rooted to the spot, to unfasten the cord that was holding Simone up. Sister Sainte-Catherine climbed up the stairs to the repository and leaned against the altar, shouting, "Don't worry, Simone, we'll untie you right away!" The rain, which was coming down harder and harder, was pinching Simone's skin, and she hid her face in her hands. She kicked her legs, spinning at the end of her rope, and she couldn't keep from screaming. Thérèse, Pierrette, Charlotte and Maurice had joined the two nuns at the altar. A statue was overturned and two flags came loose from their stands and crashed down on the steps. Simone was swaying faster and faster; at times the wind pressed her against the stained-glass window, which she was trying, in vain, to hold on to. Maurice climbed up on the altar and was trying to clutch his sister's heels. "It's too high! I can't reach her!" Sister Sainte-Philomène suddenly appeared on the slippery pediment and shouted something that no one understood. The rain had tightened the knots in Simone's rope and she couldn't undo them. All the parishioners had taken shelter inside the church, and boulevard Saint-Joseph was empty, lashed by rain in which there were now some hailstones as well. Simone screamed, "It's pinching!" At the height of the storm, as the branches of the frenzied trees were waving in a most disturbing manner, Sister Sainte-Philomène took a knife from her pocket and showed it to Sister Sainte-Catherine, who gestured to her to cut the rope. Then Sister Sainte-Catherine climbed up on the altar and took Maurice Côté by the shoulders. "We'll have to catch her when she falls .... The two of us can do it." The rope broke and for a fraction of a second, time seemed suspended. Simone seemed to be floating over the altar, her face frozen in horror, then slowly she came down, a little bundle of wet rags, into the arms held out to her.

The wind and the rain disappeared as quickly as they'd come. In the west, the sky was blood red. Simone was trembling in the arms of her mother, who was hurling nameless insults at everyone. The price was too high and Simone decided that she didn't want to be pretty any more.